Lincolnshire
COUNTY COUNCIL

COMMUNITIES, CULTURAL SERVICES
and ADULT EDUCATION

**This book should be returned on or before
the last date shown below.** MB2

To renew or order library books please telephone 01522 782010
or visit www.lincolnshire.gov.uk
You will require a Personal Identification Number.
Ask any member of staff for this.

WHO ARE YOU CALLING A VAMPIRE?

MANDI CASEY

iUniverse, Inc.
New York   Bloomington

WHO ARE YOU CALLING A VAMPIRE?

iUniverse books may be ordered through booksellers or by contacting:

iUniverse
1663 Liberty Drive
Bloomington, IN 47403
www.iuniverse.com
1-800-Authors (1-800-288-4677)

Because of the dynamic nature of the Internet, any Web addresses or
links contained in this book may have changed since publication and
may no longer be valid. This is a work of fiction. All of the characters,
names, incidents, organizations, and dialogue in this novel are either
the products of the author's imagination or are used fictitiously.

ISBN: 978-1-4401-8204-4 (pbk)
ISBN: 978-1-4401-8203-7 (ebk)
ISBN: 978-1-4401-8202-0 (hbk)

Library of Congress Control Number:2009911749

Printed in the United States of America
iUniverse rev. date: 1/19/2010

CHAPTER 1

Emergency room nurse, Katrina Drogan, preferably referred to as Kat, walked through the unlit back hallways of the hospital. She kept her eyes open for anyone lurking about, not wanting to be spotted heading towards the back entrance. She needed a cigarette bad.

As she went out the sliding glass doors to the park cold air rushed at her, causing her to zip up her coat. The sky was black with a few twinkling stars and the air was chilled but fair in comparison to the usual temperature of a Wisconsin night in February. Kat spotted her usual hideout, an unmarked door with a cement step.

Kat sat down on the cold cement, closing her eyes for a moment of blissful relaxation. Hopefully, tonight she would meet the man of her dreams and on her birthday next week he would get down on one knee, propose to her with a giant rock, and they would live happily ever after on a deserted island. The reality was that her twenty-fifth birthday would be just like any other day, without a man to share it with.

Carmen, or Carmi, is Kat's best friend. Tonight Carmi planned to take her out to a ridiculously expensive nightclub to celebrate. They planned on drinking too much alcohol and collapsing at either Kat's apartment or Carmi's house out in the county. Many post birthday celebrations ended with both women waking up the next morning with major wicked hangovers. It was part of their birthday ritual.

Sitting on the step with her eyes closed, Kat let images of the night to come and how much fun she was going to have when a soft rustling sound came from the bushes not far from where she was. Ok, that was odd, now the kid inside has me hearing things too, Kat thought. "I'd better get back inside, someone is bound to have come in from somewhere, needing medical attention," she said out loud as she stood up. The male teenaged patient inside was being treated for smoking too much marijuana and Kat assumed he was hallucinating. Kat figured the patient had her spooked. The kid kept repeating the same sentence. There were men outside waiting to kidnap him.

Then she heard it again, except this time it was definitely not paranoia from the patient inside. She really did hear noises, someone or something was making the branches moves. To make matters worse the sounds were coming from the bushes at the end of the building not fifteen feet from where she stood. It sounded like a big animal trying to be quiet and sneaky but was sucking at it. She watched as branches on the bush started to move and then separate. Kat froze, unable to move as the noisy thing in the bushes materialized into a man.

He slowly approached her; Kat couldn't move a limb. A scream of terror caught in her throat. The man coming towards her wore a military uniform accessorized by night vision goggles. Camouflage paint covered his face. He also carried a rifle with a sniper scope. His complexion was very pale. Apparently, the patient inside wasn't wrong after all. This man, whoever he was, clearly fit the patient's description. She should have listened to him better.

Kat continued to stare at the man as he approached. She was unable to move a muscle. She didn't flinch when another man, bigger than the first, jumped out of the bushes. The newcomer didn't make a sound as he silently stalked the first guy. He put his finger to his lips signaling her to be quiet not wanting her to give his position away. He moved quicker and more quietly than the first. The newest arrival took a silent leap and tackled his target. Both men landed on the snow covered ground. At that moment Kat broke out of her stupor and bolted for the door.

Kat dropped her badge before she could scan the sensor block to unlock the door. She bent over to grab the badge out of the snow and looked to her right where the wrestling duo were and saw she was suddenly alone. She didn't know how she knew, but she sensed they were both gone along with the danger that came with them. Kat decided to get the door unlocked and her on the other side of it in case either of them decided to come back.

"Theo, we have a huge problem by the park! I was just back there and there were two guys fighting, and one was carrying a gun! We need to call the police! There really could be someone after the boy in the ER just like he said!" Kat stammered as she tried to calm herself down and catch her breath. She literally ran the entire way to the security office.

"Whoa, Kat! Calm yourself," Theo said.

She reached over the security window grabbing at the phone but Theo snatched it up first.

"Go on back to triage, I'll call the cops," he said with finality, practically dismissing her. Kat looked at him suspiciously. She knew he would make the call, but she wasn't sure he wouldn't go check out the situation first, getting himself hurt or even killed in the process.

Viktor paced back and forth in his front foyer of the Council mansion. He couldn't believe what he saw tonight. During his nightly rounds in the city, he spotted one of Malice's Hunters by the hospital. Why in the hell was he after that mortal woman? Who was she? He questioned. He couldn't remember ever having seen a more beautiful woman in all of his years! Typically he didn't find mortal women appealing, mortals were only temporary. But this mortal woman was different.

Before he jumped the Hunter and tackled him back into the bushes, he sensed it, the difference in her. He got a clear look at her, she was exceptionally beautiful. Fortunately she had the sense to go back into the hospital for protection. Unfortunately, because of her perfume, he wasn't able to get a good whiff of her scent to place her origins.

"I'm telling you, that female felt different. She is definitely not full human, but the scent of perfume and the Hunter stalking her made it hard to tell for sure," Viktor said. He was confused why a Hunter would follow her, and what made them approach her now? She wasn't anyone of importance the Council was aware of. So who was she? And what did they want with her? He would find her again and make her tell him exactly what he wanted to know.

Dave, a human member of the Council, was the most sensible one. He explained in a casual tone, "Viktor, you were probably confused by the Hunter and didn't get a real good bead on the girl. She's probably just an ordinary no-body and you shouldn't give her a second thought. You have more important things to deal with."

"Ok, I get you Dave, but I still think there was something unusual about that girl, some weird vibe she gave off," Viktor said.

"Viktor, we should focus on the Hunters. For all we know, she may not have been their primary target."

"Fine, tomorrow night, we need to start talking about strategy, we need to find out what the Hunter's new project is, what all their activity has been for lately. Whatever they're planning, we need to stop it."

"Meet me here at two. I have something I need to do tonight," Viktor said as he suddenly headed out of the room. Dave followed him through the foyer to the stairs and down to the bottom level of the mansion where Viktor and his family lived for centuries. For the most part Viktor led a normal life except when the royal vampires left their underground palace. That's where he and the Council came in. They were the royal family's personal security force and escort.

"Yeah, sure you do Viktor. Just remember, you have important things you should be focusing on right now, not some girl. Malice is planning something, civilian and vampire casualties have increased and Hunter sightings have been more frequent than usual. That's what you should be focusing on," Dave said as he lit a fire in the large black granite fireplace of Viktor's private living area.

Viktor wanted to see that woman again. More specifically, he wanted to see why he was so instantly drawn to her. To find out what that unusual vibe was she wore like a second skin. He was almost sure what he sensed came from her and not the Hunter.

She was different, special somehow. Unfortunately, in Viktor's world special could mean a lot of things.

Viktor was born a vampire and had the temperament, strength, agility, and wisdom that went along with being three hundred and twenty seven years old. Ever since he was born, he had been a member of the Council. His and Dave's families long ago had both been given the honor to protect the royal family of King Alexander Caine.

The Council, also known as Delta 9, was developed to protect the royal family members of the Caine family when they left the safety of the palace. Because of Malice, the Hunter's leader, the king proclaimed a new law. All of his blood descendants were not to leave the palace grounds without his approval. That approval wasn't given out very often.

The Caine family is the second largest royal vampire family totaling around two hundred and fifty members. Once in a while a royal would go against his wishes and leave the palace alone. When this happened they were not welcomed back with open arms. A vampire didn't go against what King Alexander said. The king tended to get really pissed off when his laws were broken.

To all the rules of life and survival, there are exceptions. Viktor had a problem with knowing what was good for him and doing the exact opposite. That was where Dave came in. Dave was as loyal to the royals as anyone else. Having a human Council member was helpful since he could go out in daylight when the others could not. Maintaining the safety of the vampire royal bloodlines and ensuring the survival of the purest vampires was the Council's duty and honor by birth.

Dave and his family are protectors just as Viktor's family has always been. He wasn't mad about the job. It's all Dave has ever known. Sometimes, Viktor knew, Dave got a little tired of having to work with and coddle vampires.

Sometimes Viktor felt Dave was more of a brother to him than his own blood brothers. His real brothers were Rafe, who went missing over twenty years ago, and Grailen. The latter had turned into a lurking, brooding crab since Rafe's disappearance.

Viktor knew Grailen felt responsible about Rafe. Their vampire parents had been staked when Viktor and Rafe were young, less than two hundred years old each. Grailen was much, much older, and he had taken them both in when their parents died. Grailen trained Viktor and Rafe to be warriors and competent Council members.

Grailen guided them into being the persons they were today. Unfortunately, the word out on the street was Rafe either got staked or went rogue and was committing vampire crimes against humanity. He wouldn't be taken back into the fold until he was dealt an appropriate punishment.

Viktor's parents brought the boys to the Kensin mansion when Viktor was an infant. The mansion was located just outside the city limits of Kensin, on Lake Michigan. Their main purpose in life was to keep the Caine family safe, and secondly, to police local vampires making sure vampire existence was kept secret from humans.

Kat looked at the clock, only two more minutes left. If Sandy doesn't show up for work, she was going to scream at someone! Probably not, but she would be really ticked off. She was sick of her co-workers coming in whenever they felt like, not acknowledging it might affect her plans. Ok, so she didn't go out all that much, but still, there was the principle of the matter.

Theo, the security guard, personally came to the ER to let Kat know the police couldn't find any sign of two men fighting. He said they searched all around the area in the back of the hospital. Kat could see the doubt in Theo's eyes about what she had seen, and that angered her.

Next thing she knew, there was Sandy in all her third shift glory. Kat had to give the woman some slack. Sandy was keeping it together. She provided her kids with a good home, food, and clothing. No thanks to their slime bag father. He refused to have anything to do with the kids except when he felt like it. That included when he felt like paying child-support too.

"Hey girl, what's going on," Sandy drawled as she huffed and puffed up to the ER triage nursing desk.

"Not much. I'm only leaving you with one patient, and that's because he can't leave. His tox screen hasn't come back yet. We'll know what happy drug besides marijuana he's on when it does." She denied that the kid had any correlation to the men she saw fighting out back. They had it in for each other, she figured. She just happened to get a glimpse of their argument. Luckily she walked away unscathed. Whoever the kid was talking about was a bonus effect from whatever drug he was on, she was sure of it. Kat didn't want to admit to herself that those men had anything else on their minds except fighting with each other. She didn't acknowledge that the kid was right. It was just a coincidence, she told herself.

"I gotta go Sandy. My friend is taking me out to Jade! She got tickets to the opening, so if I hurry, I'll only miss the ribbon cutting, or whatever they do for nightclubs that open at midnight," Kat said. She handed Sandy the medication cart key and scrambled away to the locker room to grab her stuff.

Lingering suspicious thoughts continued to cross her mind. What if that kid was right? What if those two men were really after him? Probably not, they looked more like they had it in for each other.

Kat ran out through the hospital's revolving door of the ER entrance. She stopped and looked around. Wow! She was more paranoid than she thought. There wasn't any sign of commando guys so she walked up to her car in the employee parking lot. She climbed in her car, locked the doors, and took a deep breath. Geez, Kat. Get a grip on yourself!

At her apartment, she hurriedly got dressed. She put on her

new black cocktail dress she couldn't stop thinking about all day. She took one final look in the mirror. Kat didn't have as much time as she would have liked to get ready. She took a quick shower and re-straightened her hair that never fully straightened.

Kat took one last look around her apartment. She felt the top of her right thigh high stocking to make sure her driver's license was in place. She'd put her car key in the top of her left stocking when she got to the club. Money wasn't an issue. Carmi said it was her treat for Kat's birthday. Satisfied, Kat walked out of her apartment. She closed and locked the door behind her.

CHAPTER 2

The front of the nightclub building was covered with grey brick. The doorway was blocked by a thin man wearing a tuxedo. There was a line of people waiting to get in! Kat drove past the club looking for a parking spot. She knew it was going to be a night to remember. Beautiful people were swarming the entrance, trying to get in.

Carmen really came through on this one. People couldn't get into the club without a special invitation. After Kat found a parking spot a block down from the club, she nervously walked up to the man standing at the pedestal positioned in front of the door and gave her name, "Katrina Drogan." He looked her up and down, doubting that she would have an invitation. He glanced over his list. Finally, he smiled when he spotted her name. She let out a breath she didn't know she was holding.

"Ah, yes, Ms. Carmen was just out here checking to see if you had arrived yet. Please go right in," he said. The man looked at home in his black tailored tuxedo that fit his thin frame nicely. Another doorman took a little bow and opened the door for her.

Thank the powers that be her name was on the list. She hadn't brought a purse so she didn't have her cell phone. She wouldn't have been able to call Carmi which would have been a total embarrassment and the end to her highly anticipated night out. Not that Carmen would have been able to hear her phone ring. Even outside of the club Kat felt the ground thump from the bass of the music.

Kat walked down the short hallway leading to a huge dance floor jam-packed with well dressed men and women. The men had black or gray suits on with various colored shirts and ties. The women wore a variety of cocktail dresses, most bordering on the line of skimpy lingerie. Kat glanced down at her black cocktail dress. Maybe this wasn't the best choice after all. She felt a little out of place. It didn't matter. She never had the confidence these women had. Wearing barely concealing dresses wasn't her style.

The club was lit with an array of laser lights. The pulsating rhythm of the lights seemed to be timed in perfect synchrony with the beat of the music.

Kat spotted Carmen beyond the dance floor. Carmi stood at one of the four bars that lined the club walls. Kat started to make her way over to her friend. She couldn't get over how packed the club was. The noise, flashing lights, and heat were almost overwhelming.

As Kat made her way over to Carmen she bumped into someone's back. It was a tall, wide, and black jacketed back. Mr. Black Jacket smelled really good, a deep earthy smell laced with pure masculinity. Kat looked up ready to apologize and froze, unable to breathe. It was him! The guy she saw earlier tonight. He was the one who attacked the guy with the gun outside at work. She couldn't believe it. Her mouth dropped open and not one syllable came out. The urge to run verses the need to know what that was all about earlier warred within her.

"Good evening, miss. I bet you hear this all the time, but, do I know you?" He waited, wanting her to tell him her name. Viktor couldn't believe he was running into her again, two times in one night! He considered himself a lucky man, but not this lucky. He figured it was fate. When she didn't answer he leaned in close to her and said, "My name is Viktor, may I buy you drink?"

He wanted to get close enough to smell her. Singling out her scent proved difficult in this place with the humans sweating on the dance floor with their rainbow of expensive perfumes and colognes. The other, more distressing reason he did this was that he found himself unexplainably drawn to her and felt the need to be physically close to her. He planned to search for her tonight after the club opening, but indeed he liked finding her here better.

"Ah, I uh, no. No, I don't think we have met before," Kat said. She was barely able to utter a word. Kat couldn't form anything other than blubbering sounds after the short sentence she got out. Ok, she was totally confused. This guy was gorgeous in every way. His long dark hair was smooth as silk. His complexion was flawless. And his lips! What was wrong with her? Kat didn't react to men like this. He was definitely the one she saw tackle commando guy earlier tonight. What was he doing here?

Viktor smiled his most charming smile. He found her inability to respond sexy. He grabbed her gently by the elbow and guided her to the bar she was headed toward.

Kat went along without questioning herself as to what she was doing. Normally she was all about safety and self preservation. She knew when she was in danger. But she just let this stranger lead her along. He made it difficult to think clearly.

Carmi was there talking to a guy who looked head over heels in infatuation with her. Carmi's companion laughed at something she said. His eyes never wandered from her face to look at the barely dressed females gyrating on and off the dance floor. As they approached, Carmen turned and smiled at Kat. When she saw a man with his hand on Kat's elbow she frowned. Carmi knew Kat didn't do well with the opposite sex. Having failed miserably at the few relationships she involved herself in.

Kat wanted to be in a meaningful relationship but so far she had not found anyone who could hold her interest. With Kat, dating was like an experiment. Searching for a man who could peak her interest and hold it had yet to happen.

"Kat, you finally made it, we need to talk, let's go to the restroom shall we?" Carmi grabbed Kat's other elbow and gently dragged her to the woman's restroom. Once they entered the sitting area Carmen parked her bony behind on one of the maroon colored, round, couch-like chairs and pointed to the one next to her for Kat.

"Ok, Miss Secret Keeper, who the hell is that gorgeous man, where did you meet him, and does he have a brother?" Kat stared at her friend. Carmen was never without men swarming around. She was not only independently wealthy because of her father. She scored in the looks department too. Her hair was a beautiful curly, blond color. She was skinnier than a rail, yet had a chest any woman would die for. Her dress was gold and silver, showing off her cleavage. Carmi's dress didn't come out of a catalogue. Kat's friend flew to New York often to buy her clothes right off the models walking down the runways in major fashion shows.

Carmen didn't take silence for an answer. Kat decided to tell her the little she knew of him, which was basically nothing. Carmi expressed her concern about Viktor. It wasn't normal for men to hang around the back of a hospital and wrestle with each other in the snow.

Carmi said Kat clearly held the man's interest. They both concurred that Kat would hold him at bay until she found out why he showed up in the bushes at her work. They finished freshening up in the mirror and went back to the bar where the men were still standing.

Viktor, if she heard him correctly when he spoke his name, was leaning his back against the bar holding two drinks, waiting for her. Her breath caught in her throat. She couldn't get over how desirable she found him, in a mysterious and sensual way. She didn't know what to say to him, or how to speak for that matter. She giggled. This was ridiculous. It was unlike her to behave like this.

Viktor saw his woman and her friend leave the restroom heading over to where he stood. He just called her his. He decided he wasn't going to acknowledge that right now. Just as the two women arrived the pressure in the air of the club changed. He could feel it. Viktor sensed the second the Hunter entered the building. Where was he? Reality of the situation struck him like a blow to the face, he knew who their target was, and it wasn't him.

Ever since Malice held him captive and used him as a guinea pig, Viktor could sense the presence of Hunters. It was similar to his ability to sense vampires in the vicinity. Detecting a Hunter was like feeling a poisonous film on his skin. Viktor figured the Hunter's altered humanity is what he sensed.

Who was this woman? What the hell did they want with her?

Viktor leaned in close to her and murmured, "Excuse me, Kat is it? I'm sorry to end our meeting so soon, something has come up and I must go, I hope we will see each other again soon." Viktor handed her the raspberry martini he had ordered for her and walked off towards the enemy.

He knew there were at least two Hunters now as he approached them. He hoped there wasn't any more waiting outside the club. They were in a very public place with a lot of potential witnesses. Usually when Hunters wanted to take someone they waited until the target was alone with no one to witness their abduction.

Viktor stood in the darkness of the club's balcony watching the Hunters. He was surprised they had not noticed his presence yet. They were tailing Kat, most likely waiting to see where she would go after she left the club. Viktor was also interested in who she was and who she would go home with. Unfortunately, their presence meant she wouldn't be going home with him, at least not tonight. He definitely planned on seeing her again, and not just to see what Malice wanted with her.

The Hunter at the hospital stalking her and now their appearance at the club was too much of a coincidence. The Hunter may have intended on taking her earlier when she was alone at the hospital. Viktor had to ensure they didn't get another opportunity to nab her.

Viktor didn't want to be too overbearing, if he could help it. When they tailed her, he would have to follow them from a distance. That would give him the opportunity to place himself somewhere she would be. He would coincidently run into her again. He smiled, hopefully that would go well. She already had suspicion in her eyes when they met on the dance floor. She must have recognized him. Finding her later wouldn't be too difficult. He noticed the scrubs she was wearing in back of the hospital. She must be an employee.

Spying on Malice's soldiers wasn't difficult. They could do a better job at hiding their weapons too. The doormen had let them in. The Hunters had developed mind control abilities over other humans. Not as finely tuned as his own, but Viktor knew having even minimal persuasion capability went a long way.

Malice was improving his experiments, using the blood of vampires to enhance his soldiers. He was developing ways to alter his minions into super soldiers without having the same limitations Viktor and his vampire kind had. That was bad, very bad. Fortunately, the Hunter's speed and strength was no match for most vampires, unless they were caught by surprise.

The two Hunters stood together on the second floor balcony of the club looking over the crowded dance floor. Viktor knew exactly when they caught site of Kat. Their excitement was almost palpable. Their blood pressures went up, their hearts beat faster. One of them reached into his jacket inside pocket. Viktor tensed and prepared to react but the Hunter pulled his hand out holding only a cell phone.

Viktor looked to the sides of the balcony by the surrounding walls for security. He saw a man in all black with security written in white on the back of his shirt. He sent the guard a telepathic message to grab the cell phone from the Hunter's hand. Viktor didn't want to be spotted just yet, being able to trail them while they followed the woman was important. Hopefully they would lead him to Malice's hideout.

Taking Malice out would leave the Hunter's in chaos. They would no longer have anyone to direct them in their evil deeds, at least for a while. The Hunter's would have to be destroyed. Their humanity was gone, obliterated by Malice's brainwashing, experimental surgeries, and DNA manipulations.

The Jade security guard walked up to the Hunter. He tapped him on the shoulder and pointed to his cell phone. The Hunter looked at the security guard with disbelief and disdain that a simple human would have the audacity to speak to him. Malice taught all his Hunters that they were higher beings and they no longer had to abide by human rules and regulations.

Viktor pulled out of the security guard's mind just in time, he felt the soldier influence the guard. Viktor didn't want the soldier to meet him in the guard's mind. He wanted to keep his presence unknown until absolutely necessary. The Hunter closed his cell phone as the guard walked away. The Hunter then turned to his partner who was keeping his eyes on the woman. The Hunter with the phone leaned over, said something to his partner, they looked at each other, nodded, and headed for the staircase. What was that all about? Were they leaving? Were they going to make a move on the woman? He would follow and see. Viktor smiled, this night was proving to be more exciting than he expected.

As the Hunters reached the bottom of the staircase Viktor watched and waited. He knew exactly where the woman was. The woman and her friend hadn't moved far from where he had left them. Maybe she was waiting for him? He doubted it, but a man can dream. She was the most beautiful woman he had ever seen. He wanted to see her again, get to know her in every way. He knew there was something about her that drew him to her, something powerful and intoxicating besides her beauty. He couldn't quite put a finger on what it was, yet.

To Viktor's disappointment, the Hunters headed straight towards Kat. He knew when he initially saw them he should have called for backup, but decided not to. He wanted to keep her away from his brother and the rest of the Council for a little while longer. He jumped over the balcony in such a fast movement anyone around wouldn't have noticed. Over the years, Viktor's speed had developed beyond human sight and comprehension. No human could detect his movements unless he wanted them to.

CHAPTER 3

Carmen continued giving her full attention to her newest boy toy while Kat stood there half listening to their conversation and half looking around the crowd. She hoped to spot Viktor. She was sure falling in love with a man during their first encounter was a bad idea. She feared she was already under his spell whether he intended for that to happen or not. The attraction she felt for him was overwhelming.

Kat never experienced such a strong reaction to a man like this before. She hoped he would keep his word and they would see each other again. She knew he was the man who jumped the soldier guy but it didn't bother her as much as it should. Viktor was her guardian angel, her totally hot, mysterious, all lust consuming guardian angel.

"Isn't that right, Kat?" She heard Carmen say. Ok, now was the time to pretend she had been listening all along.

Kat looked at her friend and smiled. "Yes. Of course it is." Carmen and her new man leaned closer to each other to hear over the loud thumping music.

Kat smiled. Carmi really liked this man. Carmi didn't acknowledge the presence of the opposite sex often. Most men who tried couldn't capture her interest. This one did.

Kat took another feeble look around the dance floor. She noticed two men were walking towards her. They came up to her. The first one said, "Excuse us miss, is your name Katrina Drogan?" She stared at them for a moment, wondering what could possibly be the reason they would single her out in a crowd like this.

"Yes, who are you?"

"We're club security. Do you drive a red Mini Cooper?" asked the second man.

Her heart sank. "Yes, is something wrong?"

"We're sorry to tell you your car was broken into. We called the police, but we'll need you to go outside and see if anything's missing. The police should be here any minute," he said. He put his arm out to lead her in the direction of the exit.

Kat couldn't believe her terrible luck. She turned to her friend, "Carmi, my car just got broken into!" The weirdest things keep happening to me, Kat thought. "I'm just going to call it a night, but stay here and enjoy the rest of the opening, ok? Thanks for inviting me." She kissed Carmen on the cheek and turned towards the men. They led her through the mass of club goers to the exit.

Whatever the Hunters said to Katrina had her upset. Viktor overheard her name from the Hunter when they approached her. Viktor watched, leaning against an unlit wall beyond the dance floor where he could keep an eye on her. She said something to her friend and went with the Hunters. They must have made up an excuse to get her alone outside. It didn't look like her friend was going with her.

Viktor followed them from a distance. The Hunters were focused on her. They strutted out of the club, acting like they had caught the prize of the century. Their vital signs remained heightened. Their excitement barely contained. It oozed from every pore of their rancid bodies. Kat's importance to Malice must be more than he originally thought. Viktor watched Kat follow the Hunters outside. She seemed to trust them blindly. She didn't ask for any type of identification. What if she knew who they were? What was her connection to them and Malice? He had to be careful until he could figure it all out. She could be helping them set a trap to catch him. He doubted it but he never knew what Malice was up to.

Viktor teleported from the wall he leaned on out to the dark alley next to the club. When he rounded the corner of the front of the building he saw the Hunters pointing down the block towards a red Mini Cooper. That must be her car. He saw shattered glass lying on the ground next to the driver's side door. It looked like someone broke into her car. The Hunter's must have set her up. He had to admit it was clever.

Parked behind her car was a full sized van with no windows in the back. It was painted glossy white. He noticed someone was sitting in the driver's seat with the engine running.

Viktor wasn't going to let them take her. He knew how cruel Malice could be to his 'guests', having been one himself. He wasn't about to let her go through that type of torture! Not a good sign, he thought to himself. He was lusting over this woman and he felt protective of her. Protecting the innocent was second nature to him, this was different.

Viktor ran towards them and yelled, "Kat!" He waved his arm in the air to get her attention. The Hunters would know right away what he was. It was fortunate that he didn't recognize either one of them. The Hunters would sense he was a vampire, but not the vampire Malice held a deep grudge against and wanted back into his clutches.

Kat turned around, so did her companions. They didn't look happy to see him. Pointing a finger in the general direction of her car she said, "Uh, hi. Viktor was it? Now's not really a good time, my car was just broken into and I have to wait for the police." Kat tried to keep it together and not cry in front of these strangers. Hoping her CD collection hadn't been taken. It's funny, she thought to herself, the things that pass through your mind when you're under stress.

Viktor looked directly at the men who were attempting to lure her to the van they had waiting to take her captive in. "Oh, I'm so sorry to hear that."

She started walking towards her car, he followed. "Let me give you a ride home, you can't drive your car with no window, you'd freeze." Whoever broke her window left the body of the car untouched. There was glass everywhere, inside-and-out. "Once you give your report to the police, I'll call a repair shop that will have this taken care of for you by tomorrow morning, ok?" The two security guards looked at each other, simultaneously shook their heads toward the man in the waiting van, and walked away with no explanation. It seemed to Viktor the Hunters decided to delay their kidnapping attempt, for now.

Kat looked up into his eyes, surprised. "Wow, tomorrow morning? That would be fast service. Sounds like it'll cost a lot, but it's worth it. This car is my only way of getting around. Thank you for the offer. That's really nice of you." Kat smiled up at him. Her heart was pounding. She knew her physical reaction wasn't just from having her car broken into. She was reacting to this guy whom she didn't know.

Her heart beat faster when he was near her. Sweat covered her palms and thinking clearly was more difficult. And now she was going to accept a ride home from him, in the middle of the night? What could she possibly be thinking? Getting into a car with a strange man? A man she saw fighting just a few hours ago? Yep, she had definitely cracked, she thought. Throwing caution to the wind, she accepted his offer to drive her home.

The club emptied while Viktor and Kat waited outside by her car. They watched as the club goers walked out of the building, some women stumbled in their high heels.

The police never came. Kat decided to give up and go home. The two men that brought her out of the club seemed to have disappeared. Viktor waited with her.

Kat looked at Viktor and asked him to take her home. She would deal with her car and the police in the morning. She got all of her essentials out of her car. Nothing seemed to be missing after a quick search. Viktor pointed to the parking structure across the street from where they were standing. Exhaustion won out over rational thought and she silently followed him to his car.

Kat's feet were sore from wearing high heels for the last few hours. She was used to wearing her very comfortable, broken in tennis shoes. Kat silently grimaced as the narrow points of her high heeled shoes squeezed her toes painfully together with each step.

They walked up to the second level of the parking structure. He pointed to his car which was a beautiful, black Lamborghini. She knew it was really fast, and really expensive. He looked at her and smiled as they approached the stunning machine. Viktor stepped in front of her and slid the door open. She slid into the wonderful smelling black leather bucket seat. The interior of the car smelled of lotion used to treat the seats, and of Viktor. As he walked around the back of the car after closing her door, Kat inhaled all she could, trying to absorb the scent so she could remember it always.

Just as he expected, Viktor spotted the white van a few cars behind them. If they were experienced Hunters he would have trouble losing them while keeping his romantic game face on for Kat. "So, now that I have you in my car and I'm taking you home, maybe it would be a good time for us to get a little better acquainted," he said and grinned his come kiss this smile right off my face grin.

"Oh, yes, I suppose you're right," she replied. The realization of the uncomfortable position she put herself in struck her at that moment. She didn't know this man. He could be a killer for all she knew. "Um, my name is Kat," she said and held out her hand.

Viktor laughed and took her hand into his own, gentle but sure, and brought the back of her hand up to his lips. He gently brushed a feather-light kiss she could barely feel on her skin. He held her hand a little too long for her comfort and said, "Nice to meet you Kat." She became aware that he wasn't looking at the road, only at her. After what seemed like an awkward eternity, he finally glanced away, smiling, and focused back on driving.

Keeping one eye always in the rearview mirror, Viktor picked the intersection he would use to lose her would-be captors. He looked at Kat. "Why don't we go for a little drive? Enjoy some more of this glorious evening?"He said it as a statement. There was no way he could take her straight home. The Hunters would see where she lived. They somehow already knew her full name. He didn't want to give them any more information than they already had about her. He wanted to keep that to himself. He was curious to see if she invited him in when they got there. He would have to make sure he didn't leave his car parked right out front. There wasn't too many black Lamborghini's in this city.

Kat looked over at Viktor and then forward again out the front window. She was trying not to show how utterly fascinating she found him. He truly had to be the most gorgeous, sexy man she had ever encountered. "Sure, we could take a ride down along the lakefront, down Lakeshore Drive, or something."

"Sounds like a plan to me." He knew the Hunters would try to follow them. His mansion was near the lake and he planned to use his familiarity of the back roads to his advantage. That's where he would lose them.

Viktor heard Kat's heart beat speed up a little. Hearing her heart beat faster when they were physically close to each other was exhilarating and pure enjoyment to him. Never before did he feel such a strong attraction to a woman the way he did with Kat. Getting to know her personally, and hopefully, intimately, was going to be pure bliss and torture at the same time. He had all the time in the world because he was a vampire. Kat being mortal didn't.

Deep down Viktor already knew she was the one for him. He was glad over all of these years, that he waited for this moment, this woman. Not being able to read her mind was a sure sign she was different and special. Normally he could read a human's mind without much effort at all. She happened to have a natural barrier to his mind probes which made her all the more alluring to him.

The traffic light turned red as he exited the intersection. He turned left onto the lakefront road and hit the gas pedal hard. The Hunters were stuck behind four cars all waiting to take the same left turn he did. "Time to show you what this thing can do my dear. Hold on!"

Viktor raced his car down the street. There wasn't a lot of traffic. It was now a full hour after bar close. The police were back in their normal hiding spots on the busier streets monitoring for drunk drivers. That left him able to slam on the gas pedal as much as he pleased. He glanced over at Kat and saw she was enjoying herself. She wore a genuine smile of pleasure as she leaned her face towards the crisp February air. He had the heat blowing and the windows down. The wind made her hair whip around her face like dark wisps of cloud caressing a fully lit moon.

They drove around for another hour. They made small talk the entire time. Viktor found himself liking everything about this woman. He didn't tell her much about himself. He wanted to learn as much about her as he could. She had a good heart and liked to help others. She told him that's why she decided to become a nurse. She told him about her Aunt Rose and how she, a single woman, raised her. It was clear to Viktor that Kat held this female in high esteem. It was apparent Kat didn't know much about her parents. She said they died in a car accident when she was very young.

Viktor hadn't seen the white van again since he lost them down by the lake. He figured it was safe enough to drive her home. After she directed him on how to get to her apartment, he pulled up in front of her building. It was nearly 4:30 in the morning. She looked tired from all the night's activities.

"Well, here we are my lady." Viktor put on that sideways grin he had perfected over the last few hundred years and turned the ignition off.

Kat could hardly keep the light, happy feeling she felt from her face. "Thanks again, I had a really great time." She smiled back at him. Giddiness wasn't strong enough a word to describe how she felt. Deciding whether to invite him up to her apartment for a nightcap was difficult. Her common sense won out. Inviting a man up to her apartment, alone, whom she really knew nothing about, even though she was already deeply in lust with him, wasn't a great idea. It wasn't a safe one either.

CHAPTER 4

Grabbing the car door handle, Kat turned and looked at Viktor one last time. She wanted to etch the details of his face permanently into her memory. She realized she may never see him again. Never before had she met a man who made her body ache just by looking at him. When he talked to her she couldn't think of anything else but him. Even better, when his thigh brushed against hers while they stood by her vandalized car, her entire body clenched with a desire she never felt before. It was a first for Kat and she never wanted to forget it.

Kat began to look away, done memorizing Viktor's features. That's when it happened. She saw his hand come up slowly. The movement electrified her entire body as he placed his hand on the side of her face. His fingers slid behind her ear. Slowly, he pulled her face towards him. She felt his breath on her mouth. When their lips met, Kat didn't know whether she was going to pass out or melt into his hand. She did the latter. It was a very gentle kiss.

It lasted just long enough for her to have closed her eyes, and then it was over.

She would never forget it. His smell was so intoxicating. Her body was in sensation overload. His hand felt cool against her warm skin. He made her feel like she was on fire.

Viktor whispered in her ear, "Sleep well Katrina." He released her. He didn't want to frighten her. Now, after they kissed, his hormones raged and he knew that if he didn't leave, he would ask her if he could come up to her apartment for more than just a nightcap.

Katrina could only manage a half crooked smile. The kiss left her in a stupor. Its effects surprised her. She barely remembered to breathe. Exiting Viktor's car, Kat took a deep breath. She didn't want Viktor to see her stumble in her new high heels. She knew he was watching while she made her way to the entrance of her apartment building.

Kat decided to stop on her way to work at Mountain Brew and get her favorite icy caramel coffee. Hey, whatever gets you through the night, right? Because she worked second shift she felt justified indulging in the overly priced treat.

She idled in the drive-thru line of the coffee house. An odd sensation washed over her. It was the same sensation she felt last night at work right before the man came out of the bushes. Kat quickly looked around through the windows of her car. Nothing looked out of the ordinary.

Maybe she was still stressed from last night? She felt apprehensive. The man lurking in the bushes at work really had her spooked. Yeah, that was definitely it. Seeing that man come out of the bushes and meeting the man of her dreams all in one night had her wound up. She realized too late, after seeing him drive away, they hadn't even exchanged phone numbers.

Viktor came through on his promise about Kat's car. Even better, he had her car delivered to the front of her apartment building, completely repaired, and detailed. He left a single lined note attached to the steering wheel,

We will do this again, soon

Kat couldn't believe how nice he was and how much trouble he had saved her. She didn't have to take her car to the auto glass repair shop. She was appreciative.

She put the small piece of stationary up to her nose and inhaled deeply. Feeling content, she now had something to remember him by. The stationary smelled like Viktor. Kat would have to do something to show her appreciation the next time she saw him. Blushing, even though she was alone, brief scenes of intimacy flickered across her mind. No, she would do something of a non-sexual nature to show him how thankful she was for what he did for her. His kind gesture was way over the top, and admittedly, a little awkward for her just having met him. Kat wasn't used to having anyone help her like he did. It must have cost a bundle to have such speedy overnight service done on her car.

After Viktor dropped her off from the club, she couldn't sleep. In bed she tossed and turned all morning. Events of the night constantly replayed in her mind. When she did fall asleep the nightmares came. When Kat was younger she suffered from nightmares often. The premise was always the same. She would yell out for the parents she had never known. In her dreams she needed help. She knew that they were the only ones who could save her.

Last night was no different. She dreamed she was running in the woods down by the lake at night. This time she was an adult, the age that she was now. She was chased by someone or something she couldn't see, so she kept running. In her dream she wore nothing but an oversized t-shirt. She didn't have anything on her feet. Her heart pounded in her chest and her breathing labored. She constantly looked behind her to see if whatever was chasing her was getting closer. She could never see it but she could sense them and the danger. While running, she would call out to her parents for help, but they never came.

In her dreams, Kat knew they were near, but they never showed themselves. Her parents never helped her. Whatever was pursuing her never caught up to her, but last night they got closer to catching her than ever before, and that scared her. Kat's dreams were always the same scenario, just with different scenery and at different ages of her life. Aunt Rose said her dreams must be the result of Kat missing her parents. Otherwise she said it wasn't significant and to brush it off. Kat knew, or sensed, that her dreams meant something. Somehow they were related to her past but she couldn't figure out how.

Kat gulped her coffee. She needed the kick from the caffeine to help her stay awake for work. Her shift was uneventful, as she had hoped it would be. Brian, her favorite male friend and co-worker, was back to work from his mental health day off. This allowed her to enjoy work, not be bombarded with too many things to do and not enough time to get them done.

After her shift Kat drove home completely relaxed. She figured that if the creepy scary guy from the bushes was going to come back he would have done so by now, right? Kat was ready for a boring night in front of her TV after her busy shift at the hospital. She needed a peaceful night after seeing the man in camouflage and then having her car broken into.

Kat parked her car half a block down from her apartment building. The crisp air was refreshing against her skin as she walked to the door. Normally she parked in the apartment's underground parking structure but it was currently under construction. The temperature was in the thirties, which was pretty decent for February. It could be sub-zero weather right now and it wouldn't be out of the ordinary for this time of year.

She swiped her ID on the main entrance door panel. Once

again Kat felt a tingly sensation. It was the same one she had right before she saw the night stalker and then again when she was in the coffee house drive-thru.

She decided to ignore the feeling and proceed into the building up to her second story apartment. The building itself was Kensin's version of nice but cheaper living. There were four identical buildings like hers that ran along the complex property. Kat preferred the second story so she wouldn't hear footsteps above her while she slept. She slept for most of the daylight hours when the rest of the world was active. Not having to hear them stomp on their floor above her was a blessing. Her neighbors liked it too. Kat typically worked when they were home and it was relatively quiet during the night when they slept.

The steps leading up to her apartment were supported by a wrought iron framework and thick cement slabs which made up the actual steps. Kat could afford a house of her own but didn't want the responsibility of having a lawn to mow or trees to trim. So, apartment living was just right for her.

Going out in sunlight wasn't good for her skin. Kat could be out in the sun for only short periods of time, otherwise she ended up with severe sunburn no matter how much sun block she slathered on. It had been this way her entire life. Aunt Rose said she must have sunlight sensitivity from her father. Aunt Rose said she recalled Kat's father had the same problem, only worse. Aunt Rose told Kat she remembered her father not being able to go out in the sun at all.

Aunt Rose told Kat that her mom, Grace, was so in love with Kat's father, Eric, that she would have done anything for him. They were always together during the nighttime hours. Grace switched her schedule. She slept most of the day allowing her to spend time with him during the night. And her father's love for her mother was equally intense. Everyone who knew them thought they were a match made in heaven.

The two never bothered to get married. Kat's father's family would never allow it. He didn't care. Marriage didn't make his love for her mother any stronger. Aunt Rose said she remembered her father telling her mother that. He didn't care if he ever saw his family again, as long as he could be with Grace. Aunt Rose didn't know much about his family, just that they didn't like Kat's mom for some reason. His family felt the two of them shouldn't be together.

Viktor waited for Kat to get off of work at the hospital. He could never figure out what the allure was for people wanting to take care of the sick. Didn't they have enough problems of their own? Maybe that was it? Maybe they wanted to focus on someone else and be able to forget about themselves for a while? He understood dedication to a cause, him having his entire life focused on protecting others. But health care workers chose their profession, he didn't.

While waiting for Katrina to leave the hospital, Viktor wondered what he would have done with his life if he had not been born into his position of security for the royal family. He had many interests, but they tended to be somehow centered on the task at hand. Viktor loved martial arts, training, and being on a team with other men with his same interests. He didn't choose to be a member of the Council, it chose him.

When Katrina parked her car and got out, Viktor inhaled deeply. She had an unmistakable scent of lilies and something else. Never had he before smelled anything quite like her. At that moment he realized she wasn't completely human. He didn't know why after spending so much time with her in the car he hadn't noticed it before. Obviously, being anywhere near Kat muddled his thought processes. That thought caught him off guard, she wasn't human! But he couldn't place what he was sensing from her. He wasn't sure what else was in her blood. Viktor acknowledged he had a serious attraction to her, physically speaking of course, and somehow, much more.

Once he had her scent memorized, he de-materialized from his perch in the giant maple tree at the edge of her apartment building lot. He re-appeared in her apartment, drawn directly to it by her smell. Viktor quickly looked around, assessing the small but comfortable place this female called home. Finding out what the Hunters wanted with her was a priority, that's what he told himself. That was how he justified intruding on her personal space like he was. He knew the real reason. Staying away from her was becoming more and more difficult for him.

He stepped into the shadows of the living room given off by the giant book shelves lining the walls as her door opened. He saw her hesitate as she crossed the threshold. Viktor stopped breathing in anticipation. He wondered if she could sense his presence. She shrugged her slender shoulders once and closed the door behind her.

She dropped her belongings on a table close to the door, took off her coat, and went into the kitchen. As she closed the refrigerator door, he felt the cool breeze the movement gave off. Kat quickly turned and looked right at him. She looked directly into his eyes and froze. She must have sensed his presence!

Viktor noticed that she didn't move, it didn't look like she was breathing. He knew he had to say something, why was he hesitating? He knew why of course but didn't want to admit it to himself. He was so silenced by her breathtaking beauty. He didn't want to frighten her anymore than he already had. Not knowing what or who she was frustrated him deeply.

Viktor felt slightly put out because of his reaction to her. He was always in complete control of himself. He never wavered because someone of the opposite sex looked at him with interest. Not feeling completely in control because of a woman was definitely a new experience for him. He didn't like it. He always had the say whether he wanted to bother with a woman, not the other way around. And now this woman, Kat, had his uttermost attention. He yearned just to hear her talk. He felt vulnerable!

While entering her apartment, the feeling Kat had when she opened the main entrance churned in her chest and turned into one of great dread. Hesitating before stepping through her doorway, she gave into exhaustion and ignored the warning feeling coiled in the pit of her stomach. Kat closed her front door and dropped her keys into the shallow candy dish on the entranceway table her aunt had given her. As she walked into her apartment she looked around. Nothing was out of place. Kat put her trusty back pack, in which her entire life existed according to Visa and the local bank, onto the counter that separated her small kitchen and medium sized living room.

She opened the fridge and stuck her face in to find something to snack on. The dreadful feeling intensified as she began to smell a scent only to be described as pure male. She stood up and slammed the refrigerator door closed in one motion. She froze. There he was. He was the cause of her excited, erotic, and confused feelings. He was the reason why she couldn't sleep that morning.

He was just as gorgeous as she remembered, and dangerous looking. Kat sat there in her frozen state, unable to make a move in self defense. His hair was black with gentle waves that reached his collar. He wore a black blazer that hugged his extremely broad shoulders with a deep red button up shirt that was mostly left open, exposing parts of his very well defined, chiseled chest. Kat thought she caught part of an old tattoo of some sort. It looked like the edge of a wing or a blade. She couldn't quite make it out with what little of it she could see.

As her assessment continued downwards she saw that he wore black leather pants with black boots, the kind bikers wore. She liked what she saw. Her body reacted to his pure maleness. Biologically speaking, she was happy to have him here, in her apartment. She reminded herself he could be a murderer for all she knew, and all she could think of was his amazing physical attributes! Get a grip, Kat, she chastised herself.

"So, what do you want?" It was all she could think of saying. Yep, that's all she had. If he didn't have super hearing, he never would have heard her question.

Viktor liked her voice so much that he said "What?" Just to make her say it again.

She cleared her throat. Kat started to feel light headed and sick to her stomach. She said it again, this time a little louder and more firmly, "I said, what do you want?"

He stared at her. He knew what he wanted, and that was to sit there and look at her. He wanted to bathe in all her wonderful womanly qualities. Usually he was very charismatic and witty, always knowing the best things to say to women to get what he wanted. He could usually talk himself out of anything, doing things he wasn't supposed to be doing, being places he shouldn't be. At the moment he couldn't think of one brilliant thing to say.

After a long pause in silence, he decided the direct approach would be best. He asked her, "What are you?"

She looked at him now with sympathy in her eyes and he realized she thought he was ill, the head kind of ill. He decided further elaboration was needed so he said, "You know! What are you besides a vampire?" As her eyes got bigger after he said this, she gained the ability to move. She took one meaningful step towards him. He blocked her way out of the little kitchen. Viktor didn't want her to run away from him.

As Viktor moved, Kat decided she wasn't going to be the victim of this weirdo. She didn't care what his intentions were. He broke into her apartment, and for that, she was going to call the police. She took a full swing with her foot and connected with the only place on a man's body that would unquestionably paralyze him, at least long enough so she could get away. She regretted having to do that to him. Being a nurse meant that you had this unrelenting need to do no harm regardless of the circumstances. That included helping those that were mentally challenged such as this rare specimen. However, he was in her apartment uninvited, cornering her in her kitchen, and asking what type of supernatural being she was. He clearly had issues.

Maybe he was on some type of drug like the kid at work the other night was? Maybe there was a new drug that made a person hallucinate about the darker things in life, or un-life for that matter? These happenings were just way too close in time. There was definitely something weird going on. What she didn't get, or like, was the fact they seemed to keep happening around her.

While super hot, and possibly hallucinating, Viktor lay on her kitchen floor holding his just kicked parts, Kat leaped over him and into the living room of her apartment. She took a quick glance around, spotted her keys, coat, and purse, grabbed them, and dashed for the door. She took an extra moment to make sure her attacker, or whatever he was, was still lying on the floor. He was, but he was starting to get up. That made her move. She ran out into the hall, pressed the down button for the elevator, and decided the heck with it. She needed to get out of the building. She went to the staircase, heart pounding with fear, opened the stairway door, and descended.

CHAPTER 5

Viktor couldn't believe his luck, or lack-there-of. The woman kicked him so fast, he never saw it coming. Despite his suffering, he decided it wasn't a completely wasted trip. He did learn a few things about her. He also found out the Council had a big problem. He could tell from being so close to her in the little kitchen area that what he thought earlier as her being only part vampire was actually the scent of a royal vampire bloodline.

Kat gave off the smell of one of the oldest vampire bloodlines in existence. The intensity of her scent was strong enough for him to differentiate that she didn't come from an ordinary vampire family. She had to be royal blood! Besides her human and vampire blood, there was something else. Something he couldn't identify. Viktor recognized that Kat was made up of three parts. He just couldn't place the third.

Viktor wasn't sure which royal family she came from. From her scent, he could tell she belonged to one of them, he just didn't know which one. If he could, that would help him identify the age of her parents. He may even be able to figure out who her parents were. If her parents were alive she wouldn't be living alone unprotected like this. If Viktor had sensed her royal blood the night before he would have taken her straight to the mansion to keep her safe.

Could there possibly be a royal vampire family line that he wasn't aware of? That was highly unlikely, but if it looked like a duck. Viktor also figured out, yes all by himself, what the Hunters wanted with her. From the way she looked at him, and the way her scent came off so faintly in comparison to how the Caines gave off such an intense, almost palpable scent, she didn't have a clue what was really going on. She must not be twenty-five yet. But she must be close. Her ignorance was inconceivable to him! How could this have happened? Kat clearly had a royal vampire parent, but who was it? Her other parent must be only part human and part something else. That something else was what was throwing Viktor for a loop.

Vampires give off a specific scent, only detectable to other vampires and animals, like an identification tag. Most supernatural beings did. But he couldn't place the third essence that completed Kat's makeup. Viktor vowed he would find out what it was.

The older a vampire was, the more intense the scent became, not strong smelling, just intense. When vampires are younger than twenty-five, before their change, they give off a more innocent scent. Their scent was more like a hint of what was to come. The problem with this woman, and what confused him the first time he encountered her, was the complex mixture of scents she gave off.

The scent of each individual part she was made of masked and covered each other. Her scent was intense like royals, intoxicating his every breath. He couldn't get enough. That could be a sign of how powerful Kat would be once she underwent her change. When a young one hit twenty-five, they changed into a vampire and stopped aging. Their powers, what made them unique, would begin to develop. When royals were younger than twenty-five, because of their pure blood, their powers were so strong they tended to spill over before their change. People have been hurt because of it. Powers can be very difficult and complicated to control even after a vampire has gone through their change.

There was certainty that one of her parents was a royal, the other, something else entirely. Her scent intensity was of royal blood, but not directly related to any family he knew of, being there was only three. Or so he thought. Could there possibly be more still in existence? He knew he had to pull himself together, notify the team, and find her. She was in danger and she didn't know it. She was also capable of immense power she didn't know how to use or harness. Everyone around her was at risk. He was surprised all he got was a well placed kick to his you-know-what's. He counted himself lucky. Her potential for destruction on a grand scale was immense. Kat must not have been that ticked off. It was possible she had yet to tap into her inner powers. The second part of her half human parent may have had something to do with it.

Kat hit the parking lot running. Luckily she still had on her comfy work sneakers. Trembling, she headed straight for her car, jumped in, revved the engine, and sped off. Her heart raced. She realized the danger of the situation she was in. She couldn't go home because Viktor knew where she lived and was somehow able to break in. Aunt Rose would be sleeping. Kat didn't want to involve her in whatever was going on. She couldn't go to work. Viktor knew where that was too. She was afraid to go to the police. They would probably think she was the crazy one. There was no evidence of a forced entry in her apartment. There was no sign of a struggle. She even locked her door on the way out! Carmen. Carmen's house on the South side of town would be the perfect hideout. She was pretty sure Viktor wouldn't be able to follow her to her best friend's house.

Kat could hang out there and call in sick for a few days. No one would be the wiser. Carmen left early this morning and would be out of town for the next week. Kat had a key. She silently patted herself on the back for reacting in a time of panic by grabbing those keys. Carmen wouldn't mind if Kat made herself at home for just a little while. Not the best time to have her best friend out of town. Carmen had been summoned by dear old Dad. He insisted that she help entertain and manage the group of Ivy League men her father was hosting for mutual business interests.

Carmen felt obliged to go. Her father did help finance her lifestyle. Independently she didn't do too badly for herself. It was easy for Carmen to become involved in a few business adventures of her own, with the backing of her father, of course.

Carmen's house was located twenty-three miles south of Kat's apartment, close to the Illinois state line. Carmen lived in the rural area on the outskirts of the city border. Carmen's house had an indoor heated pool, a ten car garage, tool shed, and a beautiful cabana overlooking the lake. The whole property was located on twelve acres of wooded land that Carmen loved to keep more on the wild side.

Once he was able to stand up, Viktor paced in Kat's apartment while talking on his cell phone. "Dave, I'm telling you. We need to alert the field team to protect this woman from the Hunters." The feeling that he was going to vomit from her assault started to dissipate. He finished describing the details to Dave about the night's events. He already informed Dave of what transpired last night, with the Hunters almost nabbing her at the nightclub, having set up the break-in of her car.

It had taken Viktor a little longer than he would have liked to recover from her kick and he knew she was long gone by now. Where would she go?

"All right, Viktor. I've already put the call out; the team will meet at the mansion tonight when you get back. Do you have any idea where she might have gone? No? Well, since you're in the woman's apartment, do some digging, see what you can find out about her," David suggested to him.

Not knowing much about her and Viktor being the only one who had seen her in the flesh, finding her was going to be difficult. "I'll take a look around her apartment and see what I can come up with." Viktor said into the phone. "Then I'll meet up with you and the team. We have to make this quick, the Hunters could already be tailing her. I'm not sure if they know where she lives or not. My guess would be not. Otherwise they wouldn't have tried to grab her at such a public place as the club. I think that was just a bonus for them having coincidently been at the same place at the same time where she was." Viktor closed his cell phone and took a glance around the small apartment.

She wasn't the neatest person in the world he noticed. But she was definitely not a slob. The woman's dwelling was kept clean but not overly tidy. Viktor figured the desk in the living-room was a good place to start his search. He looked through the drawers for anything with local addresses on it. He hoped to find out more about her, where she hung out, what she was into. Ok, just a minute, he thought to himself. He was way too interested in her personally. It went beyond the need to protect his kind from the Hunters. He was definitely interested for baser, more primal reasons.

Viktor didn't know what it was about her. Vampires tended to believe in having only one mate, the equivalent of a human union but with absolute commitment and loyalty for life. There was no such thing as divorce in his world. His kind believed that you did not pick your mate. Everyone was born mated to someone. The biggest challenge was finding each other. When that happened, you both knew it.

Kat's reaction to him last night at the club and then again when he kissed her, he knew she felt it. He just had to figure out how he was going to explain all of this to her, and for him to accept what was happening himself. He wasn't exactly happy about it. Viktor knew he would someday want to find his mate, but didn't think it would happen anytime soon.

Viktor was the epitome of a bachelor, never really thinking that he would find his mate in a million years, again, literally. It was possible for the two persons of a mated pair not to speak the same language or be born in the same century. But when it happened, it happened. Most of the time there wasn't anything either of them could do about it, well, there was one thing. But that was pretty extreme.

Death to one or both mates was a pretty serious decision, one that Viktor wasn't even close to making. Heck, he still considered himself a teenager, regardless of how many centuries he had lived. The world was his playground, and he liked to play hard. He worked hard so he figured he deserved a little reward every now and then.

Viktor feared Kat may be that person to him. He wasn't ready for that type of ball and chain! He was only in his third century of life. Weren't people supposed to live a little before they were tied down to someone? He wasn't ready to have a perpetual nag for the rest of his life. Yet, there was an overwhelming need he couldn't get over. He needed to take care of her, protect her, and she didn't know anything about him. She had no idea what she was. This was definitely not going to be easy, for either of them. If she was indeed the one, and his instincts told him she was, they were both in for life changes they could never turn back from.

Kat was more calm now sitting in Carmen's comfy overstuffed recliner in the living room. She always felt like this was a second home. Carmen had a room set up specifically for Kat. They stayed at each other's homes frequently. Kat called the hospital and said she had the stomach flu and it looked like she would be out for a couple of days. That was as good an excuse as any. She never called in, so it was no big deal. She talked to her friend Brian, his response gave her the impression that he got the 'I'm taking a few mental health day's' vibe and told her well wishes and to not come in too soon. He was so sweet, she thought, too bad she wasn't attracted to him like she was the hunk of burning mental case back in her apartment.

Brian was a completely different story. He was more like a girlfriend to her. He was even up to date on all the latest fashions. He never made a pass at her. It was probably because he preferred men. That's what made their relationship easygoing and complete with no pressure. Kat had a few male friends but over time they usually stopped calling when she didn't return their interest or advances. They tended to lose interest and find women who would, thus ending their friendship with her.

Viktor, she thought. That was one face and body she could definitely get used to. The whole situation in her apartment went terribly wrong. But the times they spent together at the club and afterwards went great. Those thoughts kept creeping into her thoughts, trying hard to make it seem like somehow he was possibly a normal guy, or could at least be normal to some degree. Like there was even a chance they could have a relationship. He was clearly interested in her physically, as she was with him. But having a relationship with him was out of the question, he didn't seem all there in the mental department. So why did she keep thinking of him? Obviously visions of his fabulous body were trying to overrule her common sense. She should stay far away from that guy.

When he was in Kat's way, making it so she couldn't leave her apartment, she didn't feel like he wanted to hurt her. Instead, she felt a pull towards him. It felt like her molecules yearned to be coupled with his molecules, to put it into the simplest perspective. That was ridiculous. It was lust, plain and simple. She knew he wasn't a real threat to her, even though he was dangerous. He was built like a warrior, and obviously not intact northbound.

Unfortunately, that was the way her life went. She sure knew how to pick them. Out of the few men that sparked her interest he was the only one that consumed her thoughts. She almost didn't care how difficult it would be if she got involved with him. She would probably spend a lot of time visiting him at the loony bin. Surely that was where he was headed.

Kat went into the kitchen to get something to eat. Carmen

ate really well and was usually stocked with healthy food. Where to start, she tapped her finger on her chin eyeing up her options. The options were limited. Carmen didn't have much food because she wasn't going to be in town. She must have either gotten rid of all the perishables, or thrown them away. She could have given the food to her neighbor, the single mother Carmen liked to help out.

Kat groaned. She needed to go to the store. The thought of running into those guys again, either of them, scared her. Every time Viktor's image crossed her mind, her body physically reacted as if he was there in the room with her. That was a first, never before had a man done this to her. Especially since he broke into her apartment and then just stared at her like she had a big pimple on her nose. She never did find out what he was doing there, or what he wanted. The other man, the guy wearing camouflage at work, had her more worried. He would be a bigger threat to her than Viktor.

Carmen basically lived out in the middle of nowhere so Kat would have to drive a couple miles to the store. There wasn't much between the house and civilization. She never understood why her best friend, who loved to socialize, chose to live in such an out of the way place. Well, if I'm going to be holed up here for a while, I might as well hit the store, buy what a girl in hiding needed, and come right back here. Maybe even rent a few movies, seeing how she expected to be bored out of her mind. Kat planned to not leave Carmi's house again until she felt comfortable going home. Hiding out was her agenda for the next few days. She would have to go home sooner or later. She hoped Viktor would lose interest and not show up unannounced and uninvited again. That conflicting feeling hit her again. She wanted to see Viktor. She ached for him to kiss her again. But she knew he wasn't good for her, bad things tended to happen when he was around.

Staying here forever was not an option. Carmen was her most favorite person in the whole world. Kat didn't want to live with her. During their first year of college they gave that a try, and it didn't work out so well. Carmen liked to live the life of a socialite, and Kat was more a recluse, wanting to keep to herself with her odd sensibilities. Moving back in with Aunt Rose would put her aunt in danger. Kat didn't know what these men wanted from her or if they were connected. No, she would have to go back to her apartment in a few days. She could stay here until Carmen came back from her father's. Kat put her coat and shoes back on, grabbed her keys and purse, and headed for the side door close to where her car was parked.

CHAPTER 6

Kat climbed into her Mini. She put her foot on the break and reached for the ignition switch. It had definitely been a long day. When the mechanical things under the hood: gears, belts, and doodads did their job, the car was ready for travel. She put her foot on the brake once more with her right hand on the shifter. She looked up and screamed.

Another night stalker guy was standing in front of her car pointing a very deadly looking rifle at her through the front windshield. She envisioned that she probably had a red dot like you see in the movies on her chest or forehead. She slammed her fist onto the steering wheel honking the horn. She couldn't run him over, and the back of her car was parked up against Carmen's garage. She was stuck.

Kat's chest felt tight, like her ribs were squeezing her lungs tightly, she couldn't take another breath to scream again. Her heart felt like it pumped so hard and fast that she was going to pass out. Her ears rang, letting her know she was about to lose consciousness.

The other night when she had first seen super sneaky guy approaching her behind the hospital, she didn't have this kind of response. It was because Viktor was there. She was petrified. Carmen's house was out in the middle of nowhere. There wasn't anyone close by. If she screamed again, there wouldn't be anyone to hear her.

Having a gun pointed at her made her senses and ability to think straight to stop functioning. She watched a lot of movies. She always thought she would be able to react in a situation like this. Laura Croft from Tomb Raider wouldn't take this lying down. She would say something witty and disarm the man of his weapon. She would make him look like an utter fool. Well, Kat obviously wasn't Laura Croft, and her freezing from fear wasn't going to help her one bit.

As far as Kat could tell, this wasn't the same soldier guy from the other night, their physiques were different. This one wasn't as large as the one at the hospital. This one seemed more on the slim side, but he was carrying an equally effective arsenal of weapons. Some were hanging from his vest while others were strapped to his legs. It definitely was not Viktor. She was sure of that.

So now she had three fruitcakes after her? Were they related? Great, just great! She always wanted a fan club, but never thought she would get one. Ha, she realized as the internal dialogue in her head stopped, she must be losing it. That had to be the answer.

She was going to sit in her car, close her eyes, and weird guy number three, whom she figured she was imagining, would poof away. Then she could be on her way to the store. She would splurge on the fattening goodies she tried to stay away from. Well tonight was her night and she was going to get everything that caught her fancy.

She tipped her head back, closed her eyes, and took another deep breath. There was a loud thump and then she heard someone grimacing in pain. She lowered her head back down and reluctantly opened her eyes knowing that whatever she was about to see, she wasn't going to like. Yep, sure enough, she was right. Viktor had appeared. He was now wrestling with the new creepy arrival. Kat sat in her car and watched. Now that Viktor was here she felt a lot calmer, he was like watching a piece of artwork in motion.

The hard planes of his body, clearly seen through his tight clothing, were quite impressive. Viktor gained control over the man who had his gun pointed at her. When Viktor was done wrestling with the man, having one knee on the man's chest, he secured the man's hands and looked straight at her. Her instincts that had told her he was dangerous were now verified in visual form. Despite his amazing good looks and body, his eyes were now black and his eye teeth were overly long. Kat was sure those amazingly long teeth were something she would have noticed about him before, especially since he kissed her. That amazingly exquisite kiss!

Kat hoped she was hallucinating. Unfortunately what she

was seeing in front of her wasn't developed from her overly tired imagination. Acknowledging hallucinations from exhaustion would have been easier to handle than the reality of having two men fighting in front of her car. This was definitely a problem. Her heart started to beat again. It had stopped when Viktor looked up at her. Her heart felt like it was slamming up against her chest wall and again it was becoming harder to breathe. She put her foot back on the brake pedal and grabbed the shifter.

Knowing without a doubt, Kat had to get out of there. These men wanted her for something! She just didn't know what. And she wouldn't be delivered like a lamb to a slaughter. If they wanted her, they would have to come and get her. Maybe she had a little Laura in her after all? Before she could slide the shifter into the drive position, Viktor plowed his arm through the driver's side window. He wrapped his hand around her neck. She was surprised that his hold wasn't so tight that it hurt, he only held her in place in his iron grasp. He began to separate the window glass he just shattered from the door frame.

Viktor looked down at Kat, holding her in place. His groin instantly became painfully tight, just from looking at her! His manhood was immediately engorged and demanded to be set free of his restrictive clothing. He was aware of their surrounding danger but his body didn't care. He must get her to safety. He knew she would fight him tooth and nail in the process. He took a deep breath and pulled her car door open. He realized that he would have to make sure her car window is fixed again.

Next, he grabbed her with his other hand at her pant's waist band to prevent her escape. He kept her close also to prevent her from attacking him in such an evil manner as she did back in her apartment. He still had a hard time dealing with the fact that anyone could harm him like that. She had in fact been the first. He had the feeling she was going to be the person that would provide many firsts for him, even though he was over three hundred years old. He wasn't sure if he liked that or not. She was going to complicate his life in many ways, no matter who she was, no matter what blood she carried in her veins. The fact was he couldn't be without her. It didn't matter if she felt the same way about him, but he had a feeling she did.

Viktor pulled Kat completely out of the car and began to step away from it. She didn't fight him on the way out. "Hello, what the hell do you think you're doing with me? And who do you think you are grabbing my pants like this?" Kat swatted at his hand none too gently. Viktor looked at her with intrigue and something else, possibly annoyance. She wasn't going anywhere with him without a fight!

Why wasn't she following his every command? Viktor pondered on this, he had a bad feeling that fun fact was going to cause him more problems in the future than he already anticipated. Only certain individuals could withstand his power of suggestion, and they definitely were not human. Most vampires he knew he could control with the merest of thoughts. He was perplexed with her background. Viktor couldn't figure it out. He knew the majority of the vampires in the area. She said she lived here all her life. If she had been beyond her change, instead of right before it, he would have been able to sense her presence from a mile away. The power she was already giving off before her change was that strong.

He noticed power emanated from her like she was wearing a jacket that anyone could see, and not just vampires. An aura that said 'don't mess with me, I'm badder than bad'. But none-the-less, he had her in his arms and he wasn't willing to let her go, ever!

Viktor decided the direct approach, or the closest he could get to it, would be the best way to handle her. "We both need to get out of here because there are people trying to kidnap you. You need to trust me!"

"Yeah, famous last words to the girl who goes with the wrong guy. Don't you ever watch late night television? How do I know that you aren't the bad guy?" Kat questioned him in disbelief.

"Listen, we don't have a lot of time. Trust your instincts. When you are with me, do you feel calm set in? There's a reason for that and you have to trust me for now, ok?" He stared at her for what seemed an eternity.

He was right, she did feel better when he was around, she wasn't sure why. It was one of those things that you knew to be true but didn't want to put too much thought in it. Kat figured it had something to do with the insatiable attraction she had for him, who now held her in his arms pressing the entire length of her body against his unyielding muscles. His firm body pressing against hers wasn't helping her resolve to get away from him. It was really hard for her not to press her body even closer to his.

When that guy in the sneaky gear was pointing a gun at her, Kat had become immobile, unable to breathe or think. When she saw Viktor, she instantly felt better, safer. It hadn't registered in her conscience until now. Now when she was standing there in his arms, she became all too aware of how content she felt. Way to go Kat, no worries about self preservation or anything, focus on getting laid instead.

Kat took a deep breath. She decided to tell him he had her ear. She would listen to what he had to tell her about the other guys. Then she would be on her way, alone.

Viktor looked abruptly away from her towards Carmen's house. All of a sudden there was an explosion that came from the direction in which Viktor was looking. Kat swung her head toward the awful noise and the great amount of pressure they felt at the same time they heard the explosion. The area of the house where there used to be a kitchen was nothing but a big ball of smoke and flames.

"Now do you understand? We have to get out of here. The Hunters must have been watching you. They must still be in the area, more always come. There's never just one. Since I'm the only one here on the good side, you're coming with me, now!"

Viktor was becoming more impatient. He knew the longer they stayed the more danger they both were in. With Hunters having blown up Kat's friend's house, it was made clear to him that she was important to them. He didn't understand their tactic by blowing up part of the house, and he didn't care. Were they trying to hurt her? Were they trying to flush her out? Or were they sending a message to him, since they probably figured out by now that he was the one interfering on their plans? There was a lot going on around this woman, and he was going to do whatever it took to find out what Malice wanted with her.

Malice had to be behind all of the attention and effort she was getting from the Hunters. The soldiers didn't do anything without direct guidance and orders from their leader, so they were told to do this. Unless Malice gave them full reign to apprehend her using any means necessary. Hunter soldiers tended to take that literally, as in, they could do whatever they wanted, just as long as they got the job done.

"Wait just a minute, who are you guys?" Kat asked. "What do you want with me? I didn't do anything to any of you, and now you go and blow up my friends' house? I'm not going anywhere with you!" she said exasperatedly while trying to free herself from his grasp.

"Listen, I'm not with those guys. They are called Hunters

and they want something from you. I'm here to help get you out of trouble and find out what they want. So, if you want to stay here and be jumped by a group of Hunters, we can continue to stand here. You'd better be sure that's what you want, because if we sit here, they'll shoot me in the head and they'll kidnap you. And trust me, Katrina. You won't like it when they get their slimy hands on you. If not, then I'd say we'd best be on our way." He wasn't going to take no for an answer this time, normally he didn't transport anyone, not even vampires, but he didn't see any other option at this point.

Viktor quickly put both hands around her hips, pulled her close, and transported them out from being in the open at her friend's house. He had some explaining to do. He knew at the mansion there would be too many distractions, including his brother Grailen, his best friend, babysitter, and co-Councilman Dave, and any other Council members who happened to be there.

He picked a spot on the grounds of the mansion close to the lake to reappear with Kat in tow. The estate was heavily guarded by armed Council members so he figured this was the best place to bring her. The danger level would be lower, the atmosphere would be better. Oh, who was he kidding! He didn't want to bring her inside the mansion because once she was there, the Council members weren't going to let her leave anytime soon, nor were they going to let him have much quality time with her once they figured out who she was. He still wasn't quite sure he wanted to know himself, but he knew that it was her bloodline that was making her so attractive to the Hunters. He wasn't exactly sure what she had for a bloodline, they would all find out soon enough, he was sure of that.

"Tell me your name, your full name," he said. He already knew from the night before, but he hoped maybe she had a middle name he didn't know about. Usually names of royal family members hinted of their origins. His name, Viktor, came from one of his father's right hand vampires who helped rule the Council with an iron fist. He died an honorable death protecting his father during one of the earlier battles between the Council and the Hunters.

Kat looked up at him and tried to envision what she had seen earlier that evening at Carmen's house. He no longer had pure black eyes; they were more of a deep set mixture between brown and hazel. When he looked at her, she could tell there was something in his gaze. She had always been able to get a sense of emotion from others. It was like they projected their feelings at her. He was different. She did get a sense of feeling from him, but it wasn't the clear cut obvious waves of information she usually got from those around her. It was more like a subtle hint he gave off. Right now, looking into those eyes, it was obvious he felt something for her. His feelings were growing for her by the minute. Similar to the feelings she had for him.

Viktor must have drugged her. That was the only rationale explanation for how she had left Carmen's driveway and ended up here, where ever 'here' was. She didn't want to think about her friend's house and the damage that was caused because she decided to use it as her hideout. That churning, painful feeling in the pit of her stomach wouldn't go away. Kat would never be able to pay back all the money it was going to cost to have Carmen's house repaired. Great, Viktor stalked, kidnapped, and drugged her, and now she was somewhere she had never been. For all she knew, she could be in a different state.

CHAPTER 7

During her life, Kat had the occasional glimpse of men she found attractive, but never had it been on the same level as with Viktor. Even though she thought he was on the mentally ill train heading straight for a psychiatric ward, Kat found herself entranced with him. It was more like a bond, and every minute she spent with him, she felt that bond grow stronger despite her not knowing him at all.

To top it all off, he kidnapped her, or was it that he saved her from that armed commando guy? Kat wasn't sure of anything right now. She knew Viktor wasn't going to harm her, at least not for the moment. She thought now was the time to take advantage of his Mr. Chit Chatty mood and find out what the hell was going on.

"Kat, or Katrina, is my name. Now that I answered your question Mr. Secret Man, mind telling me exactly why you decided to stalk me, show up in, emphasizing on, in my apartment, following me to my friend's house, blowing it up, and then kidnapping me all the way here? Which I still don't even know where here is?" She stood there in the light of the almost full moon, waiting.

She thought she felt amazingly clear headed for someone who had just been put into a drugged haze and moved from one place to another. Wherever she was, it had to be some distance from her home city. She could see what she was pretty sure was Lake Michigan. So it couldn't be too far away. She crossed her arms, thinking she was glad she had her coat. As the night progressed, the air seemed to be getting colder by the minute. After her speech, Kat stared at him, waiting for a smidgen of information he would give to help her out of this peculiar predicament she found herself in.

"Well," Viktor said, "Again, my name is Viktor. Viktor Vasilkov, not Mr. Secret Man. There is a lot going on and I have a bad feeling you have no idea what you're in for. So, we'll start at the beginning and try to figure out how the Hunters found you and why they're after you."

"I still don't understand. Why would anyone be after me for anything? I never did anything to anyone!" Kat hollered at him.

"The Hunters usually don't send their top operatives to claim a woman. They usually start off with small potato guys and send a couple, that's what worries me. They don't see you as small potatoes, Kat," at that last remark, he quickly replied, "No offense, of course."

"None taken. Go on, explain yourself," she said. She was getting more and more pissed off by the second. It seemed whenever Viktor was around, bad things happen.

"First, tell me what you know of our people, and any holes that you may have, I'll try and fill in as best I can."

"What exactly do you mean by 'our people'? So you're telling me there are more of you, what are you, like a fraternity or something?" Kat asked.

With that omission he knew this was going to take longer than he thought. Back at that house she tried to hide in, when she saw him in full vamp face, her surprised look tipped him off. Kat didn't know any more about herself than an every day regular human on the street did. Viktor couldn't figure out how she survived in Kensin without being detected by either the Council or the Hunters before now.

Kat wasn't going to give him any more personal information than he already had. For all she knew, he already knew everything about her. The realization was setting in that this freak may have been watching her for who knew how long. He knew where she worked, where she lived, and where her best friend's house was. What the hell else did he know about her? Did he know about Aunt Rose? Was there people watching her too? She had to get out of there and warn Aunt Rose. The woman meant everything to Kat.

"Yes. I mean no, we aren't exactly a fraternity. We are more like a big happy dysfunctional family. This is going to be really hard for you to understand, I know what I'm going to tell you is going to sound crazy, like those movies I saw next to your TV."

When he mentioned that he was in her apartment she began to shiver. Not because she was cold, but reality of the situation sat heavier and heavier on her chest. Her blood felt like it was running colder in her veins, and she was starting to freak out. Kat was proud of herself. For all that she had been through it had taken this long for her to start breaking down. Kat felt like she was going to suffer a major panic attack.

Viktor sensed Kat's, he liked her full name Katrina better, emotions were starting to roll out of control again. He gave her a mental push to relax, to find inner calm. When his mind met hers, he found himself again impressed with her mental strength even though she had not reached her time yet.

Kat looked at Viktor when he did it. She wasn't sure what he was doing, but she knew it was him trying to get inside her head. From the angry expression on her face, she didn't like that at all.

Just then, they both turned at the sound of a tree branch breaking, announcing the arrival of someone else. This someone obviously was not trying to hide themselves, and for that, Kat was grateful. Lately, those that meant her harm approached her on the sneaky side with some type of weapon aimed at her.

"Viktor, what the hell are you doing?" Dave said. Viktor looked at him with a menacing glare. He knew Dave understood Kat was the woman he mentioned to the Council. Viktor also knew he was going to get shit for bringing her here to the mansion without discussing it, no matter who she was. Viktor respected Dave and his opinions, but not in this situation. Dave didn't have the capability to sense what it was to sense about Katrina. Her name felt good even in his mind. What the hell was going on with him anyways? He'd have to figure that out later. For now, they had bigger fish to fry.

Viktor looked at Kat, who was now assessing her escape options and grabbed her by the arm. "Dave, let's take Kat into the mansion, get her settled in, and we'll all have a big long chat, ok?" She swung her head to look straight into his eyes, frowning. He no longer saw fear in them that was there earlier; he saw anger beginning to take hold.

Viktor knew she didn't understand the mansion was the safest place for her. It was going to be a while before she had full understanding of what was going on. She had a major part in a war between vampires and human extremists who were trying to destroy all the vampires on the planet.

"Get your hand off me," Kat gritted through her teeth. Viktor looked at her with such intensity she took a step backwards.

"Listen Katrina, my patience is wearing thin. You aren't going anywhere. You're going to come to the mansion with us and we are going to settle this together. I understand you don't get what's going on, but you will. So let's go." Viktor took a step towards the path leading away from the beautiful view of the lake and up towards the mansion.

Dave turned around and started back up the path ahead of Viktor. Dave's shoulders slumped, knowing this was indeed going to be a very long and eventful evening. He had already called the Council operations team and they were on their way to the mansion. He didn't want to bring up that fact in front of Viktor's unwilling guest. It might make the situation worse than it already appeared. This young lady didn't know anything about who she was, and for that, Dave felt bad for her, and Viktor too. Dave had never seen his friend so enthralled by a woman before.

Kat's anxiety returned. The moment Viktor's grasp on her arm loosened, she took advantage of his lapse in judgment. She bolted backwards escaping his arm's reach when he went to readjust his grip. She ran down the path from where they came and slammed right into a tree. When she recovered from the recoil of falling on her backside, she looked up in astonishment. Viktor was her tree. She slammed right into him. But that was impossible! She had gotten away and ran down the path for what had to have been at least twenty seconds. And then there he was, right in front of her. He wasn't even breathing heavy like she was. He was all Mr. Relaxation.

The impact gave her the opportunity to feel the hard length of his body again, nothing but chiseled planes and massive muscles. Her physical draw to him was driving her crazy. She needed to get the hell away from him. Yet, she couldn't stop fantasizing about taking his clothes off, slowly, and then him grabbing her and throwing her roughly on the bed and making passionate love to her. Where the heck were these thoughts coming from anyways?

Except for the slightest trace of irritation on his face, Kat couldn't sense any emotion from him. That was odd; before he gave off a glimmer at least. Throughout her entire life she had a little bit of an edge. She had the ability to sense other's moods and sometimes their intentions. With Viktor it was different. He was like a void unless he chose to be otherwise. Besides the obvious body cues, she couldn't read anything from him at all. She silently panicked. She realized their attraction for each other may have been the reason she could sense something coming from him earlier. Her feelings could have given his a boost. Maybe it was only wishful thinking on her part, wanting Viktor to feel the same way she did? The unusual attraction she had for him and the connection she felt towards him made her feel vulnerable and uncomfortable.

Viktor reached down and picked Kat up from under her arm. She was about to step away from him when he picked her up completely off the ground. He looked at Dave and said, "Meet me inside."

Kat figured she must have blacked out again because she didn't remember the walk into the house, or mansion, or whatever the hell she was in. She didn't feel good. Her stomach felt like it was boiling from the stress.

Viktor looked at Kat. He could tell transporting hit her harder than before. She looked a little green. He turned to a cabinet in his bedroom used for supplies. He grabbed what he needed and made an old concoction used for centuries to quiet a queasy stomach. The shifting of space and time, that was what transportation was, always did a number on new vampires.

He turned around to find Kat lying on his bed where he left her. She had her head hanging off the side, pointing towards the floor. He didn't want her to get sick on his carpet. Bodily dysfunctions grossed him out. Having been born and guided through his life to be a vampire, he didn't have to deal with normal human functions like she must have. That was another reason he couldn't fathom why Kat decided to make the career choice to deal with that sort of thing all of the time.

He walked over to her, lifted her hair away from her face and told her to sit up. She did without complaint, which surprised him. Kat sat at the edge of the bed with her head hanging low. He noticed she was trying to keep it together and not vomit. Taking her cold clammy hand in his, he put the special blend of herbs mixed with carbonated water into her grasp.

While mixing up the brew, he put a tad extra of an ingredient into the mix to help her relax. She would probably be pissed off at him if she knew, but he figured she wasn't in any condition to complain. That would probably come later.

She took the glass without thinking of the contents and what they might be. Her mouth felt dry. Kat took a big swig from the glass. After a minute of silence, she looked up at her captor to find him staring directly into her eyes.

"Feel better?" Viktor knew the affects were almost instantaneous when they worked, and he was glad to see they were indeed working.

Kat nodded. "So, let's get this straight, Viktor. I'm being held captive against my will, right? I can't leave if I want to?" she asked while looking him dead in the eye.

Viktor took an aggressive step towards her in frustration, "Katrina, there is a lot we need to go over, there's much you don't understand including the fact if you were to leave you might die. You would be in a lot of danger. You'd probably find your pretty little butt in a cell, being poked at, tortured, and experimented on!"

Kat sat back, realizing Viktor was losing his temper. She wasn't sure how far she felt like pushing him.

"Those men that were after you earlier, they're not normal people. They mean you great harm. Trust me Katrina. You wouldn't like what they do to people when they catch them." Thinking of his own experiences, Viktor involuntarily shuddered.

Over the centuries, Viktor had rescued many captive vampires from Hunter jail cells. It had been after the Hunters had done their handiwork on them. Viktor remembered when he was captured and put in a Hunter's cell himself. He would kill them before that happened again. Flashbacks of his liver, pancreas, and spleen being removed from his body while conscious but paralyzed chilled him to the core. Viktor had felt every swipe of the Hunter's scalpels, every time they used a tool to cauterize his bleeding vessels. The sadistic bastards wanted to gauge his response to their manipulation of his vital organs. He never lost consciousness.

Viktor wasn't sure which would be worse. Punishment by King Alexander's demon assassins, the Judges, would be frightening. Or to be back in the clutches of Malice and his Hunters, which he already suffered nightmares from. Neither option appealed to him.

He blinked the nightmarish memories away and once more looked at his woman. "Katrina, you are not held captive here, but no, you will not be leaving the mansion anytime soon."

"Viktor, I can't be kept here like a caged animal! I have a job, people will start looking for me," Kat said with exasperation.

"I know that sounds harsh but you have to understand. The Council only wants to protect you and help you. You are going to go through things no one should have to go through alone. That is where we come in." He kept his stare level with hers while he spoke.

Viktor didn't want her to see or even sense his attraction to her or the strong pull her body had on his. That was a complication he would have to deal with later. They both would. Clarifying who she was, what family she belonged to, and what that third essence he sensed coming from her was their priorities. His wants and needs, for now, had to be put on the backburner.

His attraction to her was ticking him off to no end. Viktor wasn't ready to be tied down. He was not ready for that type of life. He was a man's man. He hadn't been looking for a mate yet, had he? Well, he wasn't ready to have one. Not right now. Viktor knew it was beyond his choice, the fates had chosen for him.

Kat belonged to him just as much as he belonged to her. There was nothing either of them could do about it. He felt the pull between them, just like his parents described to him when he was young. The sensation was unlike anything he experienced before. His family members had talked about it, how wonderful it was to find your other half. No one had bothered to tell him how awful it could be too, feeling an all consuming need to protect someone to the point of insanity. To have problems focusing because he couldn't tell what his mate was doing every second he wasn't with her. The need to protect the royal family was different. They were no longer his number one priority. The need to ensure her safety and happiness was now imprinted in his genetic makeup and it was throwing him off balance psychologically.

Viktor looked up to the ceiling of his bedroom and took a deep breath. It was unclear to him the best way to explain to her the details of her situation. He didn't want to cause her too much panic, fear, and distrust.

He lowered his head back to where she now sat on his bed and in that small space of time, he figured it out. Viktor knew it was going to piss her off, but he also knew it was going to be the surest way she would have the best understanding he could give her. He was going to bite her! He would let her know of course, you don't just go biting people without their knowing what you were going to do. Yes, smart thinking, right? Probably not!

Common vampires weren't allowed to drink royal blood without direct invitation. No one knew she was a royal yet, so he wouldn't be punished too harshly, right? With that self declaration of what he was going to do, he realized the quicker he went through with it, the better off both of them would be. He would not only sate his growing hunger only she could satisfy, her blood would help him regain focus. Focus he seemed to be losing by the minute, most likely because Kat was being so damned difficult and causing him stress he didn't need.

Drinking her blood would give him a better picture of her past. Her blood would contain images of her life, where she came from, and possibly who her parents were. One of the advantages of being a bloodsucker was whoever you fed from, you always got a little bit of whom it was you were biting. During the intimate encounter, vampires consumed both the donor's blood and highlights from their past.

Viktor sat down on his bed next to Kat, his thigh brushing

against hers. "Ok, I know this is going to sound beyond wild, but there is something that we could do to make this a lot clearer to you."

Kat looked at him as if he now had purple skin and tentacles on his head topped off with a second pair of eyeballs.

"You have to trust me Katrina, I mean really trust me. I know what you have been through makes that hard. I get that. But you just have to trust me. You are not going to like what I am about to do, but it is for the best," Viktor said as he began to move towards her in an overly slow motion.

Kat's eyes widened showing him that she did not approve of anything he was going to do to her. Taking her by surprise was the only way this was going to work. She was too mistrusting of everyone right now. Kat didn't believe a word he said when he told her what he was going to do and that it would all work out in the end.

Viktor knew it was now or never and leapt towards her, pushing her shoulders back down onto the black silk comforter of his bed while exposing her neck in one fluid motion. As he moved, he felt the knowing ache in his gums and his teeth descended in anticipation, ready to puncture her tender skin covering her jugular. He slowed down when the tips of his fangs felt resistance, savoring the moment. Kat tensed and let out a short scream before he sunk his fangs into heaven.

As his teeth pierced through her skin on the right side of her neck and into the vessel he felt like he was going to have a heart attack, or an orgasm. He wasn't sure which would come first. The experience was more than he bargained for. It was an unidentifiable mix between pleasure and pain. Viktor had given her a mental push to make her calm and relaxed as soon as her blood hit his tongue but this was almost too much for him to bear.

Viktor knew the moment her blood was absorbed into his system. Without any doubt, Kat was meant to be with him as his bond mate. He just became locked to another being for the rest of eternity, for better or worse, or however the saying went. Her blood was made for him, the absolute perfect mixture of elements that made up her genetic makeup. He would never be satisfied by anyone else. She was simply made for him. She just didn't know it yet.

When he bit her, he didn't take a lot of blood, just enough to get information he needed and to prove to her that he was a vampire. When he was done, he let her have a glimpse of his shiny, bloody, and extended eye teeth before he got off of her, letting her sit up. Just in time too. She took a swing towards his skull and missed. Viktor stepped out of the way with barely a thought. He was still a bit shocked from what he learned from her blood.

CHAPTER 8

With Kat having no reference to her history, explaining that she belonged to a race she didn't know existed, was going be difficult. Viktor was more than willing to hold her prisoner if needed. She had to understand the full scope of her situation. It was going to be a bumpy ride for both of them. Now that he knew more about her, a lot more, he wasn't going to let her go anywhere. If Hunters got a hold of her, they may actually find what they were looking for. Viktor didn't know exactly what that was, and he didn't want to know. He had thought her lineage extinct after her father disappeared twenty-four years ago. Now, he had to wonder. Was she the missing link to Malice's plans?

Now that he consumed her blood Viktor had more questions than answers. It was still unclear why no one knew she existed before now. Somehow, Katrina survived by herself. She remained undetected from both the Council and the Hunters. Someone had to know. Someone had to guide her through life. Could her

Aunt Rose have been the one to keep her a secret and never told her?

Viktor couldn't imagine a vampire fledgling being able to survive alone for so long. Kat lived unbothered her entire life. Miraculously, not one anti-vampire organization stumbled upon her. It wasn't surprising the Hunters were the ones who found her. Hunters were vampire's biggest threat. They were organized, had large resource supplies, and were the most successful at apprehending vampires. Viktor included.

Not knowing that she was going to change into a vampire, Kat had somehow flown under the radar of the entire Hunter community. Everywhere the royal family went there was always a Hunter following them, waiting for their chance to capture them. Malice getting his hands on a royal vampire once every hundred years was too often in Viktor's book. Since Viktor became the head of the royal family's security force, no one had been taken that he was aware of.

When Viktor took Katrina's blood, he had more control over her thoughts, being in such an intimate position. Viktor decided to start the bonding process. He let some of his memories, very specific and hand selected memories, flow into her mind. He did this so she could start to have an understanding. He showed her his past including images of his father and brothers. He showed her part of his own change, what he went through when he turned twenty-five. Not the painful part that seemed to last a lifetime. He decided to leave that part out. He showed her the physiological changes that he went through, the abilities that he gained, and the trial and error he went through to develop his skills over the centuries.

The ceremony his family held when one of their own successfully passed through their change was one of his fondest memories. He showed her memories that were not his, but those of his father and other family members passed on to him. He shared what he knew of the ancients, but not their locations. The many wars that occurred between the vampires and the humans have been bloody and never ending. He showed her the fall of Cade Reskin, the vampire who preceded King Alexander Caine. When Cade Reskin was slain, Alexander became the leader of America's vampires. He was the eldest of their kind within his royal family. He ruled with an iron fist to ensure the survival of all royal family members. The king's army, The Royal Army Soldiers, or RAS, gladly sacrificed their lives to protect those with the oldest and purest of blood.

At the last second, Viktor decided to show Kat the time when his father met his mother. How his father knew instantly that she was his. They belonged to each other united by a bond so deep beyond the mental or physical bond humans had as they became one in marriage. It was Viktor's way of forewarning her. He wanted her to know what was to come between the two of them. He wanted her to accept that she was cosmically bonded for all time to him, the sooner the better.

Viktor needed to convince her that she was part of a powerful community, that she was a royal vampire. Kat needed to understand what was going to happen to her as she came closer to her change, what was between the two of them, and why she couldn't leave the safety of the mansion. Once the Council found out who she really was, they would treat her like the long lost princess she was, a descendant of one of the purest blood lines known to vampire kind.

Viktor knew beyond any doubt completing the bond between them would cause major problems for both of them. When the High Council, comprised of; the king, some of his family members, close advisors, and his Judges, realized that one of their royal family members had been missing all these years, they would swoop in and take her away to the palace. Her life would be so different from what she was used to. She would never be able to go anywhere outside of their compound alone again.

Royal family members were bound to do the bidding of the king. They weren't allowed to socialize with humans. Viktor knew that was going to piss Kat off. The human woman, Carmen, was obviously important to Kat. As was her Aunt Rose. He could gauge her love for them when she talked about them. Kat's attachment to them was going to add to the complicated situation when the king told her she could never see them again.

He knew he had to do it, to take her to the palace in the next few days before her change began. He almost felt sorry for her, in a way. Her entire life was going to change forever. The freedom she had her entire life would be gone. She would always live in fear that someone was following her, trying to kidnap or kill her. He would make sure that never happened, and he would try to make the transition to her new life as painless as he could.

Making the king mad was never a good idea. The king made that clear on many occasions. He wasn't above letting his Judges have their way with a vampire who wouldn't behave. Viktor had the feeling the king was going to have his hands full with Kat, and so was he.

Judges, the king's band of demon body guards came in handy through the years. Just the threat of them hunting vampires down and punishing or executing them was enough to keep most blood drinkers in check. Unfortunately, there were a few who pushed the limit, going against the king's laws of survival. A few had been dealt the punishment of death for their actions, but not before the demons had their way with them. Each demon had different abilities and torture preferences. The Judges were very unique, very dangerous, and very scary. Viktor had only met one, Asher. He was a black demon with eyes like red lava, razor sharp teeth, and a nasty personality to match.

The compound, or palace, that he would take Kat to was a very nice place, for a golden prison. The king did a great job to make it a nice place to hang out for his snot nosed kids and their cousins. The only thing the king couldn't give them was their freedom. The king considered their safety his utmost priority.

Viktor knew Kat's every move would be dictated by her elders. She would be very powerful when she went through her change and it would be beneficial to have her cooperation before that happened to ensure the safety of herself, the Council, and anyone else around. When reality set in, the proverbial shit was going to hit the fan.

As he pulled away from her, having just experienced the most pleasurable bite of his life, Viktor didn't expect Kat to do what she did. As her fist whooshed by his perfectly angled jaw bone, he realized she may not have enjoyed the experience as much as he did.

On her second attempt, her other fist landed right where she had aimed, with everything she had. "What the hell is the matter with you? What did you give me? Making me hallucinate with all that horror movie freak show shit? And you bit me! Weirdo!"

Kat lost her cool demeanor. She never swore unless something bad happened that she didn't have control over. Perfect example, not so hot anymore freak guy here just bit her. That would make anyone swear in her mind. What was with all the vampire lore and eternal bonding crap? She definitely had to get out of here, that was all there was to it.

Kat turned toward what she assumed was the main door of the bedroom. She took one look back at Viktor, making sure he was still suffering from what was her second nicely landed attack and squeaked in horror. Viktor was standing in front of her, holding his jaw in his palm. He looked angry. He obviously wasn't happy about being knocked senseless by a girl, twice now.

Viktor felt like he was breathing fire when he returned to his position before she hit him. How dare she assault him, he didn't care who the hell she was, even if she didn't know it yet. No one gets away with that. No one! He decided to make sure that it was official, that she would spend the rest of her existence making it up to him. He, in that moment, decided that he was more than ready to declare their bond. The reasoning behind it might not be undying devotion for the moment. A mixture of obsession, anger, the possibility of her being with anyone else, and something he assumed was love would do nicely for now. Once he did this, there was nothing she or anyone else could do to unbind them. Even the High Council, led by the king himself, would have to kill him to break the bond. The likelihood of that was pretty low. Killing him would doom her to a very empty and miserable life, if she chose to live at all.

The High Council tried in the past to unbind a bonded pair. They were deeply in love and bonded without the High Council's consent. The High Council didn't like royal blood mixed with that of the more common persuasion. They weren't quiet about it either. During King Reskin's reign, a vampire prince bonded with a human and the High Council didn't approve. They contracted a warlock to undo the pair's bond. The attempt resulted in the human female's death, and the prince went feral. He could no longer recognize anyone. All he saw was blood sources. The prince exacted justice for what the High Council did, he drained his parent's blood, leaving them for death. The prince was inconsolable and heartbroken. King Reskin was forced to order punishment of death by a Judge. The Judge had left him in the sun to die by incineration from the inside out.

With fury in Viktor's mind and vengeance in his heart,

he grabbed Kat's wrists and pulled her close. She immediately struggled against his hold, but his grip was like a steel shackle. She didn't stand a chance of getting away from him, not unless he wanted her to.

Viktor looked straight into her eyes, making her unable to look away. "I hereby make you mine in all ways, forever. I hereby give myself to you in all ways, forever." The bond was complete. He sealed the deal by grabbing her head in between his hands. Viktor nicked his tongue with his eye tooth and crushed his lips to hers. He opened his mouth, making Kat open hers. He plunged his tongue deep into her warmness and let the droplets of blood swelling at the tip of his tongue soak into her taste-buds. He knew he would have the same affect on her that she did on him. She would feel the same exquisite bliss. Kat may not acknowledge what he did as binding because she wasn't raised that way. Viktor knew she would feel it though. Neither of them was able to sever the deep connection between them.

As their kiss deepened, supernatural gold and silver bonding ribbons entwined around their enmeshed bodies, tying them together for all time. Viktor felt the ribbons tying him to Kat tight. He had heard bonded vampires speak of them but didn't understand until he opened his eyes to see for himself. They were real, and so was the bond he now had with Kat. Even if Kat didn't fully grasp what he did, Viktor hoped the memories he shared with her would help her. The evil look she now gave him made Viktor think the memories may not have been as helpful as he hoped.

Kat tensed in Viktor's embrace. He did something to her, to them. When he opened his eyes and looked deep into her soul, she relaxed. Melting into his arms, another brief thought crossed her mind. The feeling that something was wrong took a tight hold on her.

She couldn't help it. She immersed herself into their mind-blowing kiss. Even as she felt Viktor press her further backwards, not registering they were both now lying horizontally on his bed. Viktor pressed harder against her, never slowing or faltering in their kiss. Somehow, Kat felt a tightening around her. Something was both pushing and pulling at her. Somehow she was closer to Viktor despite him lying on top of her. The urge to stay with him forever became scarily all consuming. She felt on a subconscious level that she could never be away from this man.

Visions of his life flashed through her thoughts. Another, stronger feeling tugged at her. Somehow, this kiss connected them. Obviously the kiss was very physical, but it was more than just a kiss. Something happened to her, to them on the psychological and chemical level. Somehow it had finality to it. Kat couldn't explain it, not even to herself. But she sensed it.

Viktor hadn't spent a ton of time getting to know and woo Kat like ordinary relationship guys did. Neither of them came from that type of cloth. Neither of them had the time for it either. In time, she would realize that what he did was right for both of them. It would take a while for her to get to that point. She would probably make it a painfully long time for him. She would no doubt remind him at every opportunity that he didn't give her a choice about the matter. He could see her holding it against him, that he gave her no choice but to spend the rest of her life with him. The alternative would be to die from a broken heart, or rather a broken bond. The majority of life bonds happened with the consent of one person, causing the other to catch up with the reality in which fate chose for both of them.

Most of the time bonds turned out well. There were a few exceptions. There was one who didn't accept the bond and felt they couldn't live as a bonded mate. They chose to end their life. The one who performed the bond chose the same fate shortly after. On the very rare occasion, it was seen as unacceptable to one of the pair to be a part of the bonded relationship for one reason or another. Sometimes they were already involved in a relationship with someone else and they chose to fight the bond, to fight fate.

Regardless, both individuals of the pair felt it, felt the pull towards each other. Felt the need to be together. There wasn't much they could do. It was once a person was bonded; the farther they were away from their mate, the weaker they became. They could not live without each other even if they wanted. The longer they were apart the weaker they got until eventually they went insane, killed themselves, or had to be put down by the Judges.

Viktor looked up to the sky. He had locked Kat in his room

to allow her time to cool off from what he had done. The night was brilliant, filled with twinkling stars. Not a cloud littered the sky. He could feel a slight chill in the air. He choked with amusement. He wasn't sure if the chill was the result of Mother Nature's doing or his newly appointed wife venting her anger through her unleashed power. It had been three days since he had bonded with her, a really long three days, he thought to himself. Even though her anger annoyed him and his patience was wearing thin, he had a great need to check on her.

He grinned, he couldn't help himself. Kat didn't want anything to do with him when it came to actually talking. Against her conscious will, her body seemed to have no problem when it came to responding to his physical advances. Viktor could feel their bond growing stronger by the minute. Every time she let him spend time with her, after their exhaustive love making sessions, he took the opportunity to tell her more of his world, her world.

When he wasn't with her, when she wouldn't let him in his room, Dave would check on her and give him reports. Kat wasn't eating much. She refused to go downstairs to the dining hall on the first floor of the mansion. Viktor wasn't forcing to her to stay in their room anymore. His only rule was that she had to stay within the confines of the mansion's grounds to ensure her safety. In a way, he felt bad for her. He never experienced the type of confinement that she would know for the rest of her life.

Viktor would go through it with her, now that they were bonded. But it still wasn't the same, his confinement would be self induced, hers would be completely involuntary. He would be able to come and go as he pleased, pending whatever punishment the king decided to give him. From what he had seen of Kat, her care-free, self deciding world, and the way she lived it was over. He bet that she wasn't going to take it well.

When Dave attempted to go over what had happened to her, what will happen, and what it all meant for her, Kat would throw the nearest movable object at him. Viktor had yet to tell Dave just how high up on the royal food chain she was. Her blood essence, the intoxicating quality of it, overwhelmed him at times. Viktor only spent quality time with the royals when they were out of the palace. When he was on guard duty he was busy making sure they were safe and sound. He didn't spend much time physically close enough to them to be consumed by their blood scent. However, he spent enough time with them to know that what he was sensing from Kat's essence was similar to theirs. Hers had a subtle difference he couldn't figure out.

Viktor had a difficult time understanding how she had managed living a completely human life. He suspected Kat paid more attention during their nocturnal visits when she gave him the chance to share with her his memories of his family and what he knew of hers. Everything he told her was real, and yet still seemed so unbelievable to her. Kat asked questions. She was beginning to accept her situation or acknowledging that he believed what he was saying, if nothing else.

Being bonded to her didn't make him a royal. It did allow him to be treated as one by the royal servants, but not by royal family members. She outranked almost everyone he ever met, almost. He still hadn't told the Council what he found out. He wanted her to know first. Once she had a general understanding of what she was, he would find the right time to explain the situation to his team.

Viktor was anxious for her change to come. Not knowing if she would survive caused him great concern. Knowing she would experience excruciating pain consumed his thoughts. He just wanted it to be over. Viktor smiled. Kat was already a very attractive, yet volatile woman. He was given quite the bond mate. Every day her scent became stronger. He couldn't tell when she would change. He only knew that it would happen soon, within the next couple of days.

He would try again. The increasing tie of their bond may give him a stronger position. Kat might listen to him and take her situation more seriously. He said this to himself, more like consoling himself, as he walked up the stairs to their bedroom. Just as he had done every night since he brought her here. Viktor stayed away long enough for her to calm down from her most recent tirade. He figured now was as good a time as any to try and talk to her again. He felt that more and more was sinking in to her thick, luscious skull. She was finally getting what was going on, little tidbits anyway. A person was only capable of hearing so much when they were busy screaming and breaking things.

CHAPTER 9

"How could you do this to me?" Kat screamed at him while looking around the room. Viktor knew she was looking for more priceless artifacts he had collected over the centuries to throw them at him. Because the housekeepers had been given the last few days off his bedroom was quite a mess.

Kat bent over a nightstand beside Viktor's overly large bed and grabbed a miniature solid oak statue of a human princess. Jasmina, who the statue embodied, lived in South America 200 years ago. Viktor met her through his travels protecting King Alexander. She was quite a lovely woman if you liked the quiet, soft spoken type. Jasmina was the total opposite of his Katrina.

Kat had no problem venting her anger towards Viktor. Right now Kat had a lot on her mind. Her entire existence depended on the events of the next few weeks. She knew there was a slight chance Viktor could be telling her the truth. Memories of her past continued to emerge into her conscious thoughts.

Kat remembered always having an unusual sensitivity to sunlight, not to mention the eerie ability to gauge people's moods around her. The realization that her Aunt Rose may have known about her true condition threw a wrench in Kat's willingness to trust him. Aunt Rose didn't have a deceptive bone in her body. Despite Kat's determination to have Viktor be wrong, the circumstantial evidence was becoming more difficult to refute.

Oh well, he thought. Kat was his princess now. The statue came barreling at him from where she stood next to his bed. Kat was breathing hard, barely containing contempt for him. Great, he thought. This was going way better than the last discussion they had. At least she wasn't crying at the sight of him, and she did let him in the room without Viktor having to break the door down. That was a good sign.

"Katrina, I know you're angry, hurt, and confused. Anyone would be in your situation," Viktor said.

"You don't have any idea how I feel! How could you? According to you, this has been the only way of life you've ever known! You said you were raised by vampires. How could you possibly think what you're telling me is real? Viktor, I know you believe what you say, but I'm just a human, not a vampire like you." Kat said.

Viktor took another step towards her, holding his hands out in front of him, "I need you to sit down and calm yourself. I need you to hear what I tell you. And..." He stopped himself, he was going to tell her that if she shot one more thing at him he was going to tie her down on his bed and make her listen. But he didn't. The thought of having her immobilized on his bed became a graphic vision in his mind, triggering his groin to tighten and ache.

Kat looked at him with vengeance in her eyes. He recognized that look. He had seen it time and again during his many years in combat. She would do him bodily harm given the chance. Viktor didn't plan on giving her any more opportunities for such acts than he already had. His testicles retracted with the memory of her well placed kick earlier. No, he would never allow her that chance again, once was more than enough.

Viktor was on guard. He had a way with women. Being able to turn their anger into pure lust with his skills of persuasion was something he used to pride himself on. He knew better with Katrina, he also knew she would put those skills to the ultimate test. Looking at her, he began to accept the fact she would be the only woman he would ever be with for the rest of his life.

Viktor needed to focus, get his head back in the game. He needed to get her to fall madly in love with him. He would never be able to let her go, no matter how she felt.

Katrina glared at him for a long time in silence. Viktor enraged her whenever he discussed details of her life. He had taken her hostage, brought her to this archaic mansion that looked like a live-in museum, and he kept her here against her will. He said he was doing everything to protect her.

The most frustrating part of the situation was her physical

reaction to Viktor every time he entered the room. Kat continued to tell herself that this was the last place she wanted to be. In spite of that, through her anger and frustration, she felt an agonizing pull toward him. She was drawn to him since that first night at her work, and it was getting stronger.

Kat couldn't believe her behavior. She was practically throwing herself at Viktor every time he came into the room. That's why she grabbed loose objects in the room. Kat was equally upset with him and herself. She couldn't figure out what she wanted to do more, pummel him with his priceless objects, or make love to him.

The tales he told her were astonishing, frightening, and exciting. Viktor believed she was somehow a long lost princess and her real father, who was a vampire prince, disappeared twenty-four years ago. Somehow she had been left unnoticed to be raised by a human family, her mother's family.

That in itself was impossible. Her parents had died in a car accident when she was just an infant. Her aunt explained this to her many times over the years. Her parents were driving back through Illinois in a blizzard at night when a car swerved in front of them. Her father veered out of the way, spinning out of control himself, causing them to slide over multiple lanes of the highway. A semi truck tried to slow down but it was too late. The truck collided with their car. The police had told Aunt Rose that both Kat's mother and father were found dead at the scene of the accident.

The timing of Viktor's story made sense, which tempted her to believe what he said. Kat hadn't shared the story about her parents and how old she was when they died with Viktor. Somehow he knew. He knew things about her life he shouldn't. Kat knew what information she shared with him, and what she didn't. Yet, somehow he knew!

Her mom's sister, Aunt Rose, raised her. Kat wondered if Aunt Rose was overly protective of her because of what happened to Kat's mom. She figured all of her aunt's maternal instincts and energies were focused on Kat because she didn't have children of her own. Overall, Kat had a pretty normal life. Her aunt was a great parent and a good role model who she learned a strong sense of right and wrong from.

Chaotic thoughts raced through her mind. Memories from the past, recent events with Viktor, and what was going to happen in the near future were all whirring in her head. Kat didn't want to think of the bond Viktor kept mentioning. Keeping that tidbit of information away from her conscience was her way of self preservation, she knew it. Viktor said she wasn't a prisoner, but she couldn't go anywhere. He evidently didn't know the meaning of the word.

Escaping the mansion wouldn't be easy, but she was determined to find a way. He said over and over again that it wasn't safe for her with the Hunters waiting to nab her. Well, how safe was she here, in this mansion with Viktor? According to him there were vampires lurking about everywhere, beings that had to drink blood to survive. She had blood of her own to protect. She didn't plan on being anyone's snack.

If Viktor was playing some weird game to win her over, he being the ultimate hero, he had another thing coming. Even though she couldn't keep her dang hangs off of his gorgeous body, she would have to reject him. The next time he advanced on her with desire in his eyes she would tell him to get lost. Kat couldn't care less if she ever saw him again. Anger, lust, concern, and fear battled each other in her heart. She told herself that she never wanted to see him again. But she wasn't sure how true that was. As her breathing started to calm, she heard more of what Viktor said.

Kat had been standing near his bed when he came into the room. She took a seat as far away from him on the bed as possible. Kat looked up at him expectantly. She would only give him this one reprieve so he better do some fancy talking before she decided to get up and grab something else to throw at him.

Viktor saw her glance around the room and knew he had to calm her. Her emotions were rising. He could feel her losing control of the semi-calm she had. He took a deep breath, figuring out what was the best way to make it all clear to Kat. This was turning out to be quite difficult for him. No one in vampire history had been brought up by humans like she had. There wasn't examples for him to go by, no how to manual to reference.

The truth was the way to go. Spending forever with her would be a really long time to make it up to her if he lied. First, he had to convince her of their eminent future together. They could have a mind blowing future together if she let their fate take its natural course.

"Ok, like I've said, you just need to listen. Don't interrupt me again. Don't say a word until you've heard everything. I need you to listen to what I'm telling you, I need you to hear the facts before you make your judgment." He looked down at her while gliding over to where she sat. Being near her and not reaching out his hand to caress her face, touch her hair, kiss those beautiful lips, was agony.

Viktor appreciated that when he was around her, he lost track of time and space. She was the one. His thoughts, feelings, how his body felt when he was with her, they had all changed in such a short time. Her soul was meant to bind with his for all eternity. Viktor knew he would never let her go. If she wanted to leave the mansion, to leave him, he wouldn't let her. For both of their sakes and his sanity, Viktor hoped Kat would accept her situation for what it was. The sooner the better, he thought.

"Fine," she muttered. Kat looked up at him, deep into his eyes and saw his sincerity. She felt a slight resignation to the situation. She felt the sincerity of his concern for her. That was one of the first emotions she could sense from him since she met him, besides the overwhelming lust. It was nice that he was blank to her, it was more like intriguing, a surprise of sorts. Only knowing what he chose to say to her made her want to hear more of what he had to say. Wow, she really had to snap out of this.

There were two conflicting internal dialogues going on inside of her. One was coming from her head that told her to run far away from him, his pointy teeth, and his ridiculous stories. The other was coming from her heart. This one told her he was the man of her dreams. He was the one who could consume her body and soul. Viktor was the man she was meant to meet and fall deeply and passionately in love with. Her heart told her to stay with him. It told her to accept what he offered, himself. By being with him she could have the happily ever after she always yearned for.

Kat felt she was falling into a trap set by him. She wanted what he said to be real, not a twisted fantastical ideal dreamed up by her extremely gorgeous psychotic captor. The trouble was she believed more of what he said. Incredibly, it was making sense to her. Particularly considering the fact that he bit her, he had fed off her blood. She saw fangs now every time during their passionate lovemaking sessions.

Viktor got a little too carried away and his long and pointies came out for a snack. It enhanced her sexual experience beyond her wildest dreams, which she didn't want to analyze too closely. No one had ever described an orgasm like that to her, and yes, she had asked a few of her closest friends.

Kat couldn't deny when he bit her at the same time he was

inside of her, she experienced the most erotic sensations she ever felt. Not that she had many to compare it to.

Viktor took a deep breath, acknowledging to himself that he had been doing that a lot lately. He sincerely anticipated doing it a lot more in the future when dealing with Kat. He described the history of his people. He described the original families, including hers. Viktor explained how her father was the last of the known Dragar royals, until Katrina was found. The similarity to Drogan, the last name she used, and Dragar was more than a mere coincidence. Her father or human family must have changed her last name from Dragar to Drogan to evade the Hunters. The name change was pretty simple, just a switch of a few letters and a new existence was created for her.

Vampires didn't normally have their names listed in the white pages of the phone book, they had too many enemies. Giving Kat her new name gave her the ability to have a normal life without the worry of Hunters finding her. Viktor wondered who had the foresight to do that. Whoever it was knew who she was, what she was, and they took steps to hide her from not only the Hunters, but the Council as well. He intended to find out the identity of that person when Kat was more comfortable with the cards of life she had been dealt. Right now he had to focus on her and her safety.

Viktor went on telling her what the Council was like, how they were a mix between a special branch of the military and a dysfunctional loving nuclear family unit. They remained close to each other, like brothers. They were hunted by the Hunters, religious groups, and anyone who thought the world would be a better place without them in it. So far Kat had escaped a life of being told exactly what she could and could not do. Unfortunately for her, that was about to change.

Whispers of human children going sick, of evil magic, and anything unexplainable was attributed to their presence. Over time the royal families made decrees to limit knowledge of their existence to only those humans who needed to know. It was easy to hide their youngest members amongst the human population because the change did not happen until the age of twenty five.

In the beginning, when all the original families existed, twenty-five was not much younger than the average mortal life span for humans. It was more difficult then to hide their existence because humans were dying all around them, and they weren't. Relocating frequently to avoid exposure became tiresome. The decision to build underground fortresses for the families became the norm. Now, with advanced healthcare and modern day sciences it was quite easy for vampires to hide, to blend in with humans when necessary.

Viktor described the role of the Council, how they protected the royal and common vampires through the centuries. No one knew how their race came to exist. They only knew the royal families and their blood lines were the source. The royal families were the origin of their immortality.

The royals were the strongest. None of the original royals were still alive that Viktor was aware of. Current members of the royal families were the closest relations to them. That's what separated them from the normal every day civilian vampires. It's also what made them so desirable to the Hunters. Their blood held the secret to what made vampires have their special abilities. That's what the Hunters were after. Somehow, although Viktor couldn't figure out exactly how, the Hunters must have unraveled the mystery of who Katrina was. That was why they were after her now. The thought of them having her made his blood boil.

For a newly turned vampire it was difficult to reach inside one's self, call on their powers, and master them. Most of the time, their strengths and special abilities were found accidentally or by necessity. Some had great speed such as Viktor's brother, Grailen, some were able to transform into animals, and some were able to teleport themselves like Viktor. However, the individual must first go through the change and survive. That was their first big challenge. The closer one's lineage was to the originals determined how strong and varied their abilities would be. Viktor wondered what Kat would be like after her change, what fantastical things she would be capable of as a changed vampire princess?

Viktor then went on to explain how every one of their race had to go through the change when they hit the age of twenty-five. He described the physical and psychological changes. He described the maturation of his physical self and the stopping of the aging process that occurred within a day's time. He described that when she saw him earlier with his eyes black and his incisors exceptionally long, that was his 'other face', as he called it.

Taking another deep breath, Viktor turned his head towards her to see if she was still paying attention and saw her watching him. He could see Kat didn't like what she heard, but knew she needed to hear it. There was no acceptance in her eyes; only acknowledgement that he believed what he told her to be true. He wasn't sure if he saw pity in her.

Taking advantage of her silence, knowing that it wouldn't hold for much longer, he went over the history of the Hunters. Their history was entwined with that of the royal families, their descendants, and the Council. He told her how those men after her the last few nights were after her for a reason. They must know she is a descendant of the originals. That she could be the one holding the key, or the blueprint, to what they were looking for. That her genetic makeup could map out the vampire secrets they were looking for. They desperately wanted that information at any price, including her life.

Obtaining super human skills as a soldier was one of their ultimate goals. Living forever and being able to control vampire and human minds were a bonus. World domination was Malice's sole objective in life. Another main goal of the Hunters was to rid the world of all the vampires, who would only get in the Hunter's way of controlling the planet.

As Viktor stood there telling her the details of a life that should have been hers all along, his gaze wavered from her face.

His eyes took in the entire sight of her. He knew initiating the bond would keep them together forever. He needed to take his time in making her emotionally bound to him, as he was already to her.

Viktor knew the High Council would try and interfere in their relationship. He even knew that he deserved whatever they were going to dish out to him for punishment. Viktor still had hope that just maybe things would turn out ok. His worst fear was the king becoming so angry that he would involve the Judges. Not only in his punishment, as was surely going to be the case, but Kat having to deal with them was a deep cause for concern and would be his only regret. It was possible the king would refuse to acknowledge his bond to Kat. King Alexander had the power to separate them physically until one or both of them died from heart break.

The need to take her physically over and over again in a very animalistic way overwhelmed him. He knew she had deep physical desire for him, no matter how hard she tried to fight it. Kat demonstrated that every night in his room with full abandon. He needed to make her accept the bond before they went to the palace. It was the only way they would survive this together.

Kat sat in front of him absorbing all Viktor had to say, again. She knew what he said felt right. She felt she could trust him, almost beyond reason and logic. The fact stood, though, that vampire families, Hunters, and vampire protector sororities just didn't exist. But Viktor believed they did, that was for sure. Her attraction to him, and of course his extremely pointy teeth that came out of hiding when he was either hungry for blood or for her didn't help clear anything up.

Desire and lust was definitely a mutual phenomenon, she knew. She wasn't sure of the severity of his mental faculty problem, or maybe she was the one with the problem. Viktor seemed pretty damned sure of himself which made her question her sanity.

Viktor looked at Kat and decided there was one sure way to show her, literally, that he meant business. Enough of her pity, Viktor couldn't stand her thinking he was insane. He told Kat what he was going to do, so this time she would have some kind of a warning and then he did it. He let his guard down and felt the beginning of the change. It came suddenly when he was about to feed or fight. But in this situation, demonstrating to someone on purpose, took a little longer.

He had to admit the theatrics of it all probably were in his favor to get her to believe him. His jaw bones began to reform into a feline structure, with elongating eye teeth. His eyes, when he was in danger or experiencing hunger shone bright red. Right now, because he felt frustration, his eyes became completely black. There was no white to be seen, just pure obsidian black.

She watched him transform into a sexy monster. The primal

essence of his being was intoxicating. She believed that at least he was a vampire. During their intimate moments he had never shown her his teeth in the process of coming out, there had not been enough time for that in the heat of passion. He didn't show her his transformation when he told her he wasn't a deranged lunatic and what he was telling her wasn't out of a science fiction or a horror movie.

Seeing Viktor mutate his face explained where his big white teeth came from and how he had been biting her. The entire story was fantastic, but the evidence was right before her eyes. She didn't believe everything he told her, but more was becoming plausible to her.

The realization that she was in this mansion with multiple creatures like Viktor hit her hard in the chest. She didn't know what she should call him, or them. Vampire, that's what he said. He fit the bill of what she would have imagined a vampire would look like. If it looks like a duck, quacks like a duck, I guess it's a duck, she thought to herself. Kat had always been logical. Logical reasoning told her she was in serious danger being here and she needed to rectify that. Her heart told her she was in the safest place available, that he would never hurt her or let anyone else do so. She needed to get away.

Kat didn't say anything when he was done transforming. She sat there and stared at him like he was a carnival freak belonging behind some caged contraption. She explored his face with her eyes and then her fingers. Feeling the contours, lines, and bony structures fascinated and terrified her. Kat stood up. Viktor relaxed his face, changing back to normal. Needing fresh air, she asked him to take her for a walk on the grounds. Viktor looked outside, the sun wasn't up, but it was on its way.

Their time would be limited. He didn't want to deny her anything as long as he could provide it. Going outside for a little while wasn't too much to ask, he supposed. He took a step towards her and she instantly put up her hands.

"Wait a minute, just hold on! I would like to walk down the steps like a normal human being," she said. She regretted that statement as soon as it left her lips. She shook her head and grabbed her coat. He was already at the door, holding it open for her. Without saying a word, Kat walked past him out into the hallway.

CHAPTER 10

Kat and Viktor passed Dave on their way down the stairs from their bedroom heading outside. That man probably never slept, having to be in charge of everything during the day and trying to keep up with the events going on throughout the night, Kat surmised.

"Viktor, the sun will be up soon," Dave reminded him. Viktor only nodded his head in response.

Kat tucked that little piece of knowledge into a corner of her mind for later. The sun was a weakness for them? She wondered if he was able to go out in it for a little while like she could, or if he would burn to a crisp like vampires in the movies. One's weakness could be another person's gain. She needed to ask Viktor what other weaknesses he had, if any.

Outside the mansion, the night air was brisk but tolerable. The sidewalk paths had been shoveled and salted. Kat and Viktor walked together in silence. Viktor saw a bench and led her to it. They were close to the location where he brought her when they arrived on the grounds a few nights ago.

The lake was beautiful to look at. The waves gently caressed the break-wall not six feet from where they sat. They both silently enjoyed the serenity of the moment. Viktor tensed, the image of her change took him by surprise.

Kat would be twenty-five in four days. That's when she would turn into a vampire, like Viktor. Neither he nor she was ready for that to happen. Kat didn't yet believe in such things, not really. Would she be strong enough to get through the change without having been prepared? She knew everything there was to know about the change, everything that was going to happen to her. But if she didn't and wouldn't believe in it, chose not to use the information he gave her, she may not be able to do what was necessary to survive it. If she didn't survive, he didn't think he would be able to survive either. Their fate, his fate, was left to this unwilling woman who refused to acknowledge what was really going on.

Kat wasn't going to accept the one way he knew that would help her change, to give her strength. He figured he had these four days to figure out how to give her the strongest tool in his armory. If he had to tie her down, so be it. Kat needed his blood. She needed to take enough of it to gain strength from him. His blood would give her an edge over the pain she would have while her body morphed into a hunter, a seductress, a vampire.

Kat already had the strength from her bloodline. The bond they shared made her even stronger, but she wasn't brought up to prepare herself for this. Going through the change was no small feat. Her body would die. Her immortal soul would take over an un-revivable carcass and give it eternal life. If one's soul wasn't strong enough, their will to live not deep enough, they wouldn't wake up. Their body and soul would stay dead.

If she had the strength of his blood, she would stand a better chance. The issue of having her take his blood would be dealt with later. Together he knew, or rather hoped they could get through anything as long as they had each other. That was what being bonded to someone was all about. Being able to lean on each other in situations they weren't likely to do well in alone. He was ready to be there for her, to help her with anything she needed. She would come around to feeling the same way about him, he was sure of it.

Viktor needed to talk to Dave about his idea in private. Dave, being a human, may give him an insight to what Katrina was thinking. He wanted to know if anything could be done to help alter her perspective of him and her situation.

After sitting silently for a while longer on the bench Viktor sensed the sun. It was about to make it's grand morning entrance to begin another day. He knew it was time for them to go back into the safety of the mansion. This time it was more for his sake than hers. He looked over at her. "Katrina, it is time. We must return to the mansion. I do not tolerate sunlight very well." He held a hand out to help her up from the bench. She didn't fight him, as he expected. She was quiet, too quiet.

Kat was tired of hearing Viktor spout off his ridiculous notions. She was sick of having to deal with the mentally ill in general. Either it was her or Viktor with the problem. She was no longer sure of her sanity and that ticked her off. She didn't have any problems in her simple life until she met him.

At work people came in to the emergency room with all sorts of problems. This type was her least favorite. She could hold pressure to a bleeding artery. She could give pain relievers for a headache. There was nothing she could do to fix Viktor and his obsession with vampires. She couldn't make him human. She didn't want to get mixed up in his dark world.

Nursing wasn't a field where you could disappear for days and expect your job to be there when you returned. Kat needed to get back to her very ordinary, very boring life. There was no room in it for Viktor or this extravagant mansion he lived in. She had a hard time thinking of never enjoying their lengthy love making sessions again. No, this was just too complicated she told herself.

The thought of leaving him, never seeing Viktor again made her feel ill. She had that awful feeling of having a rock in her stomach that would be there forever. Yes, she would miss him dearly, but she had to leave. Viktor's blood drinking habit helped her make this very difficult decision.

Her apartment was safe for now. Viktor said his brother, Grailen, paid her rent for a month so her things were safe. She would have to move to avoid uninvited guests in the future. She could deal with that.

How was Carmen going to react when she saw half of her house was blown to smithereens? Kat's car was still parked outside in the drive way, probably with the driver side door still flung wide open. Great, my best friend is going to think I either had something to do with the fire, or that I perished in it, she thought. Either way it was bad. Kat had to think up a story to pacify Carmen. Kat didn't want to implicate Viktor or his Council. She would have to avoid her best friend until she could come up with something good enough so Carmen wouldn't investigate further.

How was she going to explain any of this to anyone? It was quite a shock to her. "Hi Carmi, how's your day going? Me, oh, you know, the same old stuff going on. Oh, by the way, I stopped by your house the other night because I was hiding from large men who were hunting me. When I was leaving to go get junk food they decided to blow half your house up. Yeah, I'm really sorry about that." Talking to Carmen was not going to be easy!

Kat looked down at her hands while she walked and thought she had to get out of this self pity act she had going on and do something. Viktor said he didn't deal with sunlight very well. "Viktor, in all your worldly vampire charms, besides sunlight, what else does you in?" she asked, attempting innocent curiosity.

Stopping in place on the path, Viktor turned and faced her. All he wanted to do was take her up in his arms and feel her warm body pressed hard against his. Viktor wanted to act on the intense urge he had to show her he was very, very attracted to her. He wanted to let her feel his current state of arousal. He leaned forward, bending a little at the waist so their lips were almost level to each other.

He felt her body slowly react to his. The closer he was to her, the stronger their bond grew. It made him want to consume her more than ever. Viktor felt their souls intermingle together. He knew she was not yet aware of what she felt, that she was unable to pin point her need of him to their bond. But she would. Her heart beat increased with his overly acute awareness of her. He took it as a mutual sign of desire and lowered his lips to hers.

Big mistake, Kat slapped him across the face as hard as she could. "What the hell do you think you're doing?" She glared at him angrily, pissed off that he thought he could take the liberty of kissing her when she didn't want him to.

"What on earth would make you think that I want anything to do with you, especially right now? Yeah, Yeah, I know. The last few nights I have given in, all too willingly I admit. But this has to stop Viktor! I have a life. I have, or had, a job that I like. I have a job that I went through years of schooling to get. I have an apartment that I have to pay bills for! Viktor, I have to leave here. I'm no princess! You're a vampire. I believe you. But I'm not!"

"And furthermore, I know who my parents were, Eric and

Grace Drogan! They weren't royalty. They were normal every day people. No, I didn't know them personally, but my aunt would have told me something as important as me being a vampire. She wouldn't have kept something like that from me!"

"Listen!" Viktor bellowed. He put his face very close to hers so that she could see the anger in his eyes. There was pure anger from her assault, and lust. There was always lust.

"I can tell when a woman is aroused, especially you. I can smell it on you like perfume. Your heart beats faster with every inch closer that I come to you. You wanted me to kiss you just as bad as I did. You ache for my touch just as much as I ache for yours. Hell, you want me right now!" He screamed at her.

"I don't know what you're talking about. You keep trying to fill my head with lies and I'm sick of it! You can take your pointy teeth and shove them right up your..." Viktor snickered at that and didn't let her finish her statement.

"Unbelievable. You just can't admit it to yourself. You still think that I am a freak-of-nature. I can tell by the way you look at me. You act like I am some circus sideshow, intriguing but grotesque at the same time. I can't wait for you to go through this, for you to become like me. When you do you'll stop this denial you have going on and stop irritating the hell out of me!" Viktor was furious. He couldn't believe she slapped him. Kat caught him off guard again with her strength and quickness. If he were human, she would have broken his jaw. He turned his back on her and walked away.

Viktor couldn't even look at her. He was sick to his stomach. No one had ever done that to him. He didn't like the way it made him feel, that she was able to hurt his feelings by assaulting him. She not only kicked him in the testicles, she outright slapped him in the face. He calmly, or as calmly as he was able to, began the walk back to the mansion and expected her to follow.

Watching him walk away, Kat saw her only chance of escaping. Viktor's anger took over his senses and he wasn't watching to make sure she followed him. It irritated her that he expected her to follow along like a puppy. Kat took one last look at his glorious backside while he strode away. Scared and confused, she hoped it was the last time she would ever see him. Kat turned in the opposite direction of the mansion and ran quietly down the path leading towards the lake.

Viktor grumbled to himself the entire way to the mansion's side entrance. He was in awe at her audacity to strike him. Just before he reached for the screen door he turned around to say as much. She wasn't there! Kat was gone! He closed his eyes as fury began to build inside him. He saw nothing but angry flashes of red. After shaking his head to clear his thoughts and emotions he threw out every sensory he had to locate her. As immature as their bond was, he should be able to point out her exact location on the property. She was no longer on the property!

With a roar of anger and fear, he ran into the mansion. He

didn't stop until he found Dave and Grailen sitting in the library. At the moment Viktor didn't care how his brothers felt. He needed their help!

Viktor burst into the room, splintering the door in his wake. "She's gone, she is gone! Get up, we have to find her!" He screamed at them. He was immediately enraged when neither moved out of their chairs. "I bonded with her, she is my mate! Now get off you asses and help me look for her!" he said with such ferocity he felt like the blood vessel in his forehead was going to burst.

Once he said that they stood up, both wore dumbstruck looks on their faces. "What do you mean you bonded with her? You don't even know her Viktor. How could you do this! She doesn't even know what she is! Do you?" They traded off questioning him like two angry parents. Viktor stared from Dave to Grailen. He and his brother were once close. That ended when Rafe disappeared. Grailen had gone into a self imposed bout of misery and for the most part focused on everyone else's wrongdoings.

"Of course I know what she is. I fed from her. I know a lot more than you think I do, and I know this. I am going to bring her back here! Whether you two like it or not doesn't matter. She belongs to me, with me! I can't sense her location. Otherwise I would already be on my way taking care of the problem, now wouldn't I?" He could barely ground the words out, he was hurt that she would leave him, and that she would slap him in the face when he expected softness from her.

"She could be in danger. The Hunters have been watching

her, wherever she goes, they are bound to find her. We can't let them find her before we do. You know what they are capable of." He couldn't find it in him to tell them who she really was. The important thing right now was that she was alone and defenseless. Her being a princess was going to be quite a surprise to everyone. He wanted to keep that fun fact to himself for a bit longer.

Kat didn't let herself think about what she was doing. She hit the lakeshore and jumped in the water with no hesitation. Kat was a very strong swimmer, but the freezing cold temperature of the water overwhelmed her as soon as she was submerged. It only took a few seconds for the water to take her breath away as she struggled to break the surface. Once she did, she looked around for any sign of Viktor. She hoped he was so angry that he took a while to realize she wasn't behind him. She wasn't sure how loud the splash sounded when she jumped in. When she hit the freezing cold water she became momentarily paralyzed despite knowing that every second counted. She lost all thought processes temporarily. It felt like her body was shutting down. Her lungs burned and her chest felt tight and heavy, it was even becoming difficult to breathe.

Kat knew she had only a short amount of time before Viktor came and dragged her out of the water. Her main focus was to put as much distance between her and the mansion as she could. She knew he would come after her. The problem was she didn't know how permanently she wanted to be away from him. Concern for him bloomed in her heart.

Heading in a southern direction, the water current of the lake was strong. Kat propelled her body with the current, not wanting to hit land too soon. Her muscles felt like they were on fire and her lungs felt as if there were pins and needles sticking in them, deeper and deeper with every breath.

After what felt like an eternity the burning sensation in her legs and arms started to recede until she no longer felt them at all. Kat recognized she was starting to suffer from hypothermia and that she didn't have a lot of time to get out of the water before permanent damage to her brain and soft tissues occurred. She needed to find somewhere to warm up and dry off.

Looking towards the shoreline, Kat spotted a safe area to get out of the water. The strokes of her arms were weakening. She saw a private boat launch and swam to it. Kat thought she was hallucinating from hypothermia. Wavering shadows on the ground of the boat launch were shaped like human shadows.

Kat waded slowly in the shallow water over to the grassy area. The snow made the weeds along the shore difficult to grab a hold of but she managed. Using the last bit of energy, she pulled her body halfway out of the dark cold water onto the boat launch. Still dangling in the water, her legs were pulled at by the current. She no longer felt cold and her teeth stopped chattering. Kat lifted her head and glanced to her right. The dock light shined. She saw what was making the shapes of human like shadows. That's when she lost consciousness from hypothermia, her body taken over by shock.

CHAPTER 11

Kat woke up stiff from her endeavors in the freezing lake. Her birthday was approaching. Either Viktor was right and Kat was going to turn into a vampire princess, or he was just a vampire who she fell in love with. Time would tell which one would need psycho-therapy. Surely one of them did.

Her surroundings began to come into focus. Kat didn't recognize what she smelled and the lights were overly bright. When she saw the clear glasslike cell she was in, she figured she was hallucinating from the aftermath of being in the lake. This was pretty detailed for a hallucination. She didn't realize her imagination could be so vivid. She reached over from the cot she was lying on and touched the glass of the cell. It was solid! The glass didn't dematerialize as she thought it would. She was in a real cell!

Then it dawned on her. Viktor must really be pissed off at her to lock her up in this cage. She looked around, it was sparse.

Her cell didn't have the same amenities she was used to having in Viktor's room. She must be in the basement of the mansion. Examining the activity outside of her cell, she noticed other such cells lined the wall. They were similar to hers. Why would he keep anyone prisoner like this? Who did Viktor keep captive down here? What did he have planned for her? Surely he knew she wasn't going to be happy about this!

The figure that approached her cell wasn't Viktor. Kat felt this man was significant. Then he spoke, "Well, Ms. Drogan, thank you for allowing us to capture you so easily on the lakeshore. We've been hunting you for quite some time now."

The man wore military garb like the other military boys that chased her since the night she met Viktor. He held in his hand a curious looking syringe. The color of the solution was a dark red, the same color of blood. The needle wasn't the nice short kind. It had to be at least an inch and a half long with what appeared to be a sixteen or a fourteen gauge by the looks of it.

Reality set in with a complete and nasty thud in her chest. Viktor had been right all along! These men must belong to the group called the Hunters. The same group Viktor warned her about and told her to stay away from at all costs.

"We've taken the liberty of injecting you with our latest advancement in anti-vampire weaponry. We figured you would be a nice specimen to try it out on," he said as he held up the syringe and twirled it between his fingers.

"It would be in your best interest to cooperative with us. If you do, we may just let you live." He began to pace back in forth in front of her cell.

"I don't know what you want with me, but whatever it is, you have the wrong girl. An anti-vampire weapon? Give me a break!" Kat yelled.

The man stopped pacing and stood in front of her cell. "Your vampire powers should have already started to deplete themselves, reverting back to that of a normal human. That is if the serum works. You will report to my scientists exactly what is happening to you and any changes that occur."

"I'm not going to help you do anything," she hissed.

Ignoring her completely, he continued, "They will be taking samples regularly to monitor your body chemistry, to see if your DNA begins to shift. If you don't cooperate, we have ways to make you suffer dearly. I don't tolerate insolence," he snickered.

Excitement was written across his face at the thought of making her suffer. Kat shuddered and thought that this man was obviously a sadist.

This guy had a major problem with egotistical issues too. He looked like he was all pumped up on steroids. He could barely contain the rage that boiled under his skin. He spit every time he said anything to her, reminding her of that movie when the dog was all foamy at the mouth. He was disgusting.

There was a nasty scar on the right side of his face. It ran the entire length of his face from above his eyebrow, through his cheek and lips, ending somewhere below his chin. The scar was puckered. Either the doctor that stitched him up didn't know what they were doing, or he didn't bother getting it looked at. It definitely didn't do much for his attractiveness. His personality was ugly enough.

While he was talking, more like yammering, Kat took a look around her cell. The cell was in a line of other cells. All of them were made up of the same clear glass that hers was. The same clear walls that were in the front of her cell were also in between each cell. They allowed her to see that out of the six cells, she was the only occupant. Kat could see down the hall was a special type of cell. The door was a beige metal color. It had oversized hinges on the left side connecting it to the frame of the wall. That must be where the Hunters kept the prisoners they felt most threatened by, the most violent.

Kat's cell was the first in the line of cells. Hers was located directly in front of the Hunter's central communication area. Scientists, or whatever they were, were talking in hushed tones. The voices were a little too low for her to hear what they were saying. They looked at her once in a while as the scarred man went on and on about something. His annoying voice made her tune him out until he said the word Council. She refocused her attention back to him. He spoke about vampires, how she was part of their evil faction, and how she was a vile creature. Yeah, like this man was an angel.

Kat noticed since she had awakened, she didn't feel so hot. Flu like symptoms started creeping up on her. She began to sweat through her clothes. Even during a vigorous work out she never broke a sweat. Kat looked at the men working feverishly at the stainless steel tables, measuring multicolored liquid into different containers. They didn't seem to be hot. No one around her was dressed for warm weather. They all had long white lab coats on. Even Mr. I'm In Charge had a camouflage jacket on. She started to feel a headache brewing, and what was up with the temperature problem? This was unlike her. She never got sick.

The man talking to her noticed her discomfort because next he said, "What you are experiencing is the effects of the serum I injected." The man turned to one of his lackeys and bellowed, "Daniel! We need to take her blood." He turned back to Kat and said, "The serum is coursing through your bloodstream with every beat of you black heart. Your body must be trying to fight it off. We need a sample of your blood my dear."

He withdrew something that looked suspiciously like a dart gun. She liked action movies just as much as the next girl but this was absurd. The man walked close to her cell wall and located a small opening. He slid the object through the whole and took aim. After he fired the weapon she looked down and saw a dart with a frilly tail at the end sticking into the meaty portion of her right thigh.

She thought to herself, what do you know, it was a dart gun! Her surroundings began to spin and whirl. The lights looked like they were on a dimmer switch and someone was turning the dial lower and lower. The lights finally went completely out. She lost consciousness again.

Viktor woke up from his death sleep shuddering with the thought of the Hunters having Katrina. What he had gone through in the past with them as their captive was a living nightmare. The after affects he and his kind had from their torturous treatment weren't pretty. Those thoughts were for later, after he found his bond mate and made everything right between them. Right now, he had to focus on getting her out of there. He had to make plans to rescue her from that horrible place, away from those retched humans who called themselves soldiers of humanity.

Malice somehow brainwashed the Hunters into thinking they were fighting for a greater cause. That by getting rid of the entire vampire race would somehow make the world a better and safer place. The Hunters were the real monsters. They were the ones who should be put to judgment for what they have done. This all had to stop! He was done seeing people he cared for suffer by their hands. Viktor closed his eyes. He tried to focus, to staunch his hatred when his cell phone rang.

It was Dave. One of his friends, a local vampire, had spotted a small group of Hunters down by the lakefront not far from the mansion. He couldn't be sure, but he thought he saw the group pull someone out of the lake, possibly a female. He tried to follow them but didn't want to bring the Hunter's attention to himself. When Dave reported this to him, Viktor's heart sank to his feet.

"Dave, they must have her!" He tightened his fist in rage. Malice had to die. He had to be taken care of once and for all.

If Malice did have Katrina, as Viktor knew deep in his heart that he did, Malice just sealed his death warrant. Viktor would make sure of it, personally! Malice wasn't smart enough to keep from harming her. Keeping her prisoner was enough of a reason to pull every finger and toe nail off, one by one. That's how Viktor would start his administrations. His imagination spun wild with possibilities. He would enjoy making Malice scream in agony. Making sure his torment lasted for days, maybe even weeks. Viktor didn't care about Malice's underlings. No, they were just going to die. Malice was going to suffer.

Dave told him everything he knew what his friend saw last night. When he finished, Viktor ran to his bedroom to equip himself with armor and weapons. He chose his favorite large curved knife with a particularly sharp and nasty edge on it, a sniper rifle, throwing stars, and a few hand grenades. He pressed the name plate underneath a painting that hung on the wall; two wall panels of the closet released themselves from their locking mechanisms with a low whooshing sound. To his left Viktor kept his most valuable swords he collected through the centuries. To the right were his guns, all fully automatic with high powered scopes. Once he put on his holsters, he grabbed his set of pistols and slung his rifle with its strap on to his back.

Viktor stepped back when he finished loading himself up with his tools of death. He put his finger up to the name plate again and pressed it once more to close the wall panels. The Council had decided to lay low and focus on monitoring the movements of the Hunters. He regretted ever being a part of that decision.

Viktor considered the Hunters taking his mate the equivalent of declaring outright war. If the Council wouldn't support him, he would go after them alone. But he knew they would be behind him in whatever he decided. Once members of the High Council found out who Kat was and where she was being held captive, they would step in. That's when the Judges would become involved.

Viktor was ready to do anything necessary to get her back, even if it meant dealing with the Judges. No one wanted anything to do with the king's assassins. Those demons didn't play well with others. When the king wasn't around to keep them in line, they became mischievous in finding entertainment for themselves. When they were given an order from the king, they put their all into completing the task. As long as they did what they were told, the king didn't get involved much. They lived to ensure the pleasure of the king. They enjoyed their work and they were very good at it.

Viktor's eyes burned with anger and fear. From past experience, he knew the Hunters were capable of very evil deeds. Torture, maiming, breaking one's soul, those were their specialties. Viktor considered himself lucky, having survived Malice's hospitality and eventually escaping. Throughout the centuries others of his clan weren't as lucky as he was. The ones that did make it out alive were never the same after.

The Hunters were foul humans. During experiments, the goal was to find their victim's weakness and exploit it. The Hunters used the fear of their hostage against them, searching for more effective ways to hunt and kill vampires. You could only imagine what they made vampires go through. Viktor saw the Hunters amputate limbs to see if their body parts grew back. From his cell Viktor watched their atrocities unable to help his fellow vampires. Of course the Hunters didn't use anesthetic. They wanted to see how much pain a vampire could endure before they lost consciousness. Vampires didn't go into shock like humans did, that made the torture go on for hours, sometimes days. He could only imagine what horrible cruelties they had in store for Kat.

Dave came into Viktor's room without knocking. Now was not the time for niceties. "Viktor it may not be such a good idea for you to go after her alone. I know you care for her."

"Care for her? Dave, I love her! I can't live without her! Do you hear what I'm saying? If no one is ready to go by the time I am, then I'm going alone," Viktor stated. The problem was the Council didn't know where the local Hunter compound was located. That meant he didn't know exactly where they would be holding her.

Viktor swung around, his emotions starting to get the best of him. He barely tolerated Dave's ongoing nagging about safety. Viktor stepped up to his long time friend and put his nose close to Dave's face, "Dave, let's get one thing straight. Katrina Drogan is my mate." He felt the satisfaction of finally shutting his friend up. "And furthermore, I would rather die than have the Hunters do to her what they did to me and all the others of our kind with their little tests and experiments."

Viktor went back to checking his ammo, deciding to bring

extra clips for his pistols. Next, he began to put on his body armor. The armor was the same that he and the older vampire members of the Council still wore. It was given to them long ago, when they were soldiers of another time. The royal family had a team of blacksmiths who designed the armor. They were armor specialists employed to create protective gear to deflect Hunter weapons. Their enemies had yet to develop ammo strong enough to pierce the armor. Demon magic was used when crafting the armor. The Council hoped the Hunters would never have that resource at their disposal.

The Council started openly warring with the Hunters long ago. Viktor remembered the time when he didn't have to hide what he was, it seemed like just yesterday. He sorely missed his comrades in arms, those he had seen fall during battle with the Hunters.

When the High Council realized there was an organized group that had amassed against them was when the royals decided it was necessary to take safety precautions for the entire vampire race. Malice was not the first to lead the Hunters. Malice had somehow developed an anti-aging injection. Viktor knew Malice must be approaching two hundred years old, yet he didn't look a day over forty human years old.

Viktor remembered when he was captured and taken to their encampment for weeks. That memory was never pleasant, and he tried not to think of it often. A cold sweat broke out on his forehead, bringing him back to reality. The need to hurry and find Kat was foremost in his mind. He had to rescue his mate, save her from those abominations who believed they had the right to do those awful things they did to vampires in the name of righteousness. The Hunters claimed humans were above vampires. Hunters did not believe vampires had souls. They refused to acknowledge there was a difference between good and bad vampires. The same went for humans. Some were good, and some were evil.

Viktor closed his closet, returning the metal lined drywall partition back into place, Grailen appeared in his doorway. Viktor gave him one look and that was all that was needed. They understood each other far better than anyone else. They were there for each other in times of great need. Now was one of those times. Grailen, even though he had withdrawn from Viktor when their brother Rafe disappeared, was here now. To Viktor's relief, Grailen was already wearing his body armor that he was given by the royals. When the battle of good and evil was on their doorstep, they were there to save the day, and they did it together. He knew what humans and vampires were capable of.

Viktor and Grailen set out from the mansion, going to the location described by Dave's friend. Viktor was angry with himself for letting her run off like that. His annoyance with her confusion let him lose his better judgment. She exasperated him on so many levels. He was going to have to do something about that.

Seeing Viktor suffer like this was difficult for Grailen. He knew his brother was beating himself up for letting his newfound woman be taken. "Now is not the time for your inner battles to distract you, my brother. We need to find her, and you need to concentrate."

Viktor looked at his brother who had been withdrawn from him for so long. It was a miracle that Grailen was by his side. But when all things were said and done, they were still brothers. They had each other's backs.

"Grailen, she will turn in three nights' time. We need to find her before that happens. We do not know what the Hunters know about her. I have fed from her, from what I could tell she has no memories of vampires, the royal family, the Council, or the Hunters." Viktor explained.

"How could that be? How is it possible that a vampire, a royal vampire escaped all of our attention her entire life? And living right under our noses?" Grailen asked.

"I don't know how she came to be raised by humans, nothing in her memory showed that her Aunt Rose knew anything about vampires. We don't know who her mother was either. But when I fed from her, I could feel the calling in her. I did find out who her father was though." Viktor took a deep breath and continued, "Her father is the late Prince Eric Dragar, King Alexander's nephew."

Grailen stopped him from saying anything more, "What? You're telling me that Prince Eric had a female child with a human? That's ridiculous. The king never would have allowed that!" he said in astonishment. The story clearly dumbfounded even his brother who was older than dirt.

Viktor continued, "He must have had it set up for her mother's family to take care of her if something happened to him. Little did he know that is exactly what would occur."

It was well known the king did not approve of royals having relationships with humans. "Prince Eric must have bonded with a human and for whatever reason he did not turn her before they had a daughter. All Katrina knows of her parents is that when she was young, they both died together in a car crash. From her memories, I could not tell who the mother was. I saw her face in Katrina's memories from pictures, but she was too young to have known her. I have never seen her before, but her father was definitely the prince. I could taste his bloodline in her. Her blood was very strong, and she will become more dangerous the closer it gets to her birthday."

Grailen stood there listening as Viktor went on explaining, "I tried to explain to her what she will go through. What I did when I bonded her to me, but she thought I was crazy."

"Viktor, this woman doesn't understand what it means to be bound if she hasn't been raised by our kind. You need to give her time to come around." Grailen chastised him, as if he didn't already know this!

"No, she has no idea what she is, who she is. There's something else in her blood besides vampire and human essence.

A third species lives within her Grailen. Something I've never encountered before," Viktor recounted.

"Brother, do you realize what the Hunters have in their grasp? Your woman may have the exact blood DNA mixture they've been looking for all this time. If you're right, and she has a third essence within her, we may all be in trouble," Grailen said as he finished tying the front of his armor vest closed.

"I know. If the Hunters find out what and who they have in their clutches, she will suffer for it. That's if they let her live long enough to go through her change." Viktor turned down a path similar to the one at the mansion that led him down to the lake. He had never been on this property before, even being located so close to his home. He scowled. Incompetent feelings rising again, they badgered his confidence because he hadn't been able to keep Kat safe.

CHAPTER 12

Kat woke up in a haze. That nasty man shot her with something to make her fall asleep. She assumed it was a sedative to make her compliant. The crappy part was waking up in such a cloudy haze. She had no idea what had been done to her. Her left arm ached. She looked down and saw two puncture marks at the bend of her elbow. Being a nurse, she knew they didn't do this often. They must have dug around a bit to find her vein, she was bruised pretty badly. Her comfort was obviously not on their priority list.

The head nasty guy walked up to her cell and glared at her. He had a lump on the side of his face. The sedative started to wear off. She liked what she saw. She knew from his irritation she must have done that to him even though she was drugged. She must have caught him by surprise. He deserved whatever he got, that jerk. She didn't know who he thought he was, but she was going to get even with him for what he and his band of minions behind him were doing to her. Whatever their plans were, she wasn't going to go along with them.

The lab was up to date and seemed to be kept clean. Stainless steel counters covered the tables; there were numerous drawers on their sides. She assumed that's where the scientist lackeys kept their evil instruments. Her cell must have been cleaned when they drugged her. She had gotten angry the last time she was awake and smashed everything breakable against what she figured must be multi-layered bullet-proof glass. They didn't want her to have pointy objects at her disposal when they had to come into her cell. They removed everything that was broken when she was down for the count.

She noticed she no longer wore the clothes she had on when she was captured. The thought of being handled by these sick men made her feel like vomiting. She was now wearing light blue pajamas.

Her captor, mister lumpy head, looked a little too content about something. He stood in front of her cell, glaring at her with his vileness. The corner of his mouth was tipped up, like he could barely contain his giddiness. "Ms. Drogan, Katrina. I can't believe how rude I've been. I forgot to formally introduce myself to you. My name is Malice."

"Guess what Mr. Ugly. I don't give a damn what your name is," she said.

"Don't interrupt me again you stupid cow." Kat saw a flash of anger on his face, and then it was gone. "I figure we will be spending a lot of quality time with each other, for the next few days anyway. We should be on a more comfortable level with each other, a more personal level," Malice said in a slimy sadistic tone.

"I don't want anything to do with you. You're a sick twisted psycho with obvious problems upstairs," Kat said, looking at him while tapping her fingertip to her temple. What the hell was she doing? Was she crazy? She couldn't help but say what was on her mind. She knew it was just going to make him mad.

He decided to ignore her. "I want you to tell me everything you know about your family. Where they came from, where they live. Anything you can think of regarding your vampire world, I want to know."

"What is your obsession with vampires? Why can't you just leave me alone? They'll leave you alone. And then we'll all live happily ever after on the same planet?" Kat asked.

Malice made a dismissing gesture in the air with his hand and continued, "The serum was injected into your blood stream last night and again this morning. We aren't exactly sure what it will do to a vampire, but we have hopes. We have the antidote of course, but you are going to have to earn that by telling us what we want to know." He grinned. "Now, let us begin," he sneered as he withdrew another syringe. "We can do this the easy way, or we can do this the hard way, Katrina." He walked up the two steps that acted as a landing for the line of cells and stood very close to the glass.

"I don't know what you're talking about. You talk of vampires, locations, vampires, I don't know anything. I really think that you have the wrong girl. I'm not a vampire and I don't know anyone who is. In fact, I think you have a mental problem that needs serious attention. I can give you the number for a good therapist. You'd probably be the first for her having to treat a fixation on the supernatural, but I'm sure she would be up to the task," Kat said this as calmly as she could. Her heart started beating faster as he stood in front of her with the dart gun in his hand. It felt harder to breathe. Panic began to set in. She didn't want to be knocked out again. Heat spread down her arms and up into her neck.

She normally didn't have a problem with stress. Kat could have a patient dying in front of her at work and she never had issues of freezing up under the pressure. Kat always knew what to do, but didn't know now. It felt like her grip on reality was slipping. She was losing control of her thoughts. Her mind raced and she couldn't focus clearly to formulate an escape plan.

Every passing hour she spent here in this cell she felt worse. Breaking out in sweats one minute and feeling like she was freezing the next. Every muscle in her body hurt, like she had worked out for hours when all she had been doing was sitting in this cell getting more angry and afraid.

Being drugged for Malice's serum injections and blood tests had to be the cause. Kat didn't understand what she had to do with any of this. She knew that her current captivity was due to her falling in love with a vampire. These so called Hunters had the wrong girl and they didn't even know it. She wasn't a vampire. She was a straightforward girl from a small town who wanted simple things out of life.

Viktor thought Kat was a long lost princess. She figured Malice must think this because Viktor did. They both had a huge misunderstanding going on. They believed that her father, who passed away twenty-four years ago, was somehow related to the high and mighty vampire king. They thought this vampire king was her uncle, according to Viktor. Viktor said they were now somehow mystically bonded for all eternity. They were now married in the eyes of the vampire world.

She struggled to disprove their misunderstandings to herself. Hunted by Malice and his goons had only solidified Viktor's story. According to Malice, the serum wasn't supposed to work against humans, only vampires. That meant the symptoms she felt were happening because she did have vampire blood flowing in her veins. The thought of her being a real princess was overwhelming to think about even without all the other stuff happening. What was Aunt Rose going to say? Did she know about any of it? Questions about her past filled her thoughts. Gaps in the validity of her youth began to grow. Has her entire existence been a lie?

Kat stood up from her cot and walked over to where Malice stood outside of her glass wall. She brought her fists up and pounded on the clear barrier. "You freaks! You need to let me go! What you're doing is so illegal. You're going to pay for this!" She slammed on the glass again. Realizing that she had to be careful what she said. Kat didn't want to give any information to him. She didn't want to admit to knowing anything, even the minimal information that she did know.

"This is going to be easier than I thought my dear," Malice sneered.

"Wipe that slimy grin off your face you big jerk!" Kat turned around and went to the far side of her cage. She needed to put some distance between her and that awful man.

Kat didn't want to cry, she had been through a lot in her life without having cried, but it was too much. Tears formed in the inner portion of her eyes. Against all of her will, tears ran down her cheeks. Giving up, she stopped fighting and let them fall.

After everything that happened, she regretted leaving Viktor. Even though he told her all of those crazy things, she missed him. Kat felt the bond now that he had talked about when they were together. Kat never admitted to him that she knew the bond was real and growing. She was afraid what the bond meant to her. She felt less whole the longer she was away from him. Besides feeling sick from the experiment Malice was testing on her, the separation from Viktor was like sucking the air out of her chest.

This compound must be fairly large, she thought. For all she knew there were countless other prisoners being held here. Before Malice came back over to her cell, a female was brought out to a table sitting in the middle of the command center. The Hunters strapped her down with leather belts. Silver chains were locked across her neck, wrists, and ankles.

One of the Hunter scientists opened a wide but shallow

drawer on the side of the table. He took out a hacksaw and raised it up so the woman could see what she had to look forward to. The scientist then walked around to the end of the table where her feet where tethered. He positioned the blade over her left ankle and began to move the blade back and forth with his left hand, while the right held onto her calf to give him leverage.

The woman's scream pierced Kat's entire body. The pain the woman endured was unimaginable. Kat didn't want to think that she was possibly next.

"Malice! Make him stop! Make him stop hurting her! You are so sick!" She screamed into his eyes as Malice watched her reaction with fascination. Malice snapped his fingers and the Hunter finished his grizzly work.

Kat knew the woman's foot was completely severed from her body when the blade scraped against the metal table. A human would have gone into shock with the first few strokes of the blade. This woman didn't. To Kat's disbelief, the woman remained aware of everything the Hunter did, screaming in pain and horror the whole time. Fear and disgust rose in Kat's throat like a poisonous bile, making her want to vomit. Malice wasn't torturing the woman to see if she could handle it. He already knew she could. The demonstration of sick and twisted power was strictly for Kat's benefit. He wanted to make sure she knew he was serious.

The scientist and his helpers hacked off her remaining foot and then her arms. Kat didn't know people could grow back limbs. Apparently they could. This woman was whole again within an hour. The Hunters transfused twelve units of packed red blood cells to help the process along.

These people, these vampires, grew body parts! There wasn't any smoke and mirrors. No special effects to make her think she saw their torture. Kat knew what happened in front of her was very real. Kat noticed the growth rate was directly linked to the amount of blood the scientists gave to the woman. When they slowed the transfusion, her growth rate also slowed. Kat wondered if they had done it to the vampires and didn't give them any blood to help them regenerate. She figured those who weren't lucky enough to be given blood wouldn't grow any body parts back. Would they slowly wither away? Would their life seep out of them with the injuries the Hunters inflicted?

Kat closed her eyes. Over and over again she heard the cries of pain and agony from the woman. Hoping Viktor would come and rescue her before they turned their attention on her. She wondered what the serum would do to her ability to heal. Kat realized Viktor was most likely the only person who was strong enough to get her out of there. It seemed unlikely that someone would make a big enough mistake to allow for her to escape on her own.

She had known deep down she was safe with Viktor, even if he was a vampire. A wave of nausea hit her. Clutching her stomach, she lay down on her cot and closed her eyes. Maybe this was a nightmare, the worst she ever had, and she would wake up in her apartment? Maybe none of this ever really happened? She would wake up and it would be time to get ready for work. She sighed heavily and fell into a deep exhaustive sleep.

Viktor and Grailen found the Hunter's trail at the lakefront. Grailen, being the tracker for Delta 9, was able to pick it up quickly. "The Hunters have left a trail almost too easy to follow, Viktor. It makes me uneasy. They usually cover their tracks with more care than this."

"I see what you mean Grailen," Viktor said as he bent over to more closely examine what he figured was a size thirteen boot print in the muddy snow.

"It is almost as if they want us to be able to find them. Sloppiness like this is very unlike them, especially since they have such an important prisoner. It makes no sense to me," Grailen admitted.

Viktor grunted in frustration, letting his brother know he could do with less commentary and more trail following. Viktor knew this would take time and he would need patience, neither of which he was in abundance of at the moment.

Grailen started following the trail through the lakefront wooded area. The Hunter's trail led them to the main drive by the lake from the snow and grass covered area where Katrina must have been taken out of the water. He described to Viktor how pungent the odor was to him left behind by the Hunters. Grailen could also smell that Katrina was definitely the woman they had with them. Her fear gave off a distinct smell.

Viktor wasn't able to smell Kat's recent presence, only Grailen had been gifted with an overly developed olfactory sense. He was able to sense the Hunters. They felt like a layer of decay over his skin. It was as if they traveled with rotten meat strapped to their backs.

It didn't take Grailen long, traveling at vampiric speed, with Viktor following close behind to locate the Hunter's hideout. Grailen was sure this was where they brought Katrina. Neither brother could be sure if they would keep her here though. It was possible they may have moved her to a different location, knowing the Council would be hot on their trail. From what Viktor saw, he agreed with Grailen's assessment. It could be a trap to lure them in with Hunters waiting to take them down. Having such a protected and isolated compound so close to the mansion was very suspicious. Viktor didn't care if it was a trap. He was ready to throw caution to the wind to find Katrina. In such a short amount of time she became his sole reason for living.

Grailen was in silent awe that his brother, Viktor, would take anyone to mate. He knew when their kind took someone to mate, it was destiny. Despite that, Grailen thought Viktor was beyond the capture of any woman's snare. Viktor was difficult to live with, let alone spend an eternity with. He was moody, not that he, himself, wasn't. He almost pitied the young lady her destiny. He grinned. Viktor had his work cut out for him though. In all of Viktor's years, Grailen had never seen a woman walk, let alone run, away from his brother. Fate could be mean to her subjects.

His brother needed him to focus and help him find his

newfound woman. Fate worked in mysterious ways. Grailen wished their other brother, Rafe, was here with them to give Viktor a good razzing of his own. Grailen was sure Rafe would enjoy hunting Malice and helping take the Hunters down. Rafe was well known for his fighting and hunting abilities, which would have come in handy.

They both stopped at the top of a hill overlooking a small compound. Neither one of them suspected their task would be easy. They would have to wait for Dave to round up other Council members, of vampire persuasion, to make this work.

Viktor spied his surroundings. There was remote surveillance all around the building, cameras located above each of the entrances and probably areas he couldn't see. The compound was guarded by human-like soldiers in military attire. These men were outfitted similar to those Viktor had run into when he first encountered Kat. He noted the men had night vision goggles sitting on top of their helmets. That wouldn't really pose a problem for them or their vampire brethren. Vampire speed enabled them to pass by a human's vision without detection, even when the enemy used heat sensor visual aids.

It surprised Viktor that Malice had yet to devise something to assist him and his gang in protecting their evil lairs better. Detecting vampires would have been one of Viktor's first priorities if he were Malice. That was one of Viktor's responsibilities being in charge of his special op's unit. He had to figure out what the enemy was up to and what they were planning. Out of all the Council members, he was the best at anticipating the

Hunter's moves. Lately though, they had been relatively inactive. Sometimes Malice surprised him. Sometimes what Malice was scheming ended up backfiring on his self. This encouraged Malice to devise bigger and more evil plans. He drove his evil scientists to progress in what he called research.

Threatening his scientist's lives ensured their drive to excel and make Malice happy. Fear was a very strong persuasion aide when Malice needed something done. While Viktor spent time in one of their holding cells Malice executed an assistant for spilling the contents of a cylinder. Whatever it was, Malice must have thought it was important. It was also possible the temperamental maniac was just having a bad day.

Viktor pulled out his cell phone and hit the mansion's number on speed dial. Dave picked up on the first ring. "Viktor, what did you find out, did you find her?" Viktor could hear panic in Dave's voice. Humans were pretty easy to read. That reminded him, he had some information on Katrina's little friend, Carmen, that he needed to share with Kat. That was, if he ever got the chance. The fear in his friend's voice came from having treated Council members who experienced being Malice's guests.

"No, we didn't find her. But we did find the Hunter's stronghold. We need backup. Grailen and I are going to find a way to get into the main building while you get the guys together and send them here." He told his longtime friend where their location was and hung up. Viktor looked at Grailen. They nodded to each other in silence, knowing what they had to do. They set out in different directions to locate a weak spot in the

Hunter's security force around the compound. They needed a way in without alerting anyone. If Malice knew he had come to rescue Kat, Malice would kill her.

Their search wasn't successful. The Hunters must have been at that location longer than they originally thought. There were soldiers and cameras covering most of the compound. Neither of them could spot an easy way in. Viktor and Grailen knew fatalities were inevitable, they were about to take on an entire faction of Hunters. But that's what Council members did. They sacrificed their lives in order to save others.

Viktor's heart tightened with each waiting moment. He became aggravated as he sensed the coming sunrise. There was nothing he could do but retreat. Their backup must be coming from far away, Viktor thought bitterly. If not, they would get a real thrashing from him when this was all over.

Council units were located throughout the world, one for each of the Royal Family. There were a few more scattered throughout the world where large vampire populations existed. They all monitored Hunter's movements and watched for anti-vampire groups forming. Unfortunately, many of the American Council members had recently been deployed to various places to help the European sections. Malice and his Hunters had been quiet for so long Viktor saw no problem with lending his operatives to the other sections.

Viktor wanted to punch himself, how had he grown so lax,

allowing for this to happen? If he had all his Council members here, in Kensin, Kat wouldn't have to wait another full day until they could strike. Malice and his people had fewer limitations than Viktor and his guys due to their sunlight sensitivity. That meant Kat was at Malice's disposal twenty-four hours a day.

Viktor and his brother glided over the hill, back towards the safety of the mansion. Grailen would stay with him until this ended. Viktor knew it without having to ask. Grailen tended to float amongst the different Council sections. Lately he had taken up residence with Viktor at the mansion. He even took his turn doing patrols around the city, giving Viktor a break.

The brothers traveled in silence, each in their own set of thoughts. Viktor, consumed with visions of Katrina and what she must be going through, praying that she would survive this. Malice, the Hunter's leader, the most untraceable human-like being Viktor had ever had the unfortunate pleasure of meeting, was going to die a most painful death.

Katrina would suffer all the more if he knew she was now bonded with Viktor. Malice would ramp up her torture out of spite. Hopefully her mouth wouldn't get her in too much trouble. She was likely to say something to the fact that she couldn't wait for Viktor, her mate, to come and kick Malice's head in. Malice would figure out that he was the same Viktor she spoke of. There wasn't any other vampire in the neighborhood with his name.

Another possibility, she may insist on thinking Malice was insane, that vampires didn't exist. For her safety, Viktor hoped that was the case. That would probably be her best bet for staying alive long enough for him to rescue her. If she decided to give her captor any inkling of who she was and who was looking for her, Malice would make it more difficult for a rescue attempt to be successful. Malice had always held a sort of envy, beyond anything imaginable in the jealous emotions, against Viktor. Viktor always chucked it up to Malice wanting deep down to be a vampire, that's why he hated them so much. Malice probably hated that no one would turn him. Maybe one of the rogue vampires killed one of his family members? There was a reason for Malice's vendetta against his kind. Viktor had never bothered to find out exactly what it was.

Now, it was very personal, for Viktor. Even though Malice had treated Viktor horrendously when he had been captured, Viktor hadn't held a personal grudge against him. Now was different. Viktor thought to himself, for every hair on Katrina's head that is harmed, Malice would suffer for that many years until he was dead. Viktor had never been much into torture. The anger and helplessness he felt consumed him. The inability to go and get Katrina, to take her into his arms, he would change his ways. He would make Malice pay for everything he has done.

Viktor lay on his bed in the basement of the mansion. He couldn't stay in the room he shared with Katrina on the second floor. He couldn't be surrounded by her essence until he saved her. He went in and out of a mental trance during his unwilling rest. Visions of the upcoming mission flickered in his mind. The grave importance to the mission's success, thinking about Katrina and what she was enduring consumed his very being. Thoughts of the mission and Kat were meshed into one focus.

Viktor despised the human vampire legends, how they portrayed his kind as being unable to breathe, think, or feel during their death rest. Humans had no idea what torment he felt right now, having to lay there and wait. He struggled to endure every second while the world continued to go on without him.

The thought of having a blank mind, the ability to sleep would be much better than this. It felt like every second he lay there drove him closer to insanity. Viktor knew Malice wasn't sleeping, he knew Malice was conducting his vileness right now. Kat was probably his object of attention and Viktor couldn't do a damn thing about it.

It wasn't right for Viktor to hope Malice was focusing his evil energies on someone else, but he couldn't help it. His woman was at the mercy of one of the most vile, vicious humans walking the Earth. Malice had an army of genetically enhanced soldiers to help him. They worked obsessively to develop new ways to torture the vampires they caught. Testing the vampires, gauging what they could endure, and what would ultimately kill them was all in a day's work for them.

CHAPTER 13

When Kat woke up, she felt like another day had passed. She could feel the heat of the bright surgical lights that were kept on in her cell at all times. A thought came to her mind. Would she be alive in two days to see her twenty-fifth birthday? For some reason, that was her priority. It was important to see if what Viktor said was true. With every passing hour she felt weaker, yet she remained strong inside. The fact the serum was making her ill meant she may indeed have vampire blood running in her veins. She didn't care what happened, whether she proved Viktor wrong, or if she turned into a vampire. She was still an ordinary Kensin woman, and she wanted to see her birthday.

According to Viktor, she would have fantastic strength and abilities that she didn't have as an ordinary human. If that were true, she could take out this squad of goons all on her own. That was only if she did turn into a vampire and if she lived long enough to escape. Kat planned on letting all the other prisoners go free if she got loose. Then she would go and spend some long needed quality time with Viktor. She planned on listening to everything he had to say this time. She wanted to tell him how sorry she was for leaving. That was, as soon as she got out of here, of course.

Pulled from her internal chat, she heard a large commotion coming from down the hall. She swung her legs off the cot, walked to the wall and pressed herself up against the front panel of her cell. She was becoming used to feeling dizzy when she got up. She figured it was just another fabulous side effect of the serum. There were breather holes in her cell walls, like in that movie, Silence of the Lambs. Except in her story the bad guys were on the outside of the cell, and Clarice was on the inside.

A group of Hunters looking heavily armed ran past her cell without even glancing her way. They were all headed towards a heavy metal door down the hall. Unlike her cell with clear walls, that cell had a solid metal door with only a small window to look through. She had noticed it before but didn't pay it much attention. So far during her stay she hadn't noticed any activity happening over there. Right now there was quite the ruckus going on. Hunters were screaming in pain and yelling at each other to get the vampire.

Hunter bodies started flying out of the cell and smashing into the wall beside the cell entrance. Whoever or whatever was in that cell was causing a lot of trouble for Malice and his men. Kat felt like congratulating whoever it was for being able to hurt and fight the Hunters so strongly.

Kat wondered what unlucky soul found themselves in the Hunter Hotel, like she had. What did the Hunters want with them? Their evil leader Malice said his explanations should make everything clear to her, but nothing made sense to her. What the Hunters would gain from having her there she could only guess. The only thing Kat was sure of was that she was being held by a bunch of scary freaks that keep shooting her with tranquilizers and taking her blood. What could they possibly want from her?

Malice told her he was giving her some type of prototype drug, made right here in his own lab of horrors. Kat knew that since Malice started administering the serum she had become weaker. She sighed. Her strength was waning and she was in a perpetual state of being chilled to the bone and soaking her clothes with sweat. She couldn't eat anything they brought her, Malice threatened to tranquilize her again and feed her through a tube if she didn't try to keep something down. He said he wanted her to keep her strength up, that he needed her strong for her big day. Did he know when her birthday was? It seemed that he may know the same thing Viktor did about her bloodline. It must be why he was keeping her alive.

Watching the soldiers down the hall waiting in front of the cell door, Kat saw someone kick or ram something up against the door. It looked like it may cave in at any moment. The soldiers pushed against the door trying to keep the person in the cell from getting out. The guards sustained many injuries but in the end they closed the door to the cell. As Kat watched, a shadow crossed the viewing window of the door. A man's face came into view. His features were sharp and his jaw was angled. He reminded her of someone she knew but she couldn't place from where. His hair was long from what she could see. It was a deep rich brown color.

The man's eyes caught hers as she stared. Everything that should have been white in his eyes blazed a fiery red. When the man focused on her face, she saw his pupils dilate. He stepped away from the window and then more pounding on the door commenced. Someone in the cell behind him must have taken him by surprise because all at once, the pounding stopped. There must be holes in the cell wall like her cell. The goons probably shot him with a sedative dart like the ones they used on her. The soldiers continued to brace the door for a few more minutes until they were satisfied the man wouldn't cause them any more trouble. When they were sure the captive was no longer a threat they all stepped back except one. The soldier stepped forward and punched in a security code on the digital panel next to the door. He must be very brave, or very stupid.

Kat walked over to her cot, she needed to lie down. She didn't feel well. Maybe a short nap would help. She might be able to sleep. Watching the Hunters go in and out of the cell didn't give her any information about the man she saw through the window of the door. She heard men scream from down the hall. She could tell the Hunters sustained serious injuries. She could smell their blood and torn flesh. She couldn't get a beat on who they were keeping in the cell. His identity remained unknown to her. Too bad mister chit chatty wasn't around, he would probably brag about it to her, he seemed to have a habit of doing that about everything else.

Her ability to sense emotions from humans was becoming stronger. Maybe it was because her defenses were low. Being sick may be causing her psychic shields to be down, she thought to herself. The Hunter's thoughts were starting to make their way in a chaotic manner into her consciousness.

Right now she didn't give a damn what was going on. Maybe the prisoner would take down a couple of those jerks holding her captive? Maybe he would even rescue her when he escaped? Oddly enough, in the short moment they held eye contact, she knew there was a connection between them. Kat was certain when he looked at her face there was recognition in his eyes. She didn't want to lose hope. She was sure Viktor would come and save her from this awful place. As her thoughts turned to Viktor she fell into a coma-like sleep.

Worrying about Katrina while he could do nothing to save her was beyond any torture he ever experienced. Viktor hoped whatever they were doing to her, she would somehow be able to handle it. Physically she would be able to endure a lot, even for a yet to be turned vampire. Her royal blood would see to that. But she would have limits.

The Council had to put a vampire down because the impact

the Hunter's treatment had on the man. He was a good man, always played by the rules. The Hunters turned him into a raving monster. Ironically he turned into what the Hunters claimed all vampires were like. Viktor hoped if Katrina turned while captured the Hunters would know what to do to help her survive the change. By that time he would hopefully be with her to help her through it himself, and they would all be dead.

During her change, she would be given information. Memories of vampire history would come to her in chaotic visions. Those visions needed to be sifted through with the help of someone who had the knowledge and the patience necessary to do it. She would be given more information than non royal vampires because of her family lineage. Her rank was high in the hierarchy of their society. The visions could be overwhelming. Very few were granted the knowledge that she would be given. Kat would see the origins of the first vampires. She would see actions vampires had to take to survive, and vampire rituals in which humans were sacrificed. He wanted to be there to guide her through it all. He wanted to soothe her fear and explain those things were rarely done anymore.

There was a hefty amount of information for her to have to sift through. She wouldn't be able to differentiate between the past and present vampire lifestyles. Vampires are no longer the human hunters they once were. They have evolved alongside the humans.

Viktor feared what she saw would make her believe they were all blood thirsty monsters and that humans had every right to hate and fear them. Her physical change would be painful. Her eyes would become more angled for motion detection and enhanced night vision. Her spine would straighten making her appear taller. Every muscle in her body would heat during the change to synthesize stored fat cells. Her finger and toe nails would become thicker. Her feminine curves would become more pronounced to entice male prey.

Never before had anyone been as unprepared for the change as she was. How the hell did she end up being brought up by humans anyway? That still didn't sit well with him. A piece of her puzzle was missing.

Even if Prince Eric was worried about the repercussions of having an illegitimate child she still belonged to the royal family. The prince never should have left Katrina unprotected her entire life. Being who Kat was, she was in danger from the moment of her birth, and she was left unprotected to be brought up by a human. King Alexander would have taken care of her. They all would have.

Her childhood would have been one of entitlement. She would have had anything her heart desired. On the other hand, she would not have turned out to be the person she was now. But at least she would be prepared for what approached. Everything would have been much different for her, safer.

After what felt like an eternity, the sun finally began to set. Viktor felt his strength returning. He took his first breath of the night as he pulled back the black satin sheet and climbed out of bed. He went straight to his closet. He was readying himself for the night's events when Dave came in. "Viktor, a telephone call came through just a moment ago. It was one of Malice's soldiers. Somehow they got our number. He said he wants to make a trade. Obviously he must not know what or who he has, if he did he'd never let her go."

Viktor looked at Dave, a fresh wave of anger washed over him. "If they knew that Kat is Prince Eric's daughter, they'd keep her. There's no way in hell they'd give up an infinite supply of royal blood in trade."

Right before he succumbed to his day rest, Viktor explained everything he knew about Kat to Dave and Grailen. They were all in agreement that he created quite the mess by bonding with her before they were given approval by the High Council. They knew they had to get her away from the Hunters, no matter what the cost.

Viktor told them Katrina was a member of the royal family. That she must be the lost daughter of Eric, the prince who disappeared during the last big battle between the Council and the Hunters twenty four years ago. Prince Eric was the only one who could have had an unaccounted for offspring. If the prince was in the area, he would have been able to sense her presence and would never have left her alone to be brought up by a human woman. He would never have made her fend for herself as she did.

Typically, members of an immediate family were able to sense each other's presence when they were somewhere in the near vicinity. King Alexander would be able to sense her existence the moment she went through the change. The king may possibly be able to sense her now, Viktor wasn't sure.

He described how close she was to her change and that she didn't have a clue as to what was going to happen. They all surmised that she was a danger to herself if necessary precautions weren't taken. Her human caregiver obviously didn't know either, from what he could tell from Kat's memories. If her Aunt Rose knew anything about Kat's father, she hid it well from her. If that was the case, her Aunt Rose would be put to judgment for hiding her from the king. It was criminal for Kat to have existed all this time alone, without her real family. Viktor would have to ask Kat about that someday. He looked forward to meeting her aunt.

Viktor also reluctantly told them how he bonded with her. That he chose for them both to be married to each other for the rest of forever. Nothing anyone from the royal families could say would change it. The exception would be if they decided to order his death as punishment, which had happened in the past. Viktor presumed it was probably done long ago to prove a point. The king used the example to dissuade anyone else from committing such a treasonous act as bonding with a royal if you weren't one yourself.

Having permission from the king was highly recommended. Even if both were royals, it was still necessary to have the union approved, otherwise consequences ensued. The only person, besides the king, that had the power to break their bond was her father, Prince Eric. As far as Viktor knew, the prince had died when Kat was one year old. So that problem was solved, but not the big one, the king.

No member of the Council had ever dared to do what he had done. The connection between Viktor and Katrina, even on the chemical level, was beyond his comprehension. Viktor thought the fates must approve, for they put him by the hospital during his rounds when the Hunter approached her.

Shaking his head, Viktor cleared the emotional fog he found himself living in lately and tried to focus on the task at hand. "What do you mean trade?" he asked incredulously. Viktor knew, without Dave spelling it out, what he meant.

Malice had a grudge against Viktor on a grand scale. Ever since he escaped the Hunter's compound, Malice wanted him back. Viktor was living proof of Malice's failure. Viktor left a nasty scar along the right side of Malice's face and torso with a jagged metal pole he found while he made his way out of his cell. "He must really have it in for me bad to go through all this trouble, and that he is willing to give up a new captive, a fresh set of genes says a lot about him. Malice must not be thinking too clearly," he said as he looked at his friend. Viktor was being handed an opportunity to get Katrina away from the Hunters before her change. He had to move on it fast.

"Get him back on the phone! We need to set up the arrangements." Dave glanced at him with concern, knowing

Viktor would do anything to save this woman. He would even face death with a smile if he had to. That worried him.

"Viktor, he said he would call us back."

"Dave, what are you waiting for? Go and get that bastard back on the phone and tell him I'm ready!"

"Unfortunately we were unable to trace their location before the caller made his demands and hung up." Viktor glared at him, asking himself why everyone around him seemed incompetent.

"Don't forget, you are under a severe amount of stress and that is cause for making irrational decisions. We should wait until the men are here and make a joint decision. Do this the right way and everyone can make it out alive, Viktor," Dave said in a pleading voice. He knew Viktor was freaking out, and rightly so. Malice was a formidable and unpredictable enemy. That made their rescue mission difficult to plan. No one considered the possibility that the Hunters would offer to trade Kat for Viktor.

"Well my dear, there has been a change of plans, it seems. We're going to trade you for your friend, Viktor." From seeing her reaction at hearing Viktor's name, he continued. "Yes, we know that you two are somehow linked, we just don't know exactly how. But it no longer matters," Malice said with a wave of his hand.

"Your lab results show promising affects from the serum injections. My scientists tell me the injections you've been getting have started to take hold on your vile body. From what we can tell, you may not turn into a vampire at all. We may have just saved you from becoming the evil being you are meant to become. Wouldn't that please you?"

"I still don't know what you're talking about. All you've done is make me feel horrible. I don't think whatever you've been giving me is working at all," Kat lied. She knew something was going on, she could feel her body starting to change. Now being able to read some of Malice's thoughts and view a few of his memories, she knew what he and Viktor had been saying was true.

"The best part is being able to trade an ordinary vampire girl for Viktor. Now I'll be able to test my serum on a member of the Council. One step up from you I'm afraid," he said as if somehow he was insulting her. "Of course that's what we plan for him when he arrives, once he is secured behind that cell wall." Malice pointed to the very same cell she was now occupying.

"I'll be able to make Viktor pay for what he has done to me, not only physically, but to my pride as well," he said this more quietly, not wanting any of his men to hear that his pride could possibly be hurt. He probably didn't want to alter their perception of him.

"The Council will most likely take you back to the mansion. Not only does the serum make a vampire lose their extra-human strength and abilities, it's contagious," he said with a sneer. "While developing the mixture, the scientist was able to formulate it to make the mode of transmission airborne."

Malice barely contained his giddiness while he spoke. Ever since his research team had begun running their tests, Malice had more hope than ever that he may achieve his ultimate goal. Finally he may have found a way to rid the world of the entire vampire population. Unfortunately he wouldn't be able to see her die. He would have to be content with knowing she suffered before dying. It was too important to him to have Viktor back in his clutches. More important than keeping this insignificant female until the serum finished its course.

This woman, who fell into the palm of his hand, may turn out to be his biggest weapon yet. No one would be the wiser until it was too late. He grinned. How he had waited and committed so much of his life for this occasion. He hadn't felt this good since he captured that royal vampire now being held down the hall from her. Since they were having such a difficult time with him, he might just get rid of him. The male's blood never showed such promise as hers did. He could execute the male vampire to save him all the hassle it took just to feed the despicable being. On the other hand, it might be advantageous to keep him around for a while longer to compare this woman's blood to his. He had kept a stock of her blood infected with the serum.

Malice changed his mind. He decided to give the male her infected blood and monitor the affects that way. Then he would let him go, so he could infect all those that weren't affected by the strain Katrina carried. For reasons unknown, Katrina's chemical makeup was the catalyst they've been looking for.

The royal bastard down the hall in the closed cell never

became infected. He didn't lose an ounce of strength from being injected. They kept him around to find out why, despite all the soldiers lost when dealing with him. Although the tests weren't yielding any results, they would figure it out. Malice knew it was only a matter of time. Everything took time. Hopefully their newest version of serum would be as potent and contagious to the remaining vampires as the serum they used on Katrina.

Kat knew the situation she found herself in was dangerous and she should take it seriously. Yet, she couldn't help but roll her eyes at Malice. He seemed to really like the dramatics. Every time something new happened, no matter how insignificant it seemed to her, Malice had to run up to her cell and tell her all about it. She could envision him walking into a room, raising his arms up in the air like some great world leader. Then the vision of him entering a ballroom wearing a furry crown and cape doing the same thing crossed her mind. Except no one applauded him like he expected, they attacked. Wishful thinking she supposed.

Kat made a mental note to herself; let him think you are afraid of him. In truth, she was. Kat feared that if Malice thought differently he might really hurt her. Men like him were dangerous. She sighed. Kat knew after Malice told her of the exchange that she would be ok. Until then she had to mind her words and actions. His mention of Viktor made her fear lessen. She was able to think clearly. Tomorrow was her birthday, she was pretty sure. It was hard to judge time sitting in this cell. She would be twenty-five years old.

The infamous change everyone was talking about was supposed to happen tomorrow. If it didn't, it would prove to them that she wasn't what or who they thought she was. The thought upset her. She didn't want Viktor to be disappointed with her. What if she didn't turn into a vampire? Would he still love her and stay with her? Could he bond with a human like he said vampires did?

Once Viktor found out it wasn't true he may go and find the real vampire princess and live happily ever after. Maybe he would realize that he did have something wrong upstairs and she wasn't like him. He may be too disappointed to face her. She hoped that wasn't the case, he was kind of growing on her.

She missed everything about him including his unusual ability to piss her off. The way she got turned on just by him walking into the room or looking into her eyes, and having him tell her that she was his wife. Even though she gave him a horrible time about everything he told her, she was finally on board with the idea. Everything he told her was real to him, everything except her part in it. What the hell would he and this High Council do once they realized she wasn't anyone special? She wasn't the princess Viktor thought, was she? If she turned out to be a regular human woman, like she had said all along, what would they do to her for knowing their secrets? Would they kill her? Kat was sure of one thing. She would do anything in her measly little power to help them get rid of this vile creature.

CHAPTER 14

Malice rapped his knuckles on Kat's cell wall to remind her that yes, hello, he was still there. He couldn't figure out why this evil female spawn couldn't keep her attention on him. It seemed to him that she often fell into her own little world. Like her impish brain was misfiring and she didn't comprehend the dire situation she was in. Hello! Who's the big bad guy here? Everyone takes him seriously, everyone was afraid of him! Malice's temper flared and he began to pace in front of her cell in frustration.

No one had ever given him such disdain and disrespect as this female vampire. She had some nerve! Maybe he should keep her and Viktor. It would be entertaining to see how they liked watching each other scream in agony before he released her to the Council. It would be all her fault. He could use her to make Viktor suffer like he was never able to do before.

"Ms. Drogan, it's time for me to call your friends and set up the final details for the trade agreement. You should prepare yourself for a little journey. Who knows, you may decide that you like it here better than wherever they are going to take you."

"Not likely you piece of crap."

Malice shrugged his shoulders. "After being surrounded by vampire vermin, you may end up craving the company of normal, good willed humans. You know, you could join us in our fight to do what's right. To rid this planet of the likes of them," he said as he nodded in the direction of the hostage down the hall.

"Wouldn't you like to become an integral part of something greater than yourself?" With that, Malice walked away from her cell and went into his office. His office was located right off the main entrance of the lab. The walls of his office were lined with material that made it impossible for her to invade his mind. She wouldn't be able to hear the details of the trade.

Viktor and Grailen looked at each other after Viktor hung up the phone with Malice. Grailen heard what Viktor said to that bastard, he wasn't sure how Viktor was going to handle it. Malice told Viktor that if he brought reinforcements the woman was going to die. She was going to die anyway, if she spent another day with that madman. If Katrina went through her change without their help, she would never make it! She would require assistance to get her through the memory flashes and the pain she would experience through the change. Someone needed to be there to sift the memories, to put them into order. It was possible if she didn't have aid during that time she could end up going insane. Seeing flashes of bloody wars, human sacrifices, tortured Hunters and Councilmen. It was too much for one person to handle if they didn't have a guide.

Neither Viktor nor Grailen were sure if the Hunters had ever had a vampire during their time of change. Did they know what to do? Providing human blood was essential during that time to ensure full recovery. A vampire's body died, all bodily functions stopped, and the body had to be jump started again. If that essential step wasn't taken, the body started to feed on itself and they usually never woke up.

"Malice wants me to go to his compound. He said I can't have anyone with me beyond their outside perimeter. He said I could have a human ready on the outside to wait for Kat's release." Viktor could barely speak. "He also said that she needed help to walk out of there. What the hell does that mean? What the hell did he do to her? He is so going to pay for this!" he screamed, not at his brother but at the world. He didn't want to go back to being Malice's captive. He knew Malice would be ruthless in his administrations. Viktor's escape was a permanent mark against Malice's resume of competence. The disfiguring slice he made on his face and body didn't help his disposition either.

"Have Dave get ready. I want him to be the one to help her get out of there. If she needs medical attention he'll be able to do it. He's seen enough, he'll be able to stabilize her until the men arrive. I want you here Grailen. I want you waiting for them when he returns with her. She's going to need someone with experience, and you're it."

Grailen paced in Viktor's room. He looked as tense as Viktor felt. "Viktor, you should reconsider going in there alone. When the men come we'll figure something else out."

"Grailen, I love her with all of my soul. She is a part of me, and you better not let anything happen to her. She has strength in her, but she's still going to need your help. She has a really good chance of making it through this. Yes," he put up his hands, "I know what you're thinking. They will punish me for having bitten her and of course the bonding. But Grailen, she is the one."

"I don't doubt your devotion and love to the woman, brother. I saw it in your eyes the first time I saw you two together. Don't justify to me what you are doing. I understand. But I think you're going about it the wrong way."

"We were meant for each other. I found my mate and now she is in mortal danger. You are going to do things my way for once. If something happens because this arrangement goes bad, I don't know what I would do. If I die and she lives, you will watch over her with your life," Viktor said.

"Viktor, I want you to think about what you're doing. Being the hero is one thing, but we need you both to survive. If Malice decides to set a trap for you, to have you and Katrina both, that would ruin everything. You know she won't survive if she doesn't have the help she needs. If Malice ends up keeping you both, you will both die. I don't have to tell you how unhappy King

Alexander will be if he realizes we decided to take matters into our own hands and not inform him."

"Don't worry about the king. I'll deal with him once Katrina is safe. Right now that's all that matters." Viktor started towards the door and Grailen followed.

"If something happens to her, I can't fathom the wrath the Council will experience. I'm not just talking about what the Council will have to deal with. I'm talking about the entire human race. Ever since Prince Eric was lost, King Alexander has become obsessed with family safety. Katrina is now his family. He just happens not to know it yet." Grailen went on for what seemed like an eternity as he followed Viktor up the stairs. Viktor was getting antsy. He was sick of waiting. He needed action, and he needed it now.

"Brother, I know what you are trying to do and it is not going to work. You know how it is. Katrina is everything to me, a part of me. You know why I can't wait for backup. I appreciate your insight, but this is what has to be done." Viktor put his hand on his brother's shoulder and gave him a squeeze.

Viktor stood at the top of the hill looking down at Malice's compound. He was in the same spot he and Grailen stood mapping the compound's security. Viktor didn't see any way for his men to get in and make their big rescue once he got Katrina out. He realized he would probably die in there. He considered it a small sacrifice, as long as he was able to free Katrina. That's all that mattered to him.

Dave stood to his right. Viktor could hear Dave's heart beat. The rhythmic tempo sounded like a drum to his ears. Viktor couldn't tell if Dave shivered from the cold winter night or from fear. His friend was afraid for him. He was afraid for them all.

Dave had gone through life knowing vampires of the Council, seeing them die through the years. Some had been injured beyond healing in the line of duty. They died honorable deaths. The Council was weary due to past losses. Malice couldn't be trusted, they all knew that. Malice could only be counted on for his depravity, his inability to show mercy to his victims.

They looked at each other with an all knowing glance. They spoke volumes without uttering a word. Then Viktor started down the hill in a graceful, determined stride. His movements looked part feline.

"Ah, the great hero comes to rescue the damsel in distress," Malice purred towards Katrina as he hung up the phone. He couldn't believe his great luck! He was suspicious of Viktor keeping his word not to bring reinforcements. He knew Viktor would have something up his sleeve. That's what he would do in this situation.

Malice's captive was still in her cage. He ordered his soldiers to administer another dose of serum along with a sedative. He did this for two reasons. One was to keep her passive when they made the switch. Malice wasn't willing to chance even the slightest opportunity for her to get away before he had Viktor. The other reason was to make sure the dose of anti-vampire serum in her blood was as potent as they could make it to infect as many vampires as possible.

His science team reported the serum potency may or may not be strong enough to infect the older vampires. That's who Katrina would be surrounded by at the mansion. Malice hoped Viktor's Council members had a few young vampires in their ranks. Otherwise, his evil master plan may not work. Malice was disappointed from the news, given to him after he called Viktor and set up the trade. Of course he killed his scientist for not telling him this earlier. But the gratification he would get from having Viktor back in his cell was worth more than anything to him. If the vampire woman infected even one vampire and killed him, it would be worth it.

The contagions were not as predictable and stable as he hoped. After a few hours they seemed to lose their potency. They began to break down and cling to the original host. In this case, that host was Katrina. The scientists were unable to determine what component of her blood made her susceptible to the serum's properties. To get Viktor, Malice would sacrifice having fresh samples of her infected blood. The more vampires she infected the better, in his eyes. Malice smiled at the thought. He couldn't wait for everything to fall into place. When the vampires were in their weakened state, if the serum worked, he would strike!

With Viktor unable to guide his Council, Malice would have

a better chance to take the rest of them out. He could catch more vampires for samples too. He knew that as of right now he couldn't even get close to them, not while they had full vampire strength. He needed to even the playing field. Hopefully the serum would do that.

When the time came, he would be ready. Or, if the serum did what he hoped and took their vampire essence and strength away by mutating their DNA into a submissive state, he may just let them suffer in the human world as mere mortals. Of course he would make them suffer by his hand. After all, they had still committed their evil crimes throughout their many undeserved years of life. Malice couldn't decide what would make him happier. Kill them all, or torture them in front of each other for a very, very long time.

Malice had a team of his henchmen waiting for Viktor at the main entrance to the compound. Each of them carried of cache of weapons on their bodies. Viktor was confident he could take them out, all of them. He wouldn't, if he did, that would end the deal and Malice would kill Katrina. He slowed his pace to a more human speed when he reached fifty feet from where Malice's men stood, their guns pointed at his chest.

Viktor slowly put his hands in the air to show them he wasn't hiding anything in his hands. He slowly walked towards them. Their ringleader shouted to him when he got roughly twenty feet away from the door. He was to stay right where he was. Viktor stopped and kept his arms up. The soldiers cautiously approached him. They closed a circle around him, all six of them. The leader spoke up and said they were going to make the final length of the trip into the compound as they were. Viktor nodded in understanding. He was to stay in this formation, with him surrounded by the six heavily armed, mortal, and brainwashed assholes.

The soldier in the center threw him something that resembled a giant necklace, or dog like collar. "Put that around your neck blood sucker. I want to hear the lock click in place you disgusting creature."

Viktor caught the collar without taking his eyes off the leader. He hadn't seen this contraption the last time he was Malice's guest.

"What do you think, men? Should we shoot it in the head and put it out of its misery? Its little girlfriend wouldn't have to be released, then. Maybe the master would let us have some fun with her before we kill her," said the soldier. Disgust was written across his face. He obviously didn't like vampires very much.

"If you touch a hair on that woman's head, I won't play nice. If you hurt her in any way, I'll find you. I'll make you regret you ever met me."

"There's nothing you can do you stupid creature. She'll die if you don't cooperate, so do as you're told, dog." The soldier was really starting to piss Viktor off.

"What the hell is this for?" Viktor held up the collar. Looking at it he noticed there were electrical wires running through it. "I'm here. I said I would behave as long as Malice keeps his end of the bargain. So you can have your collar back." Viktor threw the contraption back to the man, putting a little too much strength behind his throw. The collar hit the soldier's gun, almost knocking it out of his hands.

There was no way he was putting that thing on himself, what the hell were they thinking? He would be the willing prisoner, to a point. No reason to be stupid about it. The leader rolled his eyes and pointed the muzzle of his gun towards the entrance.

Viktor and his chaperones made their way into the building. He could sense their apprehension. Being so close to him made them nervous. Good, that meant he had fear on his side. That would come in handy when he decided he had enough and it was time to leave again.

Three of the goons went in front of him through the doorway, three stayed behind him until he passed through. Viktor put his arms down at his sides as they continued to escort him through the maze of hallways. He noticed the walls were painted similar to what Viktor thought an insane asylum would be. No pictures were on the walls. He guessed this was to keep distraction to a minimum and not give Malice's guests any stimulation he didn't design himself. Nothing gave away the owner's personal choice, just the lack of one. After the little tour he got, they arrived at their destination, Viktor's cell.

He wasn't surprised Malice would choose one that was heavily equipped to contain him. That was part of Malice's error the last time he had Viktor as a guest. He underestimated Viktor. Malice didn't realize what Viktor was capable of. Not many people were privy to that sort of information.

Malice forgot to prepare some members of his squad from being controlled by vampire mind persuasion. That helped him get away. This time he wasn't sure he would be given such an opportunity. From the looks of it, the cell was reinforced to ensure Malice had a captive audience. There were large cylindrical bars crossing his prison cell door. Viktor assumed the cell reinforcement was in case Viktor felt like pounding on the walls with his super strength.

Once Viktor was positioned to be placed in his cell, one of the goons stepped forward and punched a password into a keyboard next to the door. When he finished, the screen turned green and the mechanics of the door started working. It took awhile for all the gears to unwind, depressurize, and unlock. Finally the door unhinged and popped open about an inch. Goon number two grabbed the door with both hands and slowly pulled it open. Viktor was surprised Malice didn't have him delivered through the central command area where his little minions worked their evil deeds. He figured that would be where they held Kat.

All six henchmen, still aiming their rifles at him, waited until he walked into the cell. When he was fully inside, Viktor slowly turned around towards the door. Still aiming their guns toward the door, the soldiers waited while goon number two pushed on the handle and the door clicked into place.

The tumblers of the high-tech, reinforced, locking mechanism moved into place when goon number one punched in another code. Viktor thought Malice must have upgraded features of his cell since the last time he was here. Viktor looked around, becoming as familiar with what was available to him as he could. He knew Malice would be along shortly, not being able to contain his nasty glee of happiness with his newest acquisition, that being himself.

Malice didn't disappoint him. A new sound came through the walls, opposite of where he had entered his cell. Viktor knew that all the cells, as far as he could remember, made a single line all around Malice's command center. They were positioned in the formation for easy access to and surveillance of the detainees. It was funny to Viktor, that Malice would design all of his compounds in the same manner. This compound was just like the one he was held in many years ago. The familiarity of the layout would help when he escaped. The information would be a key component to his plan. He would have to make do with the minor differences and upgrades. There were two doors to each cell, one in the front, leading straight to the command center. The other door, on the opposite side of the room, led to a hallway that circled the inner sanctum of the compound.

The sound of the door closing continued. Viktor stared at the wall, waiting. After only a moment, another set of sounds began. He turned and looked at the back wall. The bottom of the cement wall began to separate from the floor. Then slowly lifted and disappeared upwards into the ceiling, much like a garage door. Viktor took note that the segments of cement blocks were not fully attached to each other.

Beyond the cement blocks were the clear walls that he remembered. Malice kept eerily close to the design of the other compound he was held in. As he expected, Malice was waiting on the other side of the cell wall. What he didn't expect was to see Katrina standing, or rather slouching, against Malice.

Seeing her turned Viktor's heart to ice. She looked weak and beaten. Malice, on the other hand, looked as spiteful as ever. He wore a smug grin on his face, distorted by the long scar that ran the length of his cheek from the outside corner of his eye to the bottom edge of his jaw. The scar made him look twisted.

Viktor looked her over. She didn't look like she had been beaten too badly. But she did look like she had been put through hell. He was sure she had, knowing Malice. Katrina was extremely pale, thinner than he remembered. He knew tomorrow night was going to be one hell of a night for her. She needed all the strength she had to get through it. Dave and Grailen would do everything they could to help her, but he wasn't so sure that it was going to be enough.

"Katrina, are you alright?" he asked her. He didn't care if Malice knew how much he cared for her, he wanted her to know. Katrina slowly raised her head to look at where the voice was coming from. Her hair fell away from her confused eyes.

Katrina recognized Viktor. She heard him talking but she couldn't understand what he was saying. At first she couldn't figure out why he was in a cell, why was he here at all? Everything slowly came back to her. Malice's mocking words, telling her how she was going to be released to Viktor's people for a trade. Viktor! She figured this must be what he meant, seeing Viktor behind the cell wall. Now that she was no longer in a cell, she thought Malice was going to keep his word. For whatever reason, Malice seemed to be going through with his part of the deal.

Usually the bad guy in the story didn't keep their word. Or, Malice could have decided to let Viktor see her and that she was still alive. Viktor's cooperation was important. Malice didn't want two angry male vampires on his hands. His cooperation would make him easier to deal with while he tortured and interrogated him. Tears began to run down her face with the thought of Malice doing to Viktor what she saw him do to the others.

Malice interrupted their moment, "Well, Viktor, long time no see. We have a deal. I don't want anything funny to happen or else your lady friend here will suffer, and so will you. You got it?" He waited for Viktor to respond. Finally Viktor nodded his head in agreement. He couldn't keep his eyes off Kat. He knew once the Council had her safe and got her through the change, they would come for him. By now the other Council members would have arrived in the city. They were probably making a strategy right now as he looked at Malice with a cold murderous glare. Viktor had never hated any one being in all his life more than this insane malicious human.

CHAPTER 15

Katrina felt dazed. The last dose of serum and sedative the Hunters injected had left her feeling clouded and confused. She wasn't able to make out what was real and what were hallucinations. She was fading in and out of consciousness, finding herself in the most awkward positions when she came to.

Katrina didn't know she was standing until she heard Viktor say her name. His voice pulled her momentarily out of a mental fog. She again felt herself being dragged along long hallways by one of the soldiers, and not very nicely. Not recognizing her surroundings increased her confusion. She could barely stand, she felt weak and lightheaded. She hated whatever they were giving her. This last time they injected her with a whopper of a dose. She didn't quite understand what it was supposed to be doing to her, besides make her feel terribly ill. Malice mentioned something about wanting to spread some type of anti-vampire virus by exposing her to the rest of the vampire world. Somehow, just by her being in their presence, the vampires would keel over and die.

Malice motioned to a few soldiers to join in on her rough handling. He spoke quickly when he gave instructions she couldn't follow what he said. Her brain was clouded. She knew what they talked about had to do with her. But she was lost beyond that. When they finished their conversation, Malice's men led her to a door leading to the outside. When they opened the door the fresh air hit her body and she would have fallen over if she wasn't being held upright by the soldiers. They unceremoniously pushed her through the opening. They followed her through the doorway and dragged her roughly along a narrow gravel path and began to pull her up a snow covered hill.

They shoved her forward, telling her that if she didn't move fast enough they were going to shoot her. After taking two wobbly steps on her own, she turned and looked behind her. The soldiers were waiting for her to go up the path. She noticed they were armed and pointing their guns beyond her, higher up where the hill crested about seventy-five feet away from where she stood. Katrina turned her head back around to see what they were targeting. There, beside the lone Maple tree at the top was Dave. She could barely see him but she was sure it was him.

She sighed in relief. Never did she think she would find as much comfort in seeing one of Viktor's men as she did right now. Fear seared straight through her gut. She was afraid they would go against their word and kill them all.

Katrina didn't want to be the cause of anyone dying, especially Dave. He had been the only kind person at the mansion. He was the only one, besides Viktor himself, who tried to help her make sense of all the chaos of the last few days. She already felt awful for the position Viktor was in. She felt responsible. Even though she didn't understand her place in all of this, she would feel terrible if Viktor or any of his people were hurt.

One of the minions who had been holding her up took a few steps towards her, jabbed the end of his rifle into her side, shoving her forward again. She was weak to the point the forward momentum from his push caused her to fall on her hands and knees into the ice cold snow. Glancing back up at the soldier, he grunted at her as he motioned up the hill with the barrel of his rifle. Katrina barely got up off the ground, her strength seeming to seep out of every pore. Her will to get out of there and help as much as she could with whatever had to be done to save Viktor gave her the drive to push onward. She took one step forward, and then another, until she reached Dave.

Dave put his arm around Katrina to shield her from Malice's men in case they decided to take a cheap shot and shoot one or both of them in the back. He also did it to help hold her up. Viktor's woman didn't look well. He knew he must get her away from there and into the safety of the mansion as quickly as he could. Grailen didn't follow orders very well. He waited for them to come down the back side of the hill in his black SUV.

Kat began to sob when she saw Viktor's brother. Dave tried to sooth her. "Katrina, everything will be alright. We'll take very good care of you sweetheart."

Kat clutched onto his jacket as she sobbed. "Dave, they have him. They have Viktor in a cell!"

"We know he'll be alright. Everything's going to be just fine. You don't have to worry about anything. We'll take care of everything."

Kat couldn't help but sob. Her emotions came in waves and wracked her body with pain. "Dave, you don't understand, the things they to do people in there! They cut off arms and legs! Their sick and twisted leader hates Viktor. We have to get him out of there!"

Dave carefully guided her down the hill, holding up much of her weight. He stumbled once but caught them before they fell. When they reached the SUV, Grailen jumped out and helped Dave. When he touched her he was instantly surprised. With her being so close to her change, she emanated raw power. Her power was more pure than he felt from any of his kind in a long time. That one moment of contact left his fingertips and the palm of his left hand tingling from the electrical charge she gave off when he touched her. Dave was lucky, he thought, it didn't bother him like it would others of her kind.

The contact caught him off guard. It was more than just the physical strength that came from her. Kat felt different somehow, he couldn't put his finger on what it was. But she definitely was not fully human, and not fully vampire. He figured that was a question to find an answer for another time. For now, she had to survive, and he had to help her through it if he wanted Viktor to ever talk to him again. Viktor would kill him if anything happened to her. His brother was known for having quite the temper when he was pissed off. Heck, they all were, even cool headed Dave lost it every now and then.

Grailen had kept the vehicle running so when he and Dave put Katrina into the back seat she would feel the warmth from the heaters blowing at her. Grailen wasn't sure the heated seats would even work, he had never tried them. He never had a need for them until now but he turned them on anyway. Together, Grailen and Dave settled Kat in the back seat, laying her across the leather. Grailen had grabbed blankets for her, and a pillow, even though the ride wasn't much more than an hour by car.

Even with the urgency of Katrina's impending change, they would have to take precautions. They would have to drive around aimlessly for a while before they headed back to the mansion. They had to make sure Hunters weren't following them. He and Dave had talked about Grailen transporting her back to the mansion and having Dave take the SUV back. But in the end they decided that she was probably too weak and too freaked out to handle being teleported right now. So, away they drove.

Grailen expected the others to have arrived at the mansion by the time they got Katrina there. He was right. But only a few were waiting for them. The rest, the ones who had traveled from the farthest locations went out to feed in case there was action to be had that night. Traveling for vampires, whether it was the more traditional means of transportation using a vehicle or by teleportation were both draining. They would need to replenish their energy with blood.

Dave and Grailen took Katrina up to Viktor's private rooms and situated her in his bed. They tried to make her as comfortable as they could. They figured the room was the most comfortable place they had to offer her, giving her a place where she would be most at ease. At least she would be somewhere she would recognize when she woke up. Neither of them had much experience with women, they only knew how to take care of soldiers when they were injured from battle. They could give them what they needed, but having to take care of Kat was beyond both of their realms of expertise. The two men would be the ones to take care of her unless the king found out and sent a team to take her to the palace before the change occurred. But that was unlikely, there wasn't enough time.

Whatever the king decided was what was going to happen. Bad things, very bad things, happened when the king's orders weren't followed. His band of demons, the Judges, made sure of that. The threat of them was enough to keep the majority of the vampire population in their place. They gladly followed the rules and did exactly what they were told. If they did, all were happy. If they didn't, the Judges came to town for a visit.

No one in their right mind wanted that to happen. In essence, the Judges were the vampire's version of the boogey men. The Judges were the king's personal team of demonic body guards and enforcers. None of Kensin's Council members ever had to deal with them, not directly. But the stories were infamous. The general vampire society tended to behave in fear of catching their attention.

Dave and Grailen took turns watching over her. Whoever wasn't with her discussed the situation with the few Councilmen arriving. The two men talking with Dave in the kitchen were from Viktor's team, Delta 9. The others that were supposed to arrive were from Delta 6. They were a different faction of the Council but would come to Viktor's aid without question or delay. They all belonged to the Council in some fashion. It was well known that when a member of the Council needed them as a collective group, there was big trouble brewing. That's what they liked. That's what they lived for.

There was a reason why they didn't normally co-habitat the same city, or even the same country in some cases. The Council vampires were naturally aggressive. It got pretty tense when there wasn't a mission to occupy and expend their energies. Vampire males tended to not want to share the same hunting grounds. They ended up turning on each other for amusement. Sometimes it got out of hand and someone would get hurt. Or worse, someone got killed. The vampires who made up the Council were some of the nastiest vampires walking the planet. They tended not to play well with others. They tended to be vicious, have big egos, and look for action of any kind. When they worked together they were practically unstoppable.

The king didn't like it when they fought amongst themselves. He needed all of the Council members to be healthy and ready to fight, not recovering from wounds inflicted by each other. They were needed in many different locations to keep the Hunters in check. The Council made sure that all around the world peace and harmony was kept. They existed to keep the evil little mortals monitored and when necessary, decommissioned.

Viktor glared at Malice wondering what the plans for him were going to be this time. Did Malice even know himself yet? He was sure that Malice had dreamed of having this day come ever since his escape. Now he could take his retribution on Viktor. Viktor was wrong. He didn't know about the serum and how Katrina was already carrying it.

Then, there it was, a pricking sensation in his neck. Viktor, consumed with looking at Malice, failed to notice Malice's henchmen had opened a small sliding pocket window set into the wall of his cell. Viktor grabbed at what was stuck in his neck and brought the dart into his view. He looked up at Malice, realizing he was just shot by a dart gun.

As Viktor wondered what was on the tip of the dart Malice began to get excited. He didn't understand why until Malice said, "Viktor. My soldier has shot you with a sedative especially made for vampires. It worked extremely well on your female friend."

"You're going to pay for whatever you did to her."

"You should start feeling weak soon. Don't worry. It's alright to pass out. We'll do whatever we feel like whether you're asleep or not," Malice said as he laughed at Viktor and the vulnerable position he tricked Viktor into being.

Viktor took his cue to go and lie down on the cot in the corner of the cell. He didn't feel weak like Malice expected, but he didn't want his captor to know whatever he was injected with wasn't working. At least it hadn't started to yet. After he lay down he closed his eyes. After a few minutes he heard the tumblers in the door lock shift. He decided now was not the time to get frisky. He needed to be able to watch Malice and his goons for a while. Viktor needed to determine what their activities were and if they kept to any type of schedule. Schedules were good to know of your enemies.

With that information Viktor could formulate a plan of escape. The thought of taking Malice down for all of the crimes he committed against his kind, especially to Katrina, warmed him. Malice was one of the highest cronies in the world of the Hunters. The Council didn't know exactly how high on the food chain he was. He wielded a great amount of power. They gave him limitless resources for all the evil deeds his sick and twisted mind could come up with. Malice's experiments were of his design. The scientists were the ones who made those ideas come to life.

After a few hours of drowsy delirium, Katrina fell into somewhat of a restful sleep. It was Dave's turn to watch over her so Grailen could meet with Viktor's men. They needed to plan how they were going to get Viktor out of the compound alive. They all knew it was going to be a very difficult mission.

Thomas, Viktor's second in command, had taken surveillance photos of the area surrounding the compound. He also took note of the different types of security systems, personnel Malice had in place, and when they did their changing of the guard. Malice knew what he was doing when he chose his location for his nest of evilness. It was going to be very difficult to penetrate his protective forces, it seemed. But they would try. Against all odds, they would get Viktor back. Or they would die trying. The Council didn't leave one of their own to suffer Malice's tortures if they knew he had them.

Malice had killed too many vampires for the Council to let it go. Yet, he always seemed able to disappear when the Council got close to catching him. The new compound appeared to have been occupied by the Hunters for a while. The teams of outside security personnel had a pattern of checkpoints which was helpful to plan their attack. Thomas noted the soldiers comfort level was too high. They were lax in completing their rounds. But it was clear from the sophistication of the surveillance equipment that whatever Malice was concocting, he wanted to keep it a secret.

As Grailen rounded the stairway into the meeting hall of the mansion he stopped dead in his tracks. Two members of the royal family were standing in the doorway, glaring at him! Throughout his life, he hadn't had the need to interact with them very much.

He was the loner, left to brood in his darkness and despair by himself. But he knew who they were the moment he laid eyes on them. Everyone knew who they were! He also knew, without looking at Thomas, that someone had called them about Katrina. The rage of betrayal he felt was beyond words. The anger caused his blood pressure to rise to the point his ears felt hot.

Grailen didn't understand why the king would send his children. Why would the king allow them to leave the palace unguarded? Why had the king not sent a couple of their assistants or the Judges to take Kat to the palace? Someone must have told the king that Katrina was of royal blood! That was the only explanation for them being here and not in the safety of the palace. He assumed it must have been Dave. Damn humans! You could never fully trust them. Grailen knew it was all of their responsibility to do so, but betrayal burned him.

Never in Grailen's wildest dreams did he think Dave would let them know she was of royal blood. He thought the agreement was to tell them they found a vampire of unknown lineage. But the prince and princess standing before him told Grailen that Dave hadn't stuck to the plan. That had to be why the prince and princess came themselves. Whoever called from the High Council had contacted the king about the woman, Viktor's woman. Grailen didn't have the authority to keep her from them. He knew when Viktor was released from Malice's grasp he was going to be really pissed off.

On the other hand, Grailen was relieved. Now they would have help taking care of Katrina. The royal family aides at the mansion would be beneficial to her change. They were experts in assisting royal vampires going through their change.

Behind the king's children, their entourage stood in a semi-circle. Hopefully they came prepared. Considering Dave had already spilled the beans, it may have been a blessing in disguise. Grailen looked at all of them, one by one, until he saw the guilt written on Dave's face when he walked down the stairs. He was definitely the one who made the call against Viktor's wishes!

Viktor, before he left to go and save Kat, put his life on the line for her. He had asked Grailen and Dave not to say anything to the High Council in regards to her heritage. Viktor wanted to be present for that bit of knowledge sharing. He wanted to explain the situation the right way so they would understand his part in all of it. He wanted to tell the king himself they were now bonded. Grailen had mixed feelings about it. Viktor would be in a lot of trouble and would be punished harshly for what he had done. But at least with them here Katrina had the best chance at surviving the change instead of being here alone with just Dave and himself.

Prince Evan of the Caine clan and his royal snootiness sister, Anna, stood there in the hallway. They wore very expensive, extravagant clothing. Their clothes wreaked evidence of over-privileged existences. They had an air of being overly protected, having lived sheltered lives. They didn't always have it so great though. When Hunters found one of their palaces and attacked, they went into hiding. They had to give up their golden toothbrushes and platinum laced toilet paper. Ok, maybe that's an exaggeration, but you get the idea. They were forced to live the lives of everyday vampires until the king was able to erect a new sufficient holding for the family. The only drawback, they could barely go out in public.

The royal family had to rely on their aides, whom they were no longer sure they could trust given the leak of their last location. But alas, they fully recovered, having reestablished trustworthy connections all over the world. It just so happened, the Caine clan relocated nice and close to Viktor's mansion. They were only a thought away, or if you were a human, a few miles. It wasn't exactly what they were used to. Their dwelling was an extremely large golden laced underground layer. It used to be an underground factory for the military, which of course they no longer had any record of. But the royal family made do with what they had.

"Grailen, we have been notified that you are keeping one of the royal family members here hostage, how can that be? No one is missing, everyone is accounted for. So tell me, ever so carefully, why did we receive a phone call from one of your little servants to come and retrieve this relative of ours?" Prince Evan was extremely large, almost like he was the first Norsemen alive, and he looked angry about the situation. The prince, like the king, did not take having members of the royal family leaving the safety of their palace lightly. Grailen didn't know where to start. It was all so new to even him.

"Your highness, there is a woman Viktor found being stalked at St. Catherine's Hospital here in Kensin. He was out on a routine security check when he found a Hunter. The Hunter is who led Viktor to Katrina. He was not aware that she held inside her the royal bloodline when they met. They were, ah, in a situation in which he felt the need to feed from her, only to ensure her safety of course. By doing so, he found the truth in her blood. He was concerned for her safety, especially when he realized who she was. Viktor was especially concerned because the Hunters showed what appeared to be a normal human woman the utmost interest, which is alarming all in itself. You see, she has not gone through her change yet. She only has one more day until that happens. She will do well in your care," Grailen said hurriedly.

When no one said anything he continued. "Unfortunately, because she has not had you and your family to raise her, she didn't know that vampires existed. The thought of herself being one has been quite exasperating to her. Viktor could not convince her she needed to be secured until she could be handed over to you, and she ran away. The Hunters took her captive before Viktor could find her. Malice, their leader, holds a grudge against Viktor and offered a trade. Viktor willingly put himself into the hands of our greatest enemy to ensure the safety of this woman," Grailen explained.

Evan and Anna stared at Grailen, both complexly expressionless. Dave spoke up, knowing that humans were not allowed to be present when royal family members were around, let alone speak directly to them. "Your highnesses, the woman is upstairs at this time. She does not wish to stay here and she is still not aware that she is part of a royal community revered by all of us. She does not understand her role or responsibility to herself and to her people. When she was held hostage, the henchmen gave her some type of drug. She is still pretty out of it. We're not even sure if she knows what has happened to her or where she is right now. Katrina hasn't said much since we brought her here. Fevers have been ravaging her body, spiking off and on. Thankfully the vomiting has stopped though."

For the first time since their arrival, Anna spoke up. "Well, let's meet this new addition to our happy family, shall we?" Before she was done speaking she began heading up the stairs. Grailen and Dave looked at each other, they were both well aware that once one of the royal family members made up their minds, there was no going against them. They sighed in resignation, knowing full defeat. Then they followed them up the stairs.

Grailen growled at Dave. "We will talk about this later, David," he spit out. Grailen's anger towards the human male boiled his blood.

Once they all stood on the landing, Prince Evan lifted his hand. He motioned for Grailen to move forward and lead the way to Katrina's room. Grailen reached the door, raised his hand to knock and thought better of it. He didn't want to give her advance notice they were coming to her room. He didn't want her to arm herself out of fear. The element of surprise would be a good thing in the situation.

CHAPTER 16

What they saw didn't surprise Grailen or Dave. Katrina was strong willed and wouldn't be kept down for long if she could help it. As a human she must have been a very strong woman to survive alone in the world, with no one to help her but another human female. By some twist of fate, she had been able to remain off the radar of both the Hunters and the Council.

When the group entered en masse, Kat was standing in the middle of the room, obviously confused. She slowly looked towards the small entourage that entered. Her face was expressionless, only blinking at random intervals. She was still quite pale from the drug effects.

Kat didn't feel well. She was very weak. Every ounce of energy she ever had leaked out through her pores. She wasn't completely clear headed, so she sat down in the sole chair of the room by the window so she could keep an eye on her visitors. Her instincts told her that she needed to be weary of the newbie's. Not that she should be afraid, just that they appeared to want something from her that she wouldn't want to give. Their luxurious clothing didn't warm her to them either. Kat never was into the whole royalty having to wear clothing made out of gold. Their clothes were a little too shiny for her taste.

Katrina looked up at those who had entered expectantly. She sensed that somehow these people who just arrived to the mansion were going to change her life forever. It seemed like everyone she recently met had a direct hand in her fate. Or maybe the newbies brought bad news about Viktor?

When that thought crossed her mind, it felt like her heart stopped beating. The connection between her and Viktor was deeper than she could have imagined possible. It wasn't normal to feel so deeply connected to someone like she did with him. But, she guessed, neither one of them were normal, were they?

Kat's memory was sketchy at best, but she was able to remember seeing Viktor when she was let go from her prison cell. She knew that he took her place as Malice's prisoner. What she didn't know was why those men wanted her in the first place. If Viktor's story was true, what would he have to offer more to the Hunters than her? If he was right, why would they want one of the security guards more than having a princess? That comparison was similar to having a huge chunk of warm chocolate fudge brownie sitting in front of you and then you decide that you want a celery stick instead.

She didn't get that part of the story. Evidently there were some details about Viktor she didn't know. It was possible that Malice didn't have any idea who he had in his possession. Maybe he thought Viktor was worth more to him as the head of Delta 9? She got the impression there was a grudge being held there. Malice's absolute happiness was unnerving when he realized he would once again have the opportunity to torture her mate. She also knew that whatever the serum was Malice gave her, it didn't seem to be doing what they wanted it to. Off and on she was starting to feel better. She felt a little less confused. Malice mentioned that the contagiousness of the serum was more than he could have anticipated. But everyone that had been around her, especially Grailen, seemed to be fine. Yes, she could definitely use a good rundown of the whole state of affairs. Nothing like having the big picture laid out before you to understand exactly what was going on.

Still looking at them, Kat sat there waiting. Eventually Evan took a step forward and made a slight bow. Wow, Grailen was impressed. He didn't think that Prince Evan had modesty or humility in him. Grailen never before witnessed the prince being courteous to anyone but the king himself, or the king's brothers. The prince doing so now was a first. Evan may have been able to sense who she was, whose family she belonged to. Her family was revered, important, and sorely missed by the king.

"Miss, tell me your name," he said as he was still slightly

bowed, making his eyes more on the same level as hers in her sitting position.

Katrina looked up at him, directly into his beautiful crystal blue eyes that had a slight tilt at the ends. Any woman would be envious of those eyes. Looking directly into the eyes of a royal, it was just something that you didn't do. She remembered Viktor telling her that looking directly at one of the royal family members, especially in the eyes, was an insult. They were supposed to be revered. But she didn't care about protocol. Kat knew how to be polite, but at this moment such things didn't matter to her. Only Viktor mattered.

"Katrina, my name is Katrina Drogan," she said. Her throat raw, feeling like she hadn't spoken in weeks.

"Well, Katrina Drogan, I have quite important news for you, but I need you to listen and then you can ask any questions you may have," Prince Evan said.

"I'm sick of people telling me what they think is important. I already know what's important," Kat said, trying to clear the roughness from her voice.

"My dear, I'm sure this has all been quite the adventure for you and you're probably quite stressed at the moment," he said with a hint of sarcasm in his voice.

Was that jealousy Dave heard in the prince's voice? He wasn't sure, but it was well known the king loved and cared for all his family. He indulged them all with whatever their hearts desired. Kat would be no different, in time. Was it possible the prince didn't want to have to share the king's attention and favoritism? Dave suspected Katrina would end up mesmerizing the king and the rest of the royals. That is, with the exception of these two ultra spoiled, overly indulged children.

Exasperated, Kat sneered, "What is it with you people, telling me to listen to everything you have to say!" In that moment she started to feel better, demonstrated by her enthusiastic response as she grinned to herself. Yes, she was feeling a lot better indeed. Her strength was returning in waves, the dizziness subsiding. Her upset stomach was gone, and her ability to focus was lengthening.

Dave and Grailen stood back. They both knew it wasn't going to be easy for anyone, including them. Once the royals sensed Viktor's mark on her, all hell was going to break loose. They only hoped that Kat could handle herself. Even without being raised in the environment the king gave to his family, she had turned out to be a strong and independent woman. The prince and princess would have their hands full. Neither of the king's children was used to being told no, and Kat was sure to tell them just that. She would probably say no to anything they asked just because she didn't know any better. It was one more thing for her to learn, besides proper behavior and decorum she would have to pick up. Unfortunately for Katrina, she would probably learn by trial and error.

Since Viktor was the captain of the royal security team of the Council, hopefully they would make allowances for him. They hoped the king would take his commitment to the family into account when he underwent judgment. His loyalty and his centuries of service would allow for them to have some type of mercy towards him, right? Dave and Grailen hoped so.

Princess Anna walked towards Katrina slowly, her high heeled, gem studded boots making slight thuds on the carpet with every step. A normal human wouldn't have been able to make a sound on the plush material. Anna being an extremely powerful vampire did. It made her presence in the room palpable.

"Katrina, you are in a very difficult situation, we are aware of that. But you must listen. If your time of change is tomorrow as we can all tell it to be, you have to believe the impossible. Everything that you believed as your reality is about to change. No time to be fickle. There were men after you for a reason. The Hunters wanted you for your blood."

"Well, they got what they wanted. Why can't you people just leave me alone?" Kat asked.

"Katrina. You are a member of the royal Caine family. You must behave and present yourself as such. Our blood is a gift that you should cherish. We have yet to figure out how you ended up being raised by a lowly human female."

Katrina tensed. "Don't you ever say anything like that about my aunt again you bitch! You have no right. I don't care who you think you are."

"My dear, you have been through hell, so I will tolerate your tactless words this once." Princess Anna's disgust evident in her tone when she spoke of the people Kat must have had to endure throughout her life. It would be funny to Kat if the princess wasn't referring to her Aunt Rose, the only person who was there for her throughout her entire life.

The princess could only imagine what a horrible life Katrina must have had and how difficult it must have been to be by humans all the time. From the little bit of information Dave and Grailen had given Prince Evan and Princess Anna, it was a horrible thought for both of them. They could only imagine what nightmares Katrina must have had to go through to survive and endure living the humble life she lived. They couldn't believe that she had to actually make a living by taking care of mortals! The idea of being around them and their medical problems all the time was abhorrent. They had TV in the palace. They watched the emergency room and surgical shows. They knew what nurses went through, at least how the directors portrayed them. Bodily fluids were disgusting!

"Katrina, how could you have tolerated being sprayed by urine or stool on your skin? Or having something that came from the human body drip on your shoes? Ugh, ghastly! Blood on the other hand, that sounds delightful," she said to her cousin.

Katrina laughed. Obviously this woman, wearing an extremely expensive dress and boots that would make the top designers of the world melt, believed these nonsensical things that were spewing out of her mouth.

The gold and silver threaded beads that ornamented her clothing were almost laughable to Katrina. In her world, shopping at Sergi's, a designer boutique, was unthinkable to the average person. Rarely did Katrina even go to the mall because the clothes at the local chain stores were much cheaper and more practical. Katrina thought this woman was delusional to be thinking they had anything in common, even if Viktor was right and she was going to turn into a vampire. That didn't mean she would turn into a snooty, self centered person like the one standing in front of her.

Kat would still be her same logical, practical, and thrifty self. She knew she wasn't better than anyone else, and no one was better than her. That included these two, regardless if they were a prince and princess. According to Viktor, she was also a princess. But that didn't give her the right to think of an entire race, humans, as being beneath her. These two had a lot to learn. From what Kat could tell, they had the time to do it, considering they were immortal.

The thought of Kat becoming a vampire was no longer as ludicrous as it was before. The evidence was building, confirming Viktor's story. Kat wasn't overly confident that she was of the royal family. She still thought that was stretching it a bit. But Kat could feel something going on inside her body.

She couldn't explain it, not even to herself, but something was definitely happening to her. Whether it was the infamous vampire turning or the effects of the drug, she couldn't be sure. Hopefully the newcomers were a little more knowledgeable about the drug Malice kept giving her than Dave and Grailen had been.

What Viktor had been telling her these last few days had been too much for her to comprehend. When she saw his face at Carmen's house, when he looked at her after fighting one of Malice's soldiers, she knew it. She knew that he was telling her that at least he was different. Now she finally believed that she was also. Katrina supposed the red eyes and elongated chompers were a clue. She couldn't argue that point, which sealed the deal.

Ugh... That's all she could think right now. Life can be pretty overwhelming at times. Where was Viktor? What was she going to do about her job and her apartment? What was she going to say when she saw Carmen for the first time about getting half her house blown up? Was she going to be allowed to tell her lifelong best friend what happened to her? Would she be able to explain what she was becoming? What about Aunt Rose? She couldn't just leave her, making her think that something awful happened to her. In truth she was better than ever, or at least she was going to be, right?

These questions were going to be put to Viktor. Kat wanted to wait to hear the answers from him. A small part of her still believed that whatever was happening to her, he was at fault. If he hadn't bonded to her, would she still be turning into a vampire? There were still a lot of small pieces of information she wasn't sure of. Kat thought she had the overall big picture.

Vampires were real. There was a big royal family made up of vampires that governed the non-royal vampires. And she was now a part of the royal family. She also understood that it was Viktor's job to protect them, and now her. Also, he bonded her to him and whether she liked it or not, she was stuck with him possibly for all of eternity.

"Katrina!" Evan made a few attempts to get Katrina's attention down off the gloomy cloud consuming her every thought. She had to say, due to the circumstances, it wasn't getting any easier understanding all the facts everyone was telling her. "Katrina, we need to be going soon. The king is greatly looking forward to meeting you and we must make preparations for your change. There isn't much time my dear." Kat stared at the prince, evaluating him as an entomologist would study a bug.

Finally she answered him, allowing Grailen and Dave to release the breath they didn't realize they were holding. "I'm not going anywhere unless it's to the compound where they are holding Viktor prisoner doing who knows what to him. So, if you two want to go back to your royal, overly privileged from the looks of it, lives, go right ahead," she said as she stood up.

"Princess Katrina," Dave began but shut his mouth when all three royals whipped their heads towards him and stared. "Um, well, I was going to suggest that we do start formulating a plan to get Viktor out from Malice's possession. Grailen and I will be downstairs doing just that if you need anything."

"We'll all be going downstairs to work out the plans," Katrina shouted. She was already acting like a princess. In the short time Dave and Grailen had left her alone, she was able to get out of bed and see how strong she was after enduring the torture Malice put her through. She found when she got to a standing position she was still a little woozy but able to maintain her balance.

She looked down at herself and realized that she wasn't dressed for a rescue mission, let alone being in the company of royal blood thirsty pansies. She was about to ask Dave for help in the matter when he finally grew a pair and fully entered the room. All this time he stood in the doorway. He side stepped the golden couple, supposedly her family, and went to Viktor's beautiful armoire with intricate designs carved into it. The designs appeared magical. With that observation, the thought crossed Kat's mind, what if vampires weren't the only things in the world besides humans that existed? That was another item she would have to run by Viktor. Were there fairies? What about werewolves? The possibilities were endless.

Dave opened the armoire, she couldn't believe her eyes! It was full of women's clothing. Kat's spirits lifted. She approached it and started digging. With her head stuck inside the mini clothes store, the rest of the group exited to give her a smidgeon of privacy to make herself more presentable.

Katrina had no idea where her own clothes were or how many days she'd been in her drug induced nap. But she did know that her roomies being awake meant it was sometime after sunset. She needed to find something black so she could become one with the shadows on the compound. Every girl's got to have a plan.

Here we go, she thought, holding up a black turtle neck. Next she would need a black coat and pants, which she also found in the armoire. Viktor must have told someone to stock it for her, with clothes in her size. Everything fit well. Looking on the bottom, there was an array of shoes in every color you could imagine including black sneakers that would do nicely for what she needed. Anything to help her be stealthy was good. Remarkably, it seemed someone had that in mind when they purchased the clothes.

Back at the compound, Viktor began to stir after a few hours of playacting being asleep. Whatever Malice had pumped into his neck with that dart didn't affect him much more than a few alcoholic beverages would have. It hadn't lasted very long. Viktor could use an energy drink right about now, otherwise he felt fine, considering. He led Malice to believe he was down for the count when in reality he was focused and formulating a plan. The need to slice open his captor's throat inspired every ounce of his patience.

Viktor knew he couldn't drink from him. Malice didn't age as fast as other humans did. The Council was aware that he had found a way to slow the process down but not halt it completely. Whatever Malice did to himself, Viktor didn't want anything to do with it. It was possible Malice's blood was toxic to vampires, so torture and death would have to be enough to sooth his need to exact revenge. That was why Malice was still in such a pinch to get the clan's secrets. He needed to find the answer how the aging process halted when vampires turned twenty-five.

Malice was still aging, it was clear that he had yet to perfect whatever he was taking. But the aging process was slowed to a trickle. He had yet to figure out how to completely turn off the faucet.

Viktor would enjoy watching Malice slowly bleed to death. It would be a fitting end for someone who committed such vile assaults on him and his people both mentally and physically for such a long time.

Viktor sluggishly paced in front of his cell wall. Whatever the see through material was, he knew he couldn't break it. He tried the last time he was Malice's guest and found that he wasn't able to dent or crack it. The only way he knew out was through the door he was brought in. He had to wait for the opportunity to have someone open it for him. From the looks of it, that might be awhile.

The soldiers that were handling him were being overly cautious. If Viktor played his cards right and behaved for a while, the soldiers would become complacent and make a mistake. That's when Viktor would make his move. No matter how long he had to wait, he would be ready. Viktor was sure Malice educated his boys on how to keep their guests from escaping after Viktor was able to get out using one of the soldiers, making him leave the door open so he could escape. It seemed Malice had found a local witch to perform a mind guard to protect his soldiers from being manipulated by vampires. Viktor would have to find out who was strong enough to do such a thing. He would teach them a lesson for helping the bad guys.

Vampire bodies did not create waste like humans did so there was no need for bathroom facilities in the cells. They were able to see themselves in the mirror, unlike the myths implied. The vampires that tortured and played with their blood sources tended to cast a more opaque reflection, as their souls became tainted.

Older vampires only needed blood every couple of days to survive. Malice's men could administer blood to Viktor through an IV while it was daylight. He wouldn't be able to tell them no, as his ability to move would become non-existent. After a while he would become weaker, but they wouldn't let him die. They wouldn't be able to perform their experiments on him if he couldn't withstand the psychological impacts that went along with Malice's tests. Viktor noticed Malice's henchmen kept their own needs to a predictable schedule. That would be useful, eventually.

Right now Malice was down the hall harassing one of the other prisoners. That prisoner had a different type of holding cell, a type of cell Viktor didn't recognize from the layout of the last compound he was in. There seemed to be a constant station by the cell filled with Malice's henchmen standing guard with guns loaded at all times. He could see the ultraviolet pellets in the clear chamber of their guns. He assumed they were the same UV pellets they used on Viktor when he was caught the last time. Those pellets proved to be quite effective. The pain they inflicted was awful, but not deadly. Those little buggers left a nasty hole in someone that took an extra long time to heal. The marks even lasted after a vampire spent a couple of days healing in their sleep.

The effects were worse, the pain they inflicted was horrendous, and they rendered the victim powerless temporarily. It was great for when Malice found a vampire he wanted to capture. The pellets disabled them and the Hunters were then able to detain their targets with minimal difficulty. That's how it went when Viktor was taken.

Whoever they had in that cell down the hall had the guards and Malice scared. Viktor could tell by their heart beats, thumping faster and faster in their chests every time they needed to go near the door. To Viktor it sounded like a group of uncoordinated percussionists attempting to play part of a symphony. Interesting, I thought I was the scary one, Viktor thought.

CHAPTER 17

Everyone was gathered in the dining room. Katrina lifted her gaze up from the map Thomas had made of the compound. The map was sprawled out on the long dining room table which looked like something that could have been used centuries ago. Katrina envisioned ladies with their breasts popping out of their dresses and men with their long hair tied back by bows sitting all around it. All of them were giggling at the frivolous issues and latest gossip. The women were trying to impress the men with their lack of opinions, or even brains, for that matter.

The Council members had arrived while Katrina was left alone to get dressed upstairs in the room she shared with Viktor. Their names were Thomas and Spyder. They both looked menacing. From being around Viktor's kind for the last few days, she was instantly able to tell that these two were like him. They were vampires with their long pointy teeth and they both exuded a raw male sexuality that unnerved her. She wondered to herself if they too had eyes that changed to pure obsidian when they hungered for a woman like Viktor's did.

Her mind was constantly drawn back to Viktor. She missed him sorely, and yet she had the urge to scream at him for everything that has happened. Especially that he left her alone with these goofballs to deal with. She knew he put his life in jeopardy to save hers. He insisted on exchanging his safety for hers. He did it knowing the monstrous things Malice would do to him. Knowing that made her want to scream even more at him! Kat was so frustrated. She was ready to pull her hair out. To add insult to injury, she had to deal with her so called cousins. Their pompous chips on their shoulders drove her crazy!

Kat didn't want to analyze her ability to tell who was a vampire too closely. She felt different. Her sense of smell was keener. She could detect movements with clarity she never had before. There were bigger fish to fry at the moment than her growing abilities. She needed to focus on the task at hand. Her mind was constantly skipping from one topic to another.

The serum she had been injected with was supposed to infect all vampires around her. No one looked ill to Kat. Malice developed another serum for his Hunters. It must be why they had even the slightest chance fighting against vampires. Their serum made them extra strong and fast in battle. The Hunter's anti-vampire weapons and evil sneakiness made them higher threats to the Council and royal families.

Kat decided to ignore being able to hear Dave's heart beat

despite the internal dialogue running in her head. She saw beads of sweat develop on his brow. The strong urge to walk over and sniff him freaked her out. Focus Kat, focus!

Thomas was introduced to her as Viktor's second in command in their security force. His companion, Spyder, was the team's gadget specialist. That left things pretty wide open, didn't it? What was he, great at using a digital camera? Was he an iPod junky? She felt pretty punchy at the moment. Thomas was wearing similar clothing Viktor had in his closet. She assumed it was their battle garb. Kat observed that both Viktor and Thomas preferred looser fitting, floor length leather jackets to conceal their weapons from humans. The length would be useful to keep from being noticed by people while they walked among them ready to take down the enemy.

Unlike Viktor, Thomas didn't wear anything under his leather vest, which showed off the upper portion of his overly developed peck muscles. Even Hulk Hogan would be envious of his measurements! Thomas had long brown hair and it was straight like Viktor's. He wore it loose, unlike Viktor who kept it combed back and neatly tied with a leather strap. Kat couldn't help but think of Viktor. She couldn't look at an extremely sexy man without comparing him to Viktor, her almost husband. She realized, with a contented sigh, there would never be another man in her life that she would have any interest in. Her search to find someone she could fall in love with was over.

She smiled, like Viktor would ever let her be with anyone else. Just the thought of it would make him go absolutely insane.

They figured that out when they spoke of their lives, and people who were important to them while lying in bed just a few nights ago. Right now the time they spent together seemed like months or even years ago.

Kat's thoughts were going through the agonizing paces of what ifs. What if she never saw Viktor again? What if he was killed during their rescue? What if someone else was injured during the rescue and they don't make it out alive? Keep it together Kat, don't lose what little control you have and start crying again. That's all you need, to become useless and not able to help Viktor. She rubbed her face with both hands, slightly shaking her head in an attempt to rid her mind of thoughts clouding her ability to focus. Residuals of the sedative still lingered it seemed.

All the Council members at the table looked at each other nodding their heads. It may not be the sanest plan of extraction, but their options were limited. Everyone had their part to play to ensure its success. There wasn't enough time to wait for anyone else. Every second Viktor was in Malice's compound could be his last. Surely the Judges would be able to take care of Malice. But the cousins said the Judges were already preoccupied with another mission from the king. Otherwise, they would have come to retrieve Katrina instead of the king's children. That piece of information made both Dave and Grailen shudder.

How complicated could it be? Storm the castle and save the hostage. End of story. No one wanted Katrina to help. They were concerned about her safety and their own. They couldn't imagine what the king would do to them if something happened to her or his children. They were also worried about what Viktor would do to them for including her and putting her in harm's way.

Dave and Grailen knew she bore his mark. They could sense his essence on her. The royal brats had yet to figure it out, neither had Thomas or Spyder. Grailen surmised that they couldn't sense his essence on her because they hadn't met her until after the fact. The Council members discussed the severity of Viktor having taken such drastic action while the royal brats made themselves more at home in their living quarters down the hall from Kat and Viktor's room.

Clearly the prince and princess didn't know. If they did they would have called their father immediately. Thankfully they didn't know her before she bore his mark. That problem would be handled in the order in which it was received, thank you.

After a bunch of unnecessary squabbling, the team had all the details planned out. Even Prince Evan and Princess Anna would be helping.

Princess Anna couldn't be out in the open. She refused to change out of the royal obnoxious dress she had on. Putting her directly in harm's way would lead to them all being tortured brutally until their eventual death. The king wouldn't take anything happening to his precious daughter lightly. So that meant she would have to be kept in the relative safety of the mansion making sure the aides were prepared to treat incoming casualties and to be ready for Kat's change. Like princesses knew how to take care of anyone? Kat thought. She supposed, how bad could it get? They were all vampires, minus her and Dave. Even if Viktor did sustain serious injuries all he would need was to go beddy bye for awhile and drink a lot of blood, right?

Since Prince Evan had trained his entire life with the Judges, he was more than adequate to have on the extraction team. The Judges taught him to perfect his skills with all sorts of weapons; human, vampire, and demon. He was also very competent with some basic demon magic.

After everyone on the team changed into the appropriate attire they picked their weapons and equipment out of the cache Viktor kept handy in the weapon room. The team went over the plan what seemed like fifty more times. Thomas insisted on making sure there wasn't anyone that didn't know exactly what the plan was and what their part was in it. The group then gathered together outside of the mansion with all of their supplies where they went over the plan one more eye rolling time.

Everyone was in a somber mood and quiet. Knowing there could be lives lost during the mission weighed heavily on their shoulders. The hope was that those lives happened not to be any of their own. Although the likelihood of them all getting out alive was slim.

The plan was to disable a few of the henchmen on the North side of the property where they guarded the electrical box and power generator. They counted on the generator being the only power source for the entire compound. They were also relying on Malice being lax in preparedness for a sneak attack. Hopefully if he did have another emergency generator there would be a delay before it kicked in.

Even though the guards were equipped with night vision, the lack of street lighting would be an advantage to the vampires in the group. Their speed would be too quick to be detected by the human soldiers. The group would take every advantage they could. Especially considering two of the team members were not vampires, yet. No one ever mentioned turning Dave in front of Kat, but she figured that it would eventually happen. She didn't think Viktor or the Council would get along very well without him.

Katrina and Spyder were the team set to go to the North end of the compound and turn the power off. Thomas and Evan would scope out the back where the dock entrance was located and get in through the loading area. They would block all of their enemies from reloading themselves with ammo once expending the supply they carried during the initial portion of the battle.

When the soldiers walked Kat out of the compound she remembered seeing an open room with guns lining the walls and boxes of what she assumed were ammo on benches in front of the guns. She knew it was in the back near the loading dock from Thomas's map. The Hunters kept the weapons close to the dock where shipments were delivered by truck. Thomas and Evan were to block the soldier's stash once they got inside.

Malice wasn't going to give Viktor up without a fight to the death. The soldiers would try and capture or kill as many of the team as they could. The more play toys for their horrendous experiments the better.

Malice held a nasty grudge for a scar he got even though he deserved it. Katrina knew revenge against Viktor wasn't Malice's only drive for what he did. She knew he spent all of his time and energy figuring out how vampires ticked and how he could use that information against them and for himself. Kat kept thinking there was something else behind all of this madness. Something made Malice's soul burn with absolute hatred against Viktor and the other vampires. Maybe a woman was involved, maybe a member of Malice's family had died at the hands of a member of the Council? Maybe even Viktor himself did it? Something like that could surly cause a life lasting spur in a man's side.

Dave would be waiting down the street from the compound, heavily armed, with the SUVs. He would be ready to transport their wounded back to the mansion where the princess would be waiting, if needed. The plan was also designed to keep Princess Anna out of harm's way. No reason to piss off the king more than the wrath of what was sure to come. They all knew they were in hot water because Kat wasn't already at the palace.

Prince Evan was known as a risk taker. He was very old, and very powerful. He was also known for doing what he wanted even if it wasn't exactly what the king told him to do. He seemed almost cheery being able to have a little fun. Going on the rescue mission knowing full well his father would skin his hide if he knew what they were up to made it more exciting for the prince. When Evan trained with his father's demon assassin troupe the king had made a decree. The prince was never to be hurt, not permanently. His father didn't have anything against his baby boy undergoing a little self discipline learning skills. He didn't even mind Evan receiving a little punishment when he was lacking either.

The Judges knew if they really hurt him they would be ordered to submit their loved ones for the other Judges to punish until they begged for mercy. Begging for mercy by a Judge would then lead to their death. Begging wasn't allowed in the world of the Judges. Displays of emotion were unacceptable when it came to the demons who kept the entire vampire race in check. Judges never became involved in vampire politics. They only did what they were told by the king. They weren't supposed to become intimately involved with vampires either. That would be a conflict of interest and cause for instant death.

Instead of the group using the teleporting method that still gave Kat the heebee geebees, the plan was for everyone to drive in the two large black SUVs. That way they could carry extra weapons for the fight in case they ran out during the battle.

Kat and Spyder were teamed up together. Once they turned off the power to the compound they were to find a way into the building on the North side. Grailen didn't like that his brother's woman would be anywhere near either Spyder or Thomas. He couldn't find any other way around it though. Despite himself, he was a little surprised he felt protective over someone other than his immediate family. That was very unlike him. Well, Katrina was his family now. She was his sister-in-law even if she hadn't fully accepted it yet.

Thomas and Prince Evan were to gain entrance, as quietly as possible, into the compound. They were to do this before the power went off to create a barrier in between the guards and their ammunition supply. Once that was accomplished Kat and Spyder would take out the power and meet them inside. Then they were all to find themselves a way into the lab where Viktor was being held. Kat was only able to give vague descriptions of the cell lined command center and its location. That area seemed to be where Malice spent the majority of his time while she was conscious in her cell.

All four of them would meet, if all went well, in the middle of the building where the lab was. Their goal was to cause the least amount of noise as possible until they all got there. Their primary objective was Viktor and getting him out of the compound. Grailen had a different agenda. He wanted Malice, he was out for blood, and he wanted all of it.

Grailen was tired of having to watch his back in case Hunters were on his trail. It was time to finish this once and for all! He realized that if Malice was eliminated, it would only be a matter of time before someone else took his position. But if they could take out the brains of the operation, it would be a while before someone could take charge of their vile group and pick up where Malice left off. If Grailen took Malice out it would at least give the Kensin Council time to recover.

Thomas and Spyder had earlier scouted the compound for data before they went to the mansion to assist Viktor when Dave called. The situation had changed, no longer was there a damsel in distress needing to be rescued. Now it was Viktor who was the one inside the compound being held captive. The objective was still the same. Get the prisoner out, kill Malice and any of his men that got in the way, and destroy as much of the lab as possible. Ridding the building of any trace of vampire existence on their way out was imperative. In the Council's eyes the more Hunters taken out during the mission, the better. The experiments and data Malice collected needed to be destroyed. Malice was beyond the ordinary arrogant, prideful madman. Hopefully he kept his information to himself and had not shared it with the rest of the Hunters worldwide.

The Council member's fact gathering definitely paid off. While scouting the area they recognized a pattern of one of the loading dock goons. During his rounds the man routinely made his way behind one of the utility sheds to smoke a cigarette. He then reappeared by the dock without making the walk back to cover missed ground. After watching this a few times, they realized what he must be doing. There was no other explanation for it. Hunters didn't have the ability to teleport, not that the Council knew of. There must be an underground tunnel in between the two buildings. That was how Grailen would get in.

He planned on being inside the compound before Katrina and Spyder were able to cut the power. He would then locate Malice and position himself so he could take him out when the chaos started. Malice was the strongest Hunter they ever encountered and the team needed to designate one of their members to focus solely on him. That was Grailen. The other four would work together to get Viktor out of his cell and into the SUV safely. Simple enough plan. Once they were in and the lights went out, there was no going back for any of them.

Losing interest in the special captive down the hall, Malice sauntered over to Viktor's cell. He grinned. "Malice, tell me. Every time you smile, every time you chew your food, every time you kiss a woman, do you think of me? Do you feel the damaged tissue stretching across your face that I so thoroughly enjoyed damaging? The only time I ever think of you is when you are right in front of me, like now."

"Shut up you filthy creature. You're just trying to get a rise out of me so I'll do something stupid. And it won't work!" Malice accused him.

"Otherwise, when you are out of my sight I never give you a second thought. Oh, you probably don't get that much attention from the ladies, you do look pretty disgusting I must say."

Malice could barely contain his anger, he was seething with it. Fury was written all over his disfigured face. Viktor knew from experience when Malice was angry he wasn't known to think with a clear head. That's when he made mistakes. Malice's pride was injured. When that happened he would forget who he was dealing with. He would forget to take the extra precautions needed when dealing with Viktor.

When Malice became slack with Viktor's supervision, Viktor would be waiting. That's when he would make his move. Viktor knew he couldn't stay here long. Malice would eventually tire of torturing him and would press the limits. Viktor was able to live forever, but he could still be killed. There was only so much torture and injury a vampire was able to endure before they died. If Viktor was exposed to sunlight for more than a few minutes, that would be the end. Fire, decapitation, and total blood loss would also do him in.

Walking closer to the clear cell, Malice looked Viktor up and down. "Those are pretty strong words from a parasite Viktor. How do you put up with it? How does it feel to be someone else's lackey? I couldn't imagine never being able to see the sun," Malice said. He figured these would be things that would bother Viktor.

"Malice, I will admit you have been formidable for these long years, but your reign will soon come to an end. Don't you get tired of fighting nature? Don't you get tired of obsessing over me?" Viktor wasn't going to fall for Malice's attempt to piss him off. He was already pissed, but nothing Malice said would make it worse.

Malice turned and looked around the lab. His scientists stopped what they were working on and looked at him. Malice looked back at Viktor with suspicion in his eyes. He turned back when a loud noise erupted from down the main hall. Viktor knew the hallway led off to one of the supply rooms towards the back.

"What the hell is going on? One of you go and check the dock," he said, pointing to a group of Hunters standing by the hallway entrance. Malice marched over to the many rows of refrigerated drawers and bubbling brews the Hunter scientists had been working on around the clock. It was clear Malice always got his way. Barking orders at random like that, not specifying who was to do what was pretty self assured behavior. The Hunters were known to become unorganized during a crisis. Idiots, Viktor thought.

Malice stood in the middle of the command center. The lights went out and didn't come back on as they should have. Malice walked over to Viktor's cell. Through his experiments he had found a way to see in the dark just as well as Viktor could. "Your Council better not have anything to do with this. I'll get that woman friend of yours and kill her right in front of you. This I vow!" Malice growled at him.

"You will rot in hell before you ever lay a finger on her again," Viktor assured him. Malice walked away from his cell towards what was probably his office off to the right of the command center.

Viktor knew his host would have major problems soon if the power wasn't restored. For one, all of his lab specimens kept in incubators of evilness would die. Then he'd have to start from scratch. Viktor was doubtful that Malice had the original hosts who he got the samples from. He would have to go out and collect all new sample sources for his experimental research.

Another issue, possibly the worse of the two for Malice, if there was no power, the electrically run hydraulic door reinforcements would fail. All the prisoners, Viktor included, would be able to escape. Without the huge amount of pressure holding those doors in place, the locking device would only be able to keep a human contained in their cell. Thank his lucky stars he wasn't human.

Viktor saw from Malice's expression frenzied thoughts raced in his mind. The realization of the situation settling in on his face was pure pleasure for Viktor. Now it was Viktor's turn to grin in satisfaction. Even if he didn't get out of the compound alive, being able to see the fear on Malice's face was unrivaled. Viktor experienced pure satisfaction. His only regret if he died would be leaving Kat alone to deal with her change. He would also miss being able to serve the king with his brother.

Viktor started to turn to see if his theory on the hydraulics would work when Malice screamed in frustration. Viktor glanced back towards the middle of the control room. Malice grabbed a microscope and threw it across a stainless steel table. It slid off the table and shattered into a thousand little pieces when it hit the floor. Viktor sensed fear from Malice. Even through the thickness of the cell walls he could feel it like a sheen of sweat on Malice's pale skin.

Viktor turned back to face the front of the cell. Grailen was here? Viktor was able to sense his brother's presence in the compound. He had to be in the building for Viktor to sense his essence! Viktor couldn't see him, but he could sense the sibling blood-bond they shared.

Hunters began yelling from down the hallway the explosive sound came from just moments ago. Malice looked towards Viktor's cell again. The contemplation of killing him crossed his mind. That's when all hell broke loose.

Gun fire erupted out of nowhere. Hunters were shouting orders to each other. Their goals were to restore the power, contain the captives, and take out the intruders. Strangely, no one seemed to be paying any attention to Viktor or what he was doing. He verified that as he walked over to the door and started pounding on it with all of his strength.

Without the hydraulic pressured cylinders running across and through the door, it became pliable. Every time he punched the cell door it gave in a little more. Without the bars crossing the door he would be able to get out in no time.

CHAPTER 18

After they figured out how to eliminate the men guarding the perimeter of the compound grounds, they executed their plan. Spyder came up with the idea that if they could lead the soldiers individually down the other side of the hill they would be able to dispatch them. The soldiers would be too far away from anyone who may hear them yell out while they were being suffocated and dumped behind the very large tree at the base of the hill. When all the soldiers were taken out Spyder and Kat would work on shutting the lights and power off to the compound. They had to wait a little longer than anticipated, but their patience paid off.

The soldiers kept to a regular scouting path, it didn't take long to figure out a simple distraction technique. Throwing an empty can of soda, making enough ruckus to have the soldier check it out was efficient. It turned out to be enough to peak the soldier's interest. Spyder jumped them from behind when they came one by one to investigate. Spyder then ended their miserable existence. Katrina helped him carry them behind the tree.

Quietly as they could, Spyder and Kat scurried over to the generator box located fifty feet away from the side door. Three large wires ran from the box to the building. They were the compound's main energy source. Spyder grabbed the three wires in his hand. He yanked on them causing the outer casing of the box to bow towards them from the force of the wires being crudely separated from the inside.

Afterwards, they made their way slowly down the hill and hid behind one of the compound trucks. Spyder signaled to Kat each time letting her know when it was safe to move. Even though she now had super senses, she wasn't used to them. Spyder's skills were much more advanced for now. She had to rely on his abilities, too unsure of her own. Spyder moved without making a sound. Katrina on the other hand didn't have time before they left the mansion to perfect her cat-like sneaky skills. It seemed as if she found every dry leaf and twig on the ground and stepped right on them.

They both crouched down against the compound wall behind one of the delivery trucks. Kat tried not to breathe too deeply because her breath steamed up in the frigid night air. She was afraid one of the remaining guards would spot them. The truck they hid behind had an opening in the back and Kat was about to crawl in when Spyder grabbed her arm and pulled her back to a squatting position. He signaled for her to stay right where she was.

They heard footsteps on the pavement slowly making their way to where they were hiding. Kat and Spyder waited for the guard to walk past them so Spyder could jump on him and disable him. This was the official plan he described to her only seconds earlier. Once the guard was down for the count with a big nasty knife in his neck, they moved on.

Of course, when something seemed to be too good to be true, or too easy to accomplish, it usually was. The door the guard was watching was locked by a chain that was linked around the door handles. The chain was held tight by a padlock. Malice and his men wouldn't just leave it open for their enemy to stop by and make an unannounced visit. Good thing Spyder, mister gadget guy, was so handy. From one of those pockets you don't know is there until someone pulls something out of it, he pulled out a little device. It looked like a small wrench, but not an actual wrench, with a little light on the top of it.

Spyder worked on the lock with delicate skill. Apparently the chain was made of silver because he was having trouble keeping his swearing to himself. Kat saw every time the chain touched the skin on his hand, a little smoke was emitted. There were lines on his skin bubbling into raised welts. That looks painful, she thought. Another fun fact that hit the bottom of her gut, she wasn't going to be able to wear her favorite silver earrings given to her by her Aunt Rose.

Kat vaguely remembered someone at the mansion saying something about silver being a hindrance to vampires. She never bothered to pursue more information from whoever said it, finding out what they meant. It was funny, the thoughts that cross a person's mind when they were stressed out.

About sixteen seconds later Spyder had the lock open. He quietly slid the chain through the handles of the door. Kat took it from his burning hands and tucked it under a bush that grew alongside the building six feet away from the door. She went back to where Spyder was crouched and together they slowly entered the building. Once they were both in, Spyder carefully closed the door behind them.

Kat took a step forward. She wanted to rush in and find Viktor as quickly as she could. When she felt Spyder's outstretched arm across her chest she realized her plan wouldn't do. He held her back. Kat knew he was right and they needed to use caution. She looked at him, her visual acuity enhancing by the second. "Hey Spyder, I can see in the dark!" Kat blurted out. Spyder held up his index finger to his lips for her to be quiet.

He then motioned his outstretched hand for them to lower themselves. Once she too was in a crouched position, he motioned for her to press up against the other wall. Then they began to move along the walls reducing the chance of detection.

They turned around to sneak down the hallway. Sure enough, chaos had already started to spread throughout the compound. Shouts and gunfire were coming from up ahead. Kat and Spyder heard more shouting as they slowly crept forward. They continued to move forward down the hall only to see Malice's body being thrown across the room in front of them. They looked at each other. Both of their foreheads raised in excitement. They then stood up and ran forward to join the party.

Grailen waited high in a tree. The soldier he was stalking stood smoking a cigarette. Grailen waited for his chance to drop down and kill the human. The soldier had made a few rounds while Grailen watched and learned his pattern. He was quite predictable.

The soldier dropped his cigarette and stomped it out with his boot. He began to walk towards where Grailen had figured was the tunnel entrance that would lead him to the inside of the compound. Grailen dropped out of the tree, silently landing on the snow covered gravel drive.

He trailed the Hunter until he was close to the entrance of the tunnel. Grailen had the information he needed to get into the compound. He no longer needed the soldier. Grailen unsheathed a knife out of his vest. He silently walked up behind him and grabbed the soldier from behind by the chin. He slowly slid the razor sharp knife across the man's neck, covering his hands in warm, sticky blood. The smell of fresh blood excited Grailen's lust for blood.

Grailen lifted the round tunnel entrance. He looked around to ensure he wasn't being watched by any other Hunters. He descended the stairs and landed on a cement floor. Running down the hall, he felt Viktor's essence. Viktor was still alive!

He came to a metal door. This one had an electronic keypad

for a lock. Grailen lifted his fist and smashed the entire unit off the wall. It left bare wires sticking out. He grabbed the green and red wires and tied the exposed copper tips to each other. When he was done connecting them, the door popped open enough for Grailen to stick his fingertips in and pull it all the way open.

Behind the door was a stairwell going up. He didn't hesitate and took the steps four at a time. Grailen's speed impressed even himself. Too bad he hated everything else about himself.

At the top of the stairs was a hallway with two doors. One was at each end of the hall. He tried the door on the left. Not surprising, it was locked. Grailen used his vampire strength and twisted the door handle against the lock, it came apart like butter. He looked inside of the room. There was nothing in it but a kitchenette, a small card table and a few chairs. The table had an ashtray full of cigarette butts on it. This must be the soldier's break room. He left the room not bothering to shut the door.

Grailen grabbed the handle of the door on the other end of the hallway. This door wasn't locked. He went right through to the other side. It was a room with two desks positioned against each other in the center of the room. Sitting at the desks were two Hunters. They heard him come in the room but didn't budge from their chairs. Grailen used his vampire speed, running to the Hunter closest to the door. When he got to the Hunter Grailen grabbed him by the head and twisted with great force. The head came away from the body like a child's toy. He let the Hunter's head go as the body slumped over in the chair. The body's face hit the computer keyboard before it bounced to the floor.

The second Hunter had his hand on the pistol in a holster on his right hip. The Hunter never had a chance. Before the first Hunter's body finished slumping onto the desk, Grailen's hand was already loaded with three long pointed throwing stars. The Hunter worked to unsnap the holster to take out his gun. He did this not realizing that he already had the three throwing stars lodged in his body; one in his left carotid artery, the second penetrating his left temporal artery, and the third in his chest above his heart. The Hunter fell from his chair with his hand still on his holster. That's when the lights went out.

Viktor pounded his way through his cell door. It took longer than expected, but he was able to dent the door enough to get out. Viktor never wanted to see the inside of one of Malice's cells again. Once outside of the cell, Viktor ran over to the door of Malice's office and stopped. There was something in the walls making it impossible for Viktor to get a read on what was going on inside the room. He was sure that Malice was in there. Throughout both of Viktor's stays with Malice he had never been inside the room Malice used for an office. He wasn't quite sure what Malice kept in there but he didn't want to rush in and get shot with a UV pellet or something worse. Viktor had plans for Malice and he intended to see them through.

To Viktor's relief, he didn't have to wait long. Malice whipped open his office door and roared when he saw who was standing on the other side. Malice stepped back and began to bring the gun he had in his hand up to take aim. Before he could finish the motion Viktor was on him. Viktor grabbed the gun out of Malice's hands, snapping the rifle strap in the process. He grabbed it in both hands and broke it in half, throwing the pieces to either side of him.

Malice put his hands up in front of him, "Viktor, if you kill me you won't be able to save your woman. I've injected her with a serum and only I know where the antidote is. It will kill her and the rest of you if she doesn't take it by the time she changes." Fear contorted his face.

Disgust consumed Viktor. He grabbed Malice's jacket in both of his hands, tightening the material around Malice's neck, "What are you talking about? You better talk fast. My patience has run out with you!"

"My scientists injected her with a serum that will either stop her from changing into a vampire or kill her. Once it has done its job, she'll become contagious to all vampires. All of you will die if she goes through her change."

"How could you do this? Vampires aren't the filthy beings you speak of you piece of garbage. You are far worse than any vampire I have ever met! You and your Hunters killed thousands of innocent people."

"They weren't innocent, not one of them deserved to live. Your kind is vile, disgusting insects living off the human race. You all deserve to die," Malice said, trying to appear as if he were the one in control.

Viktor changed his grip from Malice's jacket to the upper

part of Malice's arms. Viktor was so angry he could barely control his emotions. There were two loud cracking sounds as Viktor realized that he had kept squeezing Malice's arms until the bones snapped like two dried twigs. Malice's face turned ashen. Viktor continued to apply pressure to the broken appendages not allowing Malice to pass out yet. Viktor found pleasure in knowing that he was causing pain to this sick, twisted, creature as he had to his woman and himself. An eye for an eye, right? Viktor tried to justify his own cruelty to himself.

"Where is the antidote Malice? You will give it to me right now. Or so help me I will bite you and make you into what you hate so very much."

With that threat, Malice said, "It's there, in the drawer lying on the floor. It should be ok. We kept it in a foam liner."

"If you're lying to me I will find every member of your family and kill them in front of you before you die by my hand." Malice took a swipe at Viktor's head with a dagger he had hidden in his sleeve. Viktor put his arm up to block the cut of the knife to his face. The blade cut into his arm but not deep enough to hinder Viktor from using it.

Malice bellowed out in frustration, "You will never be rid of us you vermin! It is you and your kind that will all die." Viktor took a hold of Malice's jacket, dragged him out of the office doorway and threw him across the room. Malice hit the wall with a loud smack. When he slid to the floor his body slumped over and didn't move. Viktor felt retribution seeing Malice's spine snap when he collided with the edge of the counter before he landed on the floor. Viktor began to feel at peace as he heard Malice's heart beat slow down to fewer than five beats a minute. The human would be dead in a matter of seconds.

Viktor walked over to the drawer that Malice said held the antidote for the serum he injected Kat with. He looked inside of the drawer. It was lined with black foam as Malice described. Viktor leaned over and picked up the two glass vials holding a neon green liquid.

Seconds after Kat and Spyder watched Malice's body sail through the air, a group of Hunters ran into the command center room wearing night vision goggles. Their attention wasn't on them. The Hunter's guns were pointed toward someone else in the room. Someone they couldn't see from where they stood. They ran forward to help whoever it was. Entering the large room, Kat saw that Malice's body lay on the floor with his back against some fallen lab equipment among broken glass spread over the ceramic tiled floor. Malice didn't look too comfortable. His body was contorted at abnormal angles. Then she saw Viktor with something green in his hand.

Grailen entered the room behind the Hunters and attacked. Viktor ran at the Hunters from the front taking two down with a slashing motion of his fingertips. Grailen took two more out before they even knew he was there.

Kat ran over to Viktor while Spyder and Grailen finished up

with the last of the soldiers. Viktor grabbed Kat up into his arms, holding her tightly to him. One hand wrapped around her back and the other cradled her head and neck. He squeezed her close. He could barely contain his relief at seeing her up and doing well. He was also greatly concerned about her being back here in Malice's compound.

Who the hell decided to let her participate in his rescue? If he knew her at all, he knew she wouldn't have had it any other way. Viktor was sure she would have fought with anyone who had the nerve to tell her she couldn't come with. Being so physically close to her now, he could sense immediately that the change was about to overcome her. He also knew they had to get the hell out there fast. The Council members had to make sure the insides of this compound were completely incinerated before they left. Then they needed to get themselves back to the mansion so they could prepare for her change as soon as possible. It was going to start very soon!

Viktor was beaten up. Malice had not been kind to him during his stay. Viktor had broken bones all over his body that had yet to fully mend. The Hunters only gave him enough blood to live, not to heal his wounds. His strength was low, and he didn't know if he would be able to walk out of the compound on his own but he would try. He didn't want to ever let Katrina out of his arms again. Viktor used most of his energy pounding the door open, confronting Malice, and then fighting off the last of the Hunters. He felt like collapsing where he stood. Spyder and

Kat each took one of Viktor's arms. They supported him as best they could.

Grailen led the group down the hallway saying that he couldn't wait to get away from such evilness. He said it felt like insects were crawling all over his skin. As they approached the exit door closest to where Dave was parked Viktor heard a clicking noise. Similar to a noise you hear in movies when a booby trap is triggered. Nothing happened.

They all silently acknowledged the noise to each other and decided to carefully move on. Grailen was the first one to the door. As he put pressure on the crash bar to leave, explosives set inside the door and all around the arch of the hallway where they stood went off. One of Malice's soldiers must have set off an alarm system when they realized their compound had been breached by the enemy.

The impact from the explosion caused such a concussion all the team members were thrown backwards. If Spyder didn't have his vampire strength, Viktor and Kat would have been knocked completely through a wall! Unfortunately, Grailen's legs suffered from flying debris caused by the explosives. The flying debris had torn deeply into his flesh. He instantly started to bleed. Spyder pushed Viktor against the wall and went to help Grailen.

Blood pooled out of the wounds at an alarming rate. Spyder pressed his hands above the wounds on Grailen's legs but the blood continued to pour out. Spyder looked up to Viktor and

Kat, "This isn't good. We need to get him blood. He won't survive this if he continues to lose blood this fast."

Viktor pushed himself off the wall and staggered forward. His brother could die because he came to rescue him! That's when Viktor saw something glowing on the floor. "Spyder, grab some of that debris from the blast. We need to look at that closer when we have time. Pick my brother up and carry him outside. I can try and transport him to the mansion once we're outside of these walls." They all looked and saw the exit door was now blocked off by chunks of concrete.

Viktor and Spyder had sustained minor lacerations all over their bodies from the flying debris. Luckily Spyder had pushed them up against the wall away from the main part of the explosion. His reflexes were better than most, even better then Viktor's. Kat was at the back of the group when the bomb went off. Viktor was relieved that she experienced the least amount of injury from the explosion.

Grailen suffered the worst of the injuries. Blood poured from both of his legs and a multitude of other sites on his body. Vampires had superb coagulation rates when injured. Spyder's wounds stopped bleeding after a short amount of time. Grailen, because he lost such a large amount of blood so quickly, was still bleeding and was now unconscious.

The group turned back to find another way out of the compound. They moved carefully, not wanting to set off more explosives. They considered themselves lucky having endured only one casualty from the first trap they encountered. Having a second one go off probably wouldn't go as well.

As they entered the main cell area again they saw a shadowy figure pass through one of the other hallways. The figure was moving slowly and quietly. They assumed it was a lone soldier trying to escape. They paid no mind to him and continued on. There shouldn't have been any troops left. The team did a pretty thorough job of dispatching the Hunters they had run into on their way in.

Kat glanced down the hall to cell number seven. That's where Malice kept his extra special guest locked up tight when she was his prisoner. He was the one who made the guards extra tense. She remembered listening to the soldiers wager with each other, trying to goad each other into dealing with whoever it was. None of the Hunters wanted to do it themselves. That cell was more secure than the one Malice used to contain both Kat and Viktor.

Half the door for cell number seven was hanging off the frame. The other half was missing entirely. Hydraulic fluid dripped from the piping that held the door in place. The piping had been sheared off during the prisoner's escape! The sheer power it must have taken to do that kind of damage was absolutely amazing! Luckily the occupant of the cell was nowhere to be found. No one wanted to have to deal with that kind of encounter at the moment. They needed to find a way out of the compound and get everyone to the safety of the mansion.

Obviously, whoever was kept in that cell was a bigger threat to them than Malice or his goons. Kat could feel the fear and excitement whenever the lackeys had to deal with him. They had always taken extra precaution with that prisoner. Precautions they didn't bother taking with Viktor or Kat. Maybe the sedative darts didn't work on that particular guest. Or maybe, the darts did work and they didn't want to take the chance the prisoner would wake up early and retaliate.

The team went down the hallway that led towards the back of the compound to the dock where Prince Evan and Thomas had entered the building. The group went into the loading dock where they still were. Thomas and Prince Evan were dispatching the final pair of Malice's soldiers who were trying to escape with little effort. The group in the lab gave a brief rundown of what happened to the duo. Together they all headed for the exit. Everyone seemed to be satisfied with the way the mission was executed and that no one was killed in battle. Prince Evan was in high spirits. He was covered in blood and wearing a smile from ear to ear. It seemed he would be perfectly comfortable as a member of Delta 9 as much as he was being a prince.

Once they were all outside and standing on the hill overlooking Viktor's recent prison, everyone took pause to look back one more time at the compound and all the vileness that took place within its walls. Tonight, there would be a large explosion. It would be bigger than the one that injured the group when they were trying to leave. Malice and his men's remains would be incinerated in the blast, extinguishing all evidence of Malice's long reign of terror on the vampire community. It would finally be over, at least for a little while.

There was always someone ready and willing to take over. When the head of one of the Hunter factions was killed there was always someone waiting in the shadows. But it took time to set everything up again and train a new regime of soldiers for their bloody and horrific cause.

When the group left the main lab, Malice was still crumpled, lying on the floor looking life-less. Spyder made the call while they approached the hilltop to have the compound, everything and everyone inside of it, incinerated. It would get done tonight, as it needed to be. Spyder called in his group of special friends that would take care of it. For the moment they were pre-occupied with another mission for another division of the Council in Chicago. When they were done with that they would transport to the mansion.

Spyder and Thomas would take them back to the compound to finish the night's work. They couldn't afford having evidence unprotected for overly curious humans to find. If a human made their way inside the building and saw all of the experiments and the video tapes of torture, they would immediately go to the police. Everything Malice had kept to prove vampires existed was too high of a risk to have lying around.

Everyone reached the SUV Dave had parked inconspicuously on the side of the road. They all poured in filling both vehicles.

None of them had the strength to transport themselves or Grailen back to the mansion. Kat needed the small reprieve the ride home would give her to mentally prepare herself for the days to come. She needed to phase her mind out from what was happening around her. She sat there and tried not to think of anything in particular.

Kat was in no shape to be of much help for Viktor or his brother but she wanted to be there and do whatever she could. She didn't want to get in the way while the others took care of Grailen and his injuries. Her need to be near Viktor made her almost nauseous. She could barely keep her eyes open she was so tired and weak. Katrina's turning would begin in the next hour or so. She could sense it; she could feel her body getting ready for something she had no clue exactly what that was. With that thought, she felt a little awkward not knowing if anyone else in the SUV could tell what was happening to her.

Viktor once told her that vampires could sense when the young ones were about to change. Kat wondered if it was similar to dogs going in heat. Did it drive the boys crazy? She really didn't want to think about that.

Dave drove Kat, Viktor, Grailen, and Spyder back to the mansion. Prince Evan and Thomas took the other SUV. Dave told the staff at the mansion to leave the grounds and take the next few nights off, paid of course. The royal aides that had come with the prince and princess would provide them with the help they needed. Their knowledge on caring for injured vampires and helping young ones go through their change would be more than enough and they wouldn't need their human counterparts around.

The entire house staff was gone by the time the two groups in the SUVs got there, which was a blessing. Katrina's temperature started to spike and Grailen was still unconscious. Both needed some serious medical attention. Unfortunately, when the group gathered their supplies for the mission, no one had the foresight to grab bags of blood in case someone was injured. They were vampires! That was just as bad as an asthmatic not carrying their inhaler with them, Kat thought.

With the type of enemy they were dealing with they didn't know what was going to happen. The Hunters always had new weapons they developed, that made them unpredictable. No one knew who would get injured or even come out alive. They did the best they could under the circumstances, she supposed. But one would think extra blood would be the first thing on the supply list. Men! Why did they always think they were indestructible? Human or vampire, it didn't seem to make a difference. Viktor was usually the one in charge of planning for what was needed. He was the one who always made sure the group was well prepared for the task at hand so there could be allowances for oversights.

Kat, Prince Evan, and Princess Anna stood back and watched while Viktor, Dave, Spyder, and Thomas ran around the mansion like wild animals. The whole time they were yelling something to one another. From what Kat heard it was obvious none of them were listening to each other. The aides were trying to accomplish what needed to be done while staying out of their way. From their ramblings, Kat figured out their care plan. Viktor and Dave would be in charge of Katrina during her change with the help of the royal aides. Thomas and Spyder were in charge of caring for Grailen.

They had both watched young ones go through the change. They were never in charge of taking care of them before so they hadn't paid much attention to detail. They were both regretting their lack of interest on the matter at the moment. This was similar to a passer-by having to deliver a baby in the back seat of a car. You could watch it fifty times on TV, but doing it yourself was a completely different story.

CHAPTER 19

Thomas and Spyder took Grailen to the basement of the mansion, half of the aides following behind them. They were ordered by the prince and princess to do whatever was needed. Down in the basement, they would treat Grailen's wounds and transfuse him with blood. Hopefully that would be enough to save him. However, optimism was not in any of their hearts. Thomas and Spyder had both seen and experienced serious battle injuries. What they saw in Grailen's face and the fact that he lost consciousness was a bad sign. Grailen, extremely weak from the explosion in the doorway and his injuries, would be lucky to survive. Thankfully, Grailen was an old vampire. The strength he gained over his many centuries of life would give him an edge.

Katrina told everyone during the trip back to the mansion about Malice's serum he injected her with and what it was supposed to do to all vampires. The assumption was that Malice used it on Viktor as well. The serum was probably the cause for

Kat's unconsciousness when they brought her back to the mansion after the switch. It could also have something to do with why Viktor's broken bones weren't healing as quickly as they should.

Grailen groaned out in pain every time Thomas and Spyder moved him. His right arm and left ankle were bent at wrong angles, and there were still chunks of concrete stuck in his body that needed to be removed.

Viktor's men put Grailen on the table in the center of a room in the basement. This area of the mansion was where the vampire inhabitants kept their main blood supply. Various sets of intravenous pumps, transfusion tubing, and stock of ancient herbal ingredients to help young vampires with their change, were kept in refrigerators and cupboards around the room. All of this was kept away from the few humans employed to keep the mansion clean, the grounds manicured, and the refrigerator in the main kitchen stocked with food for Dave and themselves.

Dave was the only human allowed down into any part of the basement and certain other rooms throughout the mansion. When human servants started to ask questions that weren't pacified with simple answers, it was time to replace them with someone a little less curious and a little more thankful for their job. That was another one of Dave's responsibilities. He was in charge of the human employees. He did all the hiring, firing, directing, keeping the mansion running smoothly during the day, and keeping the activities of the vampire residence out of the interests of prying eyes.

"Thomas, get the tubing, the first thing we need to do is give Grailen blood, then we can focus on re-setting his bones and taking the cement out of his legs, arms, and stomach," Spyder said quietly as he pointed towards Grailen's legs. "We don't want to have to re-set those bad boys when Grailen wakes up so we need to move fast. Better to do it now when he won't remember," Spyder said as he busied himself going through the closet fridge picking through the blood. Finding the freshest of the stock, checking the expiration dates on the labels. The blood with the newest expiration dates would be the most beneficial to Grailen. It was more recently acquired and would have the most healing properties still left in it.

Even though Thomas was Viktor's second in command, Spyder had far more field experience dealing with injuries. That gave him full reign, telling Thomas what he needed to do. Thomas was expected to comply without question. Hopefully, Spyder had enough experience from past battles to deal with Grailen and his injuries, Thomas thought. Thomas would do anything to help Viktor's brother survive. He had the highest respect for his friend and commander's brother.

Thomas had never met anyone so focused on their duties as Viktor and Grailen. When it came to protecting the royal family they always put their lives, plans, and desires on the backburner. Organized chaos happened whenever the royals came out of their palace. The brothers always insisted on being present when any member of the royal family decided to make a jaunt away from the palace. Viktor could have delegated the job to anyone on his team, but he never did. It wasn't because he thought they were incompetent, he and his brother felt that it was their personal duty to take care of them.

Viktor and Grailen had been at the royal family's beck and call since they were given their positions a few hundred years ago. They still took it as seriously as the day they started. Their parents had both perished doing their duty as Council members. The brothers assumed they would also die in the line of duty. If Grailen didn't make it, he would have died an honorable death. They were also very serious about training. They made sure Viktor's team members were as competent with all the weapons they could get their hands, which was everything known to man, and vampires. Neither of them asked anything of Viktor's team they weren't willing to do themselves. In Thomas's eyes, that was an awesome quality for leaders. Viktor and Grailen deserved the respect they received from his men and all the other Councils. Thomas and the other men would gladly follow the two brothers to the very gates of hell if need be!

Katrina lay in her bed feeling quite sick. She was bundled up in blankets Dave and Viktor wrapped around her. She fell in and out of a restless sleep. On the way to the mansion she had fallen asleep while Grailen lay across her and Viktor's legs in the back seat of the SUV. The rest of the team decompressed from their mission silently, no one said much about what they had seen. The evidence of what Malice had done to other vampires, the tools used for torture and maiming had been strewn about the room after the battle ended. It reminded them of the most gruesome hack-em-up horror movie they ever saw. Except this was no movie, it was their reality.

Viktor and Dave had taken Kat up to the room she shared with Viktor. Dave sat with her after Viktor helped him make her as comfortable as they could. They made a cocoon of blankets around her and wedged pillows at her sides, anticipating her to go through thrashing fits during the change. Otherwise they weren't really sure what else to do. They didn't know how to make the awful experience any better for her. They were both at a loss. She was pouring out sweat and her body temperature kept rising. The royal aides were currently down in the kitchen preparing herbal brews for both her and Grailen. Because of the serum no one knew what they could give Kat. What type of interactions would the herbal brews have with the serum still flowing in her veins?

Dave and Viktor were afraid for Kat's life. They worried that her lack of preparation and knowledge would hinder her change. They feared that she wouldn't come out of it the same person as she went into it. They both hoped Viktor was right, and the strength of her bloodline would push her through it unscathed. The unknown factor of the situation was how the serum would affect her body during and after the change.

Dave leaned over the side of the bed from the chair he pulled up close to her and wiped her forehead with a cool wash cloth. He felt rather helpless. He wasn't sure what else to do but wait.

Soon, Kat's organs would begin to shift inside of her, redesigning her body to become the perfect predator. He knew the process was quite painful. Not being able to receive sedation would make it even worse. The human form was ineffectual. From the design, the human body lacked certain animalistic qualities. During the physical portion of the change Kat would be at her most vulnerable. Organs could shift into the wrong position, become deformed, or lose their function all together. It was possible the organs would become confused and not be able to sustain life. That part of the change was when most young vampires didn't make it. Their organs no longer functioning as they should because there was too much confusion at the most basic, cellular level.

There was no medication they could give her that would help through this part. Normally young ones were sedated. Because of the serum, no one knew what interactions their herbal remedies would have with it so Viktor and Prince Evan decided she would have to go through it on her own. She would have to suffer without the help of pain killers and numbing agents. This would be the most excruciating pain anyone would ever have to endure. No one envied her that challenge.

Viktor came in to her room carrying bags of blood he got from his personal stash from the cooling unit in his bedroom located in the basement of the mansion. He threw them into the black mini fridge that stood by her bed on the opposite side from where Dave was sitting. Spyder was next, he came in carrying more bags of blood while carrying his cell phone wedged in between his shoulder and ear. He was jabbering to someone, making sure the final details of the compound would be covered. He made sure there wouldn't be a trace of what went on in there to be found by inquiring minds who wanted to know.

Kat giggled, Spyder had the qualities of an obsessive compulsive patient when it came to mission details. Although this mission was very important to the entire vampire community. Evidence of their existence was always handled with the utmost of care and discretion. When excessive force was required, that's what was used. Taking down one for the greater good of many was the way of life in the world of vampires. Sometimes humans ended up being in the wrong place at the wrong time. The king considered civilian human deaths related to vampires a personal failure. He felt there was no reason for humans to die because of vampires, so the Council used the least force necessary to minimize the repercussions from the king's anger. An unhappy king was an unhappy Council.

Spyder gave the team specific instructions, making sure they brought the right equipment to incinerate the contents of the building without completely demolishing the structure. A large explosion detectable by humans would bring unwanted attention to the area and to them. With Grailen currently out of commission, that was one more thing in which they didn't need to deal with.

Prince Evan and Princess Anna were last to arrive to Kat's room. They too were carrying in armfuls of bagged blood. Everyone in the mansion had an idea of what was to come with the exceptions of Evan and Anna. What they had in mind, of course, was totally different from the other blood bag Santas that came in. Princess Anna was the first one to speak. She was clearly insulted. "Excuse me, but what the hell do you think you're going to do with this bagged blood?" She cringed as she said it while almost dropping it onto her brother's arms. She could barely tolerate having the plastic of the bag touch the precious skin of her arm. The only reason why she helped bring more up to Katrina's room was because her brother, who was older by a few minutes, told her to do it. Damn titles, Prince Evan didn't use his power over her all that often. He knew if he did she would probably start to rebel. So he savored it for when he really wanted or needed her to do something.

Distaste was written all over her face, it was so obvious she had never touched a bag of blood in her life and Kat could hardly keep from laughing at her. Kat's new princess cousin was a total twit. "You're not actually going to feed her this are you?"

"What did you have in mind your majesty?" Dave asked with obvious ignorance. Viktor knew right away what she was implying. He happened to be present when a royal member underwent his change a few hundred years ago. Royal vampires didn't feed from a bag. They were the only ones allowed to feed straight from the hoof, so to speak. Only during their change, otherwise they were served their blood, warmed, in a glittering goblet of gold encrusted with precious jewels. When a royal vampire made their change, if they survived it, they didn't have any control over the thirst. Civilian vampires didn't either. The donor was a sacrifice.

Some humans felt it was an honor to be chosen to be the royal's first meal. Some didn't.

Sometimes, if you pissed off a royal bad enough, and the timing was right, you ended up being the donor whether you wanted to be or not. The changing Viktor witnessed didn't turn out well for the donor. They didn't walk out of the room. But, you never go against the wishes of a royal. Because of this, the donors rarely had to be tied down. They usually willingly submitted themselves and their bodies for whatever the changeling needed. But for mercy's sake, the donors were given a sedative to relieve their fears and relax them. When a vampire changed they woke up very thirsty. The first human in sight tended to be ripped apart to shreds. The one Viktor witnessed was no different.

Princess Anna looked at Dave as if he was from Mars. "You don't intend to give her, a royal vampire princess, blood from a bag, do you?" Dave and Viktor stared at the royal siblings. Both Council members realized exactly what the princess had in mind.

Viktor stepped in at this point and addressed the issue at hand. "Your highnesses, we don't have time to find a proper donor, she's going through the change as we speak. The blood we have in these bags is her only chance at making it through, her best chance."

"I think not, Viktor. While you were away at the compound, putting the princess and my brother in harm's way, I made a few phone calls. I can sense, as can my dear brother, Katrina is starting her change. So, I have a donor being delivered. Also, the king would like to have a word with you and your brother when you have time. I suggest the sooner you respond, the better it will be for both of you. He sounded a little peeved, shall we say." She sneered at that last sentence.

Viktor was confident Princess Anna enjoyed watching others feel the wrath of her father. The king was quite the force to reckon with, even if you were his darling little angel Anna. She was known to be an insolent spoiled brat and he had to deal with her using a heavy hand once or twice, so she enjoyed seeing others suffer at his hand. Viktor heard stories of her life and how she had found ways out of the palace without her father knowing it. She proved to be quite the handful, even for their king.

Katrina looked pitiful laying there in that huge bed all bundled up. Viktor wanted nothing more than to curl up next to her, wrap his arms around her body, and absorb all the pain and agony she would soon experience. Kat was coming in and out of consciousness, moaning about the pain, and what Malice had done to her and Viktor. She had sweat beading on her forehead yet she was shivering. Viktor knew the pain would only get worse.

Once that started, it was a done deal. The pain signaled the beginning of her body transformation. Her cellular structure would begin to shift itself into perfection, hopefully. Viktor could only imagine how beautiful she would turn out to be. Young ones were born beautiful in their human form, but when they went through the change they became even more so. Her hair would thicken and grow longer. Her eyes would develop a permanent glisten to them. Her skin would look like she had never suffered from acne or a day of stress in her life. Her breasts would become firmer, grow a cup or two in size, and remain lifted and perky for all of eternity.

It was said that royals had it the worst. Their change was the roughest because their blood lines were the purest. They suffered longer and more severely than non-royal vampires. Their blood made the change more efficient and potent. That's why it was believed the royals were the ones with the most unique abilities out of all the vampires. Their bodies were given more time to develop all sorts of neat capabilities.

Just then, while the royal twins and Viktor sat arguing, not paying much attention to her, Kat sat up in bed. She let out a low painful moan. Her face was beat red, she could feel the blood pounding in her temples. It felt like she had her own team of drummers walking a chaotic pattern around in her head.

"I think it's time the human slave was dismissed. This is no place for a lower being. He should not be allowed to see a royal vampire go through their change," Princess Anna said, pointing at Dave.

"Princess Anna, Dave is a member of the Council. He is knowledgeable of these things," Viktor said.

"I don't think so. What will happen when my father hears how you treated his beloved niece so inappropriately during her greatest time of need?"

"Dave is our friend princess, he should be allowed to stay and help her," Viktor said, standing his ground.

"Well, I suppose he could be of some assistance. He could be her first meal," she said with a wicked smile.

"Fine. Dave, it would be best if you went to the basement and sent Thomas up here to help. You can stay with Grailen and make sure he's ok." Viktor gave up. He didn't like that the princess was right. If Kat woke up from her change while Dave was in the room she could attack him in her first blood rage. Dave silently bowed his head towards the prince and princess then left.

Everyone stopped their discussion of how she was going to be fed for the first time after her change and stared at her. She looked ethereal, Viktor thought. She was obviously in pain, yet she looked fantastic. Her long dark hair was wet, tangled, and snarled all around her head. Some hair stuck to her forehead from the fever that was trying to claim her. Kat's eyes opened and she looked around at all of them.

When she looked at Princess Anna her eyes changed. She didn't know it, but everyone else could see it happen. Her eyes gave away her strong dislike for her new cousin. They turned completely black. Kat already had issues with the princess because she knew that Viktor would be in very serious trouble with the king. That, and the pretentious attitude she carried around with her, which Kat thought was stuck very high up her ass. Princess Anna and Prince Evan looked at the others and decided now was a good time to pull Viktor out in the hallway to clarify some things that seemed to be out of place. They wanted an explanation regarding Viktor's and Kat's feelings for each other.

Once they had Katrina's door closed behind them Princess Anna started in. "What the hell is going on here, Viktor? Why does our new little cousin feel the need to be so protective over a simple security guard? There's obviously something more going on between the two of you than what you have decided to share with us, so spill it right now!" she shouted. Prince Evan looked at him with curiosity. He was eager to hear what the little imp was going to say and how he was going to try and get himself out of the mess he created.

"Princess Anna, Prince Evan, I tried to explain before but we didn't have time. With everything going on; Malice capturing Katrina, me being locked away, and now the beginning of her change, there hasn't been much time for any discussion," Viktor said in apology.

"If there is something going on between you two, you already know what will happen. My father will never accept your relationship. He'll have you judged and executed for treason."

"Princess Anna, I know there are consequences for what you are suggesting. I will deal with that when the time comes."

"I hope I get to see my father's face when you tell him," Princess Anna said with a sinister grin.

Viktor went on to explain how one night he was tracking

one of Malice's soldiers when he realized the soldier was tracking someone else, a human female. Viktor decided to figure out why the Hunters were so interested in a particular human female. The human female turned out to be Katrina. And so, if it wasn't for the Council and their efforts, she could still be stuck in Malice's compound even now. Everyone agreed that if she went through her change at the compound she would never survive. Not to mention, the Council and the royal family never would have known she existed because Prince Eric hadn't bothered to share with them that he had fathered a daughter.

Since he was on a role, Viktor thought it was as good a time as any to explain why he consumed royal blood. He told them he had to take extreme measures to ensure Kat's comprehension of the situation. While explaining what and who she really was, he bit her.

He left out the part where he knew by biting her he would end up bonding them together. Once he realized that she was a lost royal, Viktor knew he was in deep shit. He kept certain portions of the story out for now. He wanted to discuss issues with Grailen before the High Council became involved. Grailen's hide was also on the line for allowing involvement of the king's children during the rescue mission.

When Viktor finished explaining all the events leading up to them bringing Katrina back to the mansion, their royal pain in the asses looked content, for now. This was for two reasons. One, the royals would do anything to protect their newest family member, and have shown just that in their actions. The second reason; the king was going to come down hard on Viktor and his brother, and they knew it.

The king's children loved when others were in trouble, consuming their father's attention. It never boded well for whoever it was, but it was better than having his attention on them. Better to blend in than be looked at too closely.

Thomas walked around them and opened the door to Katrina's room. He waited a few minutes for a respectable gap in the group's conversation as was appropriate for he was servant to the royals.

Thomas stepped into the hallway allowing for them to enter. "I think everyone should come back into Princess Katrina's room, there's something I think you need to see," he said. He clearly thought something was wrong. The group went in to evaluate Kat. Unfortunately, Thomas was correct.

Katrina was out of bed, walking around, and angry as hell. She should have been lying in her bed moaning unconsciously while her body went through the change. She cursed Viktor's name as she paced the room. She bumped into the inhabitants as she passed by without caring. She was obviously on fire, in the pissed off sense. It was surprising she didn't have smoke coming out of her nose. She looked directly at Viktor and Thomas. "How could you people do this to me? What exactly is it that you've done?" She stood directly in front of them with her feet spread apart and her hands on her hips, barely containing her anger.

Viktor stepped forward ready to embrace her in his arms.

"Katrina, I'm so glad to see you walking about my love." With that, he did grab her and squeezed her to his chest.

"Viktor, what is happening to me? Why are these people here, and what do they want?" she asked as she pointed a finger in the prince and princess's general direction.

"Kat, they're here because I've been telling you the truth all along." Viktor put a hand on each side of her face and kissed her softly on the lips.

Her confusion controlled her temper, the moment his lips touched hers, she calmed. "Viktor, I'm not going anywhere with them!"

The prince interrupted. "Hello, sweetheart. I'm glad you could join us. And we didn't do anything to you at all, ask them," Prince Evan said then pointed to Viktor and Thomas. Katrina glared at them in expectant silence.

"Dearest cousin, we've come to take you home, to the palace, where you belong. Viktor and his men didn't mistreat you did they?" Princess Anna asked. She prodded Katrina into saying that Viktor had, in fact, treated her poorly. The princess seemed to have something against Viktor and the Council. Or maybe she was a sadist and enjoyed watching others suffer. Who knew? Either way, Kat didn't like her much. Princess Anna was too snooty, too privileged, and too overall annoying to be around for extended periods of time. It was clear that the overly entitled princess had never worked a day in her life, never having worked for what she wanted or needed. From the princess's cavalier attitude, Kat was sure she was given everything when she asked for it, and probably when she didn't.

No one realized Kat had consumed half the blood supply brought into her room when they first arrived at the mansion. She put all the empty plastic bags in the garbage in the connecting bathroom, out of their direct view. They were amazed she was in an upright position instead of lying in bed screaming her head off. That fact made it difficult for them to figure out what they could do to help her.

Kat looked at Viktor and saw something green glowing from his left hand while he searched a cabinet with his right. He found what he was looking for and walked back to where she stood. Grabbing her hand gently in his, he led her to their bed. He sat down near the bedside table and guided her to do the same. "Katrina, when we were in the compound, Malice used a serum he injected us with. When I had the last discussion with him, he gladly led me to the serum's antidote," he said as he held out two vials containing a bright green solution in the palm of his hand.

Kat grabbed one of the vials and held it up to the light of the lamp on the bedside table. "Viktor, are you going to use this on us? How do you know that's what this really is?"

"We don't know. Not yet anyways. I want to have Thomas analyze the solution and see if it will counteract the serum or if it's another one of Malice's attempts to kill us." Viktor took the vial from Katrina's hand and stood up.

"Where are you going?"

Viktor looked into her eyes, seeing his love for her reflected back at him. He knew they would be ok, if she made it through her change. "Kat, I need to give this to Thomas and check on Grailen. I'll be right back, I promise." With that, he left the room.

While standing in Viktor's bathroom Kat freaked out. When she looked at herself in the mirror, the reflection looking back at her was an altered version of herself. Kat considered herself to be a plane girl, not hideous, but not gorgeous either. The woman she saw in the mirror was beautiful. Even her eyebrows looked like she was at the salon twenty minutes ago. They were a perfect shape she would never have been able to achieve with tweezers. Her boobs were bigger, her skin almost flawless, not one pimple. There was a magnificent glow to her whole being. Must be the lighting, she thought.

Princess Anna spoke, pulling Kat from her thoughts. "Katrina, we should really discuss leaving this place. You need to prepare yourself for a trip to the palace."

"What are you talking about? Cousin? Palace? I'm not going anywhere with you. I'm fine right where I am!" Kat said as she looked at the prince and princess with a new reserve of venom. Kat's eyes changed when her anger peaked. It seemed to happen every time she glared at her cousins, which was unusual. Normally a young vampire's eyes didn't change until they had lived for a few years consuming blood. Just then, at that very moment when Kat wanted to appear intimidating to the group standing in front of her, she screamed out in agony and bent over onto the floor in pain.

Thomas and her new royal cousins looked at each other. No one knew what to do. This was obviously a delayed part of Kat's change. The t-shirt she wore was covered in sweat, sticking to her back. Her skin, bones, and muscles began to ripple underneath her clothes at odd angles. No one knew what to do, moving her didn't seem to be an option. It would probably cause her more pain than she was already in. They didn't want to touch her in fear of manipulating tissue into doing something it wasn't supposed to.

"Where is he, where is Viktor? I need him!" Kat screamed. She dug her fingertips into the plush carpeting, and mashed the side of her face into the floor.

"Kat, Viktor went down to the basement. I'm sure he'll be back as soon as he can. He's helping them with Grailen who needs blood for injuries. He'll come up here as soon as he can I promise. He wouldn't stay away from you if he absolutely didn't have to, especially not right now," Thomas answered softly. He felt sad for this woman. She loved Viktor deeply, and right now she probably felt the need to rip the hair from Viktor's head for what she was going through. Somehow she still thought Viktor was the cause of all this.

The rumbling underneath her clothes had stopped after a few torturous minutes. Kat was finally given a reprieve from the pain.

She slumped to the floor and passed out. The pain consumed her. Her body, which had begun to transform, caused her extreme agony while it underwent the changing. Her bones were broken and reset. Every cell in her body began to starve and die.

As she lay on the carpet, her skin started to heal from where marks developed on her chest and thighs from stretching in such a short amount of time. Thomas bent over and as carefully as he could, picked her up off the floor. Not wanting anyone else to touch Viktor's woman, he positioned himself to be the only one to administer her care. He laid her once again on the bed.

"It must be a side effect of the serum Malice gave her. I wonder what other complications it will cause?" He started unraveling tubing, setting up equipment to give her a blood transfusion.

Some blood would help her. Thomas went to grab the blood out of the fridge and noticed there were barely any bags left. He looked up at the prince and princess with a questioning glance. Thomas looked around; he didn't see any bags full or empty, lying around. When he went into the bathroom, he grabbed the four empty blood bags from the garbage and brought them back into the bedroom suite. She was in no state to drink from a bag, and certainly not straight from the 'hoof' as her cousins suggested. She needed the healing properties it would give her, and the strength. He would give her a few units intravenously while she slept. It must have been her that drank the blood. He was surprised she was able to get herself out of bed alone to get it from the fridge. Maybe the serum inadvertently would change the process of her turning? They would soon find out.

CHAPTER 20

The prince and princess finally accepted what Thomas was doing and understood the need for him to proceed, despite their distaste. They realized that if they didn't allow Katrina to receive the blood transfusion and something happened to her because of it, Viktor's ass wasn't going to be the only one on the line. Their donor had not arrived, and Katrina needed all the help she could get. Once Thomas primed the blood and saline tubing, he put an IV in her vein. He connected the primed tubing and unclamped the tubing clips, allowing for gravity to draw the blood down into her body. Thomas pulled a chair up to the side of her bed and settled in so he could watch over her.

Thomas didn't move until it was time to switch the bags. The prince and princess had come and gone a few times, saying nothing. Their concern was curious to Thomas. He hadn't realized the prince and princess were capable of caring for another person besides themselves. Viktor had come in when they were gone. He checked on her as much as he could. Knowing there was nothing he could do to help her he focused his energies on helping Dave and Spyder figure out why Grailen's injuries hadn't stopped bleeding. Kat hadn't woken since the time she was up walking around and then collapsed.

Everyone waited for word from the king and what he wanted them to do. They were all apprehensive about what the consequences were going to be regarding what Viktor had done and how it was going to affect them all.

The really scary part was Grailen hadn't woken up yet. If King Alexander decided to take Katrina before he did, there would be hell to pay on both ends. Viktor and his Council members had never gone against the king in any fashion in the past, but now was a totally different story. Kat was Viktor's woman, his bonded mate, and Viktor would fight to the death to keep her by his side. Because of their loyalty to Viktor, the members of the Kensin Council would stand by him in battle. That meant that if the king wanted Viktor dead, his men would also die protecting him.

Viktor had finally found her. Kat was his bond mate. Even if she wasn't his biggest fan at the moment, he knew the instant she woke and looked at him with those feral eyes, she was his, and he was hers. She may fight it for a while longer, but they were destined to be together. Viktor would make sure of it. For now, they had bigger fish to fry. Kat may finally come to terms that they are on her side. It would happen when the king got involved and decided to keep her at his palace for the next decade, or even century. It would all be a matter of how ticked off he was about what happened. They'll just have to see, and do whatever was necessary for everyone to stay alive.

Spyder came into her room holding his cell phone in one hand and his head in the other. Thomas noticed the phone was open, which meant there was a caller on the line. "It's the king. Princess Anna insisted on calling him to give him an update on our newly found Tinkerbelle." Thomas rolled his eyes. The Council would call her by that nickname for the rest of her days. Thomas put the phone to his ear and took a deep breath.

"My king, this is Spyder of the Kensin Council unit Delta 9. How can I be of service to you?" He pulled the phone away just in time to save his ear drum from being blown. The king demanded they bring Princess Katrina to the palace at once. "My King, I don't think that is a wise decision. She is currently undergoing her change, and nightfall is almost over. It is not a safe time for her to be moved, she isn't even conscious," he said this as he looked down at their charge with concern.

Katrina's change wasn't going as any of them expected. She had drank blood from the fridge, that meant she was up walking around before they saw her, at least for long enough to get blood for herself when no one else was in the room. She was back in the bed, unconscious, and consumed by pain from the changes. Damn, it seemed like every second things were becoming more and more complicated.

"We will come to the palace when the princess's change

is over. It may be a few days. I believe that your children have been here too long. It's not safe for them to be away from the palace like this when Grailen, one of the Council's sergeants has been gravely injured. Our numbers are down and we don't think it wise to have the prince and princess here. We are unable to protect them and Princess Katrina adequately at the same time. I ask you to call them back. When it is safe, we will bring her to you." Spyder could barely speak the words. He knew Viktor would never give her to them and walk away. He would never condemn her to be confined to the palace. Without her bond mate, as rich of an environment as it was, it would be torture for both of them.

They knew there was a chance Viktor would never be welcomed to the palace again, after they found out he had fed from her. Or, when he went to the palace, he may never be allowed to leave. The king was quite the intimidating kind of a guy. He was often unpredictable in his decisions. Whatever those decisions were, they had to be followed. It was on an or else basis.

No matter how ridiculous those decisions seemed. The Judges were overly vile demons. When the king ordered the Judges to give out a punishment, everyone cringed. They felt sorry for the person that was their target. The Judges had quite the imagination and array of magical torture skills. Not to mention the rotten oozy stuff a few of them tended to leave behind on their victims.

After his discussion with the king, he closed the phone and

put it in his pocket. "So it's true? All of it? I'm supposedly a long lost princess who happens to be a vampire too? And you were just talking to the king who happens to be a relative of mine?" Spyder looked down in surprise when Kat started talking. He hadn't expected her to hear his conversation. The last he saw, she was out cold, writhing in pain. He hadn't noticed during his conversation the moaning stopped and she began to listen to him.

He hadn't really wanted her to hear what he said, but the cat was out of the bag. Spyder knew he and the rest of the Council had to bring her back. It was the king's order whether she liked it or not. All of their lives depended on it.

Katrina would spend the rest of her life being hunted because of what and who she was. Everyone wanted to get to know the royals, even if the royal in particular didn't want to get to know them. It was similar to being a celebrity. The Hunters and some of the common vampire community were the paparazzi, chasing them, trying to get a glimpse.

The royal family members were celebrities within the vampire population, only coming out for special occasions. Threats to their safety caused their visits to the outside world to be less and less these days. Malice and his group made sure of that. The vampire fanatics and other seekers of the royal families didn't help the situation either.

The king was strict on royal's movements. Ever since the family was relocated to the palace, he hadn't been open to the idea when his kids wanted to leave the nest. That was the only desire he would not grant them.

"You don't really think you're taking me to the king, do you? I don't know how to act in front of a king! Forget it, I'm not going and none of you can make me!" Kat said as she sat up in bed and crossed her arms in defiance. She realized she looked like a child throwing a tantrum in the middle of a store. "And besides, where's Viktor? I want to see him. Right now! He won't let you people do anything to me and he's going to be ticked off when he hears you said you were going to take me somewhere," she said while glaring at Thomas and Spyder.

"Katrina, ugh..." Thomas threw his hands up into the air in frustration and got up from his chair next to her bed. "We have to take you to the palace at some time. You'll be safest there as you learn things about being a vampire. Things you'll need to know to survive. And there you'll be protected from all those that would do you harm. It's something that has to be done. You may not understand how dangerous it is for everyone here if we keep you and not do what the king said. Katrina, he will kill us all, and he will still have you taken to the palace with or without your consent," he said that last word more pointedly then he meant to.

"If you are this well tomorrow when the sun sets, we will be leaving, so be ready. And it doesn't matter if Viktor is ready to go with, it is what has to be done, no matter if any of us like it or not," Spyder added, and with that, he and Thomas left the room to go and check on Grailen.

Kat sat there in awe at what Viktor's soldier said to her. How could he do this to her? She had gone through the biggest event of her boring life and Viktor's men were going to hand her over to some freaky guy with an obvious power trip, not even looking back on their way out? Didn't they care that she loved Viktor? Didn't they care she didn't want to leave, and that even now she felt the pull towards Viktor, the need to be by him?

She knew what her emotional storm was about. She didn't want to lose Viktor when she had just found him. Never in her life had she been so deeply attracted to someone like she was to him. And what happened between them before she took off, well, that was obviously not going to happen again with anyone else, ever. The deep passion they shared between each other. The feelings he invoked in her. She didn't think anyone else would ever be able to achieve that.

Love um and leave um she supposed, what a jerk! She knew it wasn't Viktor's fault. If he knew what they were planning, he would never let her be taken away, right? He would be her champion. He would stay with her and take care of her forever. Just like he said he would, and she would take care of him too.

What a total and complete manipulative jerk. She actually started to believe he cared for her like she did for him. Or, at least, was starting to with the potential for more. Way to give your heart away girlfriend. You idiot! Now he wasn't even coming up to see her. Did she believe Thomas and Spyder when they told her that he was so busy that he wasn't able to come for a two minute visit? Was it that he just didn't want to ever see her again?

Her heart felt like someone had put their hand into her chest and squeezed it, making it harder and harder for her heart to beat or her lungs to expand.

Her brain was working on overdrive. Kat never really had a lot of self confidence, she was sure that's why all this questioning was going through her mind about Viktor. Was she questioning his feelings for her because she didn't feel she deserved them? Over analyzing things was what she did best. She couldn't help it.

Kat stood up out of bed. She felt the sun was getting ready to make its presence known to her side of the world. Energy was seeping out of her, leaving her body. She was feeling the effect of everything she had gone through, and now she was feeling the energy sapping pull of the sun.

She had to do it. Kat had been waiting for a moment like this when she was completely and utterly alone. She could leave the room without any of the big brothers watching over her every move. She was scared out of her mind at what was to come, having to meet the king and all. She had to see for herself. She was never very good at social situations, always preferring to be the loner.

That was one perk of working second shift. There weren't as many supervisors to tell you what to do and what you were doing wrong. She was used to making due with more work, less nursing staff, and a lack of resources. That was the way of things in the medical field.

She missed Viktor greatly and she was tired of everyone telling her she couldn't go and see him. It was never a good time. Thomas and Spyder told her that she was too sick and would only make things worse for both of them. Well, she was tired of waiting and having to listen to what everyone else had to say about what she could and couldn't do.

Spyder and Thomas continued giving Grailen more blood with little improvement. Grailen was coming in and out of consciousness but the wounds he sustained during Viktor's rescue weren't healing. For some reason the healing process was taking a lot longer than normal. No matter how much blood they gave Grailen he continued to bleed.

"Viktor, come and look at this," Thomas yelled, motioning Viktor over to a microscope he had been looking through in another room down the hall in the basement.

"What are we looking at, Thomas?"

"Do you remember the sample of cement we picked up after the bomb went off in the hallway?"

"Yeah, the cement was everywhere. Do you have a point to this?" Viktor's patience was wearing thin. His brother would die if they didn't find out why he wasn't healing, and his bond mate started her change where she could also die.

"Well, I've made a slide from the sample of cement. Look what happens when I add a drop of vampire blood to the slide."

Viktor leaned over and put the ocular piece up to his eye to watch. Thomas grabbed a dropper preloaded with blood. Viktor motioned that he was ready to see what had Thomas so excited. Thomas put a drop of blood onto the slide with the cement sample.

Viktor couldn't believe what he was seeing. The cement molecules attacked the blood. "Viktor, I think Malice had a new use for his UV pellets. I think the cement blocks in that hallway were laced with the pellets."

Seeing what he needed to see, Viktor stood up and looked at Thomas. "That's why Grailen's wounds won't stop bleeding. Thomas, we don't have the capability to deal with this here. The UV pellets must have penetrated his bloodstream. The UV won't allow his blood to coagulate before he's dead."

"I know Viktor. There is only one way that I can think of to save Grailen."

"Yes, I agree. I know what you're thinking. We have to bring him to the palace. The royal doctors will know what do to. They're the only ones who can save him now." Viktor turned and looked at his brother. For his entire life, Grailen had been there for Viktor and Rafe. He had to make a decision and he needed time to think. Time he didn't have.

Kat walked down the stairs as quietly as she could. She didn't want to bring any unwanted attention to herself. The stairway was one of those old fashioned types that hugged alongside the wall. Fancy maroon carpeting with gold designs swirled in various patterns covered the wooden steps. There was a large engraved wooden banister that ran the whole length of the staircase. She crept down to the bottom without hearing anyone.

Kat didn't know where to look to find Viktor, but she wasn't going to stop looking until she found him. There was no more keeping her away, she decided. Kat wanted to see him and make sure he was all right. She was afraid they wouldn't tell her the truth if he wasn't. It was possible they would keep bad news from her to ensure her compliance on going to meet the king.

Walking towards the kitchen, she spotted Dave passing by her with his arms full of blood bags. He must be going to re-supply someone that needed blood, and that person was probably just the man she was looking for.

Kat heard Prince Evan and Thomas talking in the sitting room off the kitchen. It sounded like they were arguing. Thomas sounded more heated than Prince Evan. Sticking around to get the scoop would make her loose whatever direction Dave was going in. Have vampire will need blood, right? Follow the guy with the stash, find your honey vampire.

Dave carried his load down the hall from the kitchen and entered the main entryway that held the main staircase. He passed by the stairs and went into the library. Typical, Kat thought. He would probably go right into the library, pull on a book, and a big book shelf would move to let the person into a secret room or something.

Kat stepped into the library in time to see Viktor's comrade in arms punch a code into the digital wall panel. A really thick metal pocket door slid open with a whoosh. When the door was fully open, Dave disappeared through it without looking back.

Kat discovered a new skill. She was able to catch the door before it slid shut. She ran at a fantastic speed across the room without making even a scuffle sound on the fluffy carpet. Grabbing the door before it locked back into place, she held her breath for a moment and stood there. She hoped Dave hadn't noticed not hearing the pocket door lock into place behind him. She gave Dave enough time to get to where he was going before she slid the door open wide enough to pass through.

Spyder was holding Grailen on the table when Dave entered the room. Grailen was still running a fever. They were worried that his wounds were infected and that's why the fever was able to keep a hold on him. Fever was never a problem for vampires except for some going through their change. The UV in the cement must be causing it.

Dave had just set down his bundle when Katrina entered the room. The silence was thick in the air. She ran over to where Viktor was standing, holding his head in frustration.

Grailen lay on the table, moaning. Slowing down when she got close enough around the table to see Viktor's face, she felt sick inside. Lifting her hand to his face, she brushed his hair away from his eyes. That black glorious hair was all out of place from the bond he tended to wear it in. His face twisted in agony. She wished there was something she could do to help him relieve his pain. Ironically, she noticed a lessoning of the intensity of his painful expression when she touched him.

"What has happened to him? Why isn't he healed? He should be all better by now Viktor, right? He's a vampire with vampire strength, what's the problem?" she asked all the men now standing with her around Grailen's table.

"Katrina, we're doing what we can for him, you know that. Malice laced the concrete with UV pellets and Grailen's blood is unable to clot. The UV has taken a hold of him and is fighting us every step of the way. I think he will be ok, it may just take more time than expected, and a lot more blood," Spyder said in a low tone. From working with this woman when they got Viktor out of the compound, he knew she cared deeply for both brothers. He respected her for that. Not many women could fall in love with a male vampire, with all their egotistical, bossy ways. Falling in lust with them was a lot easier, and a lot more temporary.

"Well, do more! There's got to be something you're not doing, something you're missing," Kat said. "Have you thought of giving the serum to Grailen? It feels like whatever the serum is made of, it's helped me, not hurt me. Look at Viktor. He looks ok, and he's already a vampire. Maybe you could give Grailen some and see what happens."

Dave chimed in, "Unfortunately, nobody grabbed any samples of the serum Malice was using. I'm afraid it was all destroyed in the fire the Council had set on the inside of the compound."

Viktor put his arm around Kat's shoulders and said, "Katrina, we don't know what the effects of the serum are. You are right. If the serum was as bad as Malice said it was, I would be dead by now. You haven't fully gone through your change yet, so the effects on you are still unknown. I don't know what to do."

"Hello people, you can use my blood. He injected me so many times with that stuff I should be glowing right now. With the mixture of my blood and the serum, maybe it would help? Malice said the properties of the serum could change a vampire into a human."

"Kat, Grailen was never a human."

She stared at Viktor. It dawned on her then that he was right. None of the vampires she had met were humans made into vampires. They were all born that way.

"Viktor, if the serum could change Grailen into a human, then he would be able to heal his wounds and get rid of the UV pellets. When that's over just change him back into a vampire. It seems pretty simple to me really."

"We still don't know what would happen if we gave him your blood Katrina. With you being so close to your change right now, it wouldn't be wise to take any from you. You are kind to offer, but I must decline."

Dave and Spyder looked at each other. Neither one of them had thought about using her blood to help find an antidote for Grailen. It was possible from her blood they could create an anti-UV solution to help him get through it. That was, if they could figure out what they needed, and if it worked. Spyder went over to the mansion intercom and beeped for Thomas. Thomas was a scientist of sorts, and he was the only one in the mansion who could figure it out.

"How about I just give a few vials of blood for them to work with, I promise to replace it right after?"

"I don't like this one bit Katrina."

"Viktor, now's not the time to be overbearing. Ok? Spyder, let's get the show on the road."

"Katrina, as long as you feel ok, we'll keep you down here with Grailen. We'll need to take a few samples of your blood and see if Thomas can figure out a way to use it to help him."

At Kat's look of dismay, Dave smiled a little. "It will be ok, even if we don't find a cure for him, he is getting better. The timing is what we are concerned about. The longer it takes for his body to heal, the longer his brain and cognitive skills will be permanently affected. But eventually he will be alright. He does have all the time in the world."

Thomas came down the hall and into the room they were keeping Grailen in. He had already gathered some of the supplies he needed and told Spyder to go and get the rest. First things first, he needed Katrina's blood to work with. Kat was sitting in a chair at the head of Grailen's table. Thomas went to a table against the wall while Kat silently followed.

Kat was barely able to hold it all in and not cry at the

helplessness she felt. She knew Viktor was worried about Grailen and the danger they were all in. Kat didn't want to think of Viktor not having his tougher than nails, big brother around. Regardless of Viktor's self sufficient exterior, she knew he cared for Grailen greatly. The man who seemed to have brought her into all of this mess was looking a little unsure of what Thomas was about to do to her. None of them knew what the outcome of their efforts would be, but they had to try something. Grailen could die if they didn't. She just hoped that he would be ok, that he would end up safe and healthy. That was all that mattered. Kat would do everything in her power to help him. If that meant giving blood, that was the least she could do.

Thomas was ready to begin withdrawing her blood. Meanwhile, Dave set up a chair for her to sit in next to the table with Thomas's supplies on it. Even though she was a nurse, she wasn't a big fan of needles. Surprisingly, Thomas was gentle through the whole process. He was almost nice to her, in his gruff vampire security sort of way. He took three small vials. Each of them had a different colored top. Interesting, was it possible the vampire community followed the same procedure for running blood tests as humans did? She had never seen these colors on blood tubes she used at work. It was possible Thomas knew more about blood chemistry than she gave him credit for.

CHAPTER 21

Prince Evan and Princess Anna remained on the first floor between the kitchen and the living room the majority of the time until Dave called for Thomas. They didn't have much to offer in the care of wounded soldiers, the palace staff dealt with that sort of thing. So they left their aides to do what they did best. The royal cousins did what they did best, which was standing by watching while everyone else took care of what needed to be done. The aides acted more as gofers to Spyder and Thomas than actual healers. They stayed out of everyone's way but were available to run for supplies when needed.

The prince and princess followed Thomas down to where Grailen was being tended to. They were talking to everyone now, trying to make the group understand what was to come, what they were risking by not bringing the princess immediately to the palace which the king was demanding. They explained that their father may become impatient with all of them, including his own children. Not returning to the palace the next night with Princess Katrina and Viktor would be a huge mistake. It would likely result in a visit from the Judges. That would be bad.

The Judges didn't care what they had to do to carry out an order from their king. They got the job done anyway they deemed necessary. They were above all laws, human and vampire. The only being they had to answer to was the king himself. If the king told them to bring Katrina and Viktor back to the palace, they wouldn't care whether Viktor's brother was injured or not. The Judges would only take a bit of extra care when it came to Kat. The Judges weren't well known for their ability to discriminate which targets needed to be handled with care. They only understood the mission. The intricate details had to be explained so they wouldn't kill someone the king didn't want to die.

Princess Anna told the group of the horrible story she heard when she was younger about the Judges. She was never sure if the story was made up by her father to keep her, her brothers, and cousins in line, in fear that it may happen to them. He may have used the story so they knew if they didn't do exactly what they were told he would order the Judges to take care of them also.

Princess Anna's aunt, Kendra, decided to make a run from the palace where she was being kept before King Alexander was crowned. Kendra's father, King Reskin, found her and punished her repeatedly for her disobedience. She was always the one going against the king's orders. Princess Kendra didn't want to be a vampire. She never appreciated what she was given by being born a vampire royal. She wanted to live a human life, among the humans. She enrolled in a local college, taking classes at night with human students without her father's knowledge. Of course that wasn't allowed. Vampires were not to interact freely with humans. It was against logic to establish intimate relationships with humans as she so desired and had attempted over and over again.

King Reskin sent a group of Judges to retrieve her and to expel residual loose ends she created with the humans she interacted with. The Judge's perspective of the order was to exterminate every single human Princess Kendra was in acquaintance with and their entire families. King Reskin didn't take that lightly. The princess caused him to create a huge death toll among the humans. They were humans who did nothing to deserve it besides being in the wrong place at the wrong time. King Reskin respected humans as a race and did not want to create a war with them. His goal was to have his race live peaceably, but separate, from the humans.

Any human who knew vampires existed and who wasn't under their direct control were considered to be a liability. They were a possible cause for discovery, and that was unacceptable to him and his brethren. The secrecy of their existence was the highest priority to them all, even more important than any one individual. That included his daughter.

The king decided to deal with the princess once and for all, tolerating her attempts to leave his palace no more. He felt she was becoming too defiant and dangerous. To interact with the humans, she had begun to take greater risks. The possible exposure of the vampire race by her actions was becoming too great. She had to be stopped.

He loved his daughter very much. But as king, he had no choice but to eliminate the constant threat of humans discovering their existence. The king knew there was only one group of beings that could keep a constant watch over her. He saw only one other option and he couldn't imagine having his own flesh and blood destroyed. To protect his people, he decided to give his youngest daughter to the Judges. He made rules of course. He insisted the head of the Judges pick his most deserving demon to be assigned only to her. That Judge would then be held one hundred percent responsible for her actions and her care. That would be his only job until she died.

The Judge chosen was Rowden. He was their meanest demon, and had shown Princess Kendra no mercy in his care of her. All Judges wore a black robe to cover themselves. Royalty wasn't accustomed to seeing hideous creatures walking among them, and Rowden was no exception. Rowden specialized in making people do what he wanted them to do. He used all sorts of nasty techniques. He pulled body parts off that would heal overnight. He infected his victims with his venomous bite to ensure their compliance. The venom burned until it finished completing its cycle through the body's circulatory system.

The king left her to the demon's ministrations. His only job was to make sure she stayed alive and safe from her own self. The king said it no longer mattered how he had to get the job done.

No one has seen her since Rowden took her away from the palace. Rumors surfaced that Rowden killed every human he could smell her essence on, totaling eighty-four. When the king was killed, that line of communication was lost, and so were Rowden and the princess. The last time anyone heard from them was over nine hundred years ago.

Princess Morgan, Princess Kendra's young daughter, was recently sent to King Alexander for protection. That was the only hint that told the Caines Princess Kendra and Rowden were still alive.

After performing every possible test he could think of, Thomas thought he may have developed an antidote to Malice's UV pellets for Grailen. He processed it into an injectable form. When he was done, he went over and reviewed what he did with Katrina's blood and what he hoped would happen when he gave it to Grailen. He couldn't guarantee what this blood antidote would do to Grailen.

Katrina's first response was yes, do it, give it to him right now. But then she wasn't sure. No one was sure what to do. How would it affect him? They needed to do something! Finally Viktor said to go ahead with it. It was Grailen's only chance, right?

It was daylight and Katrina sat lying on a sofa with a blanket covering her in the same room as Grailen. Viktor was also there, never leaving his brother's side. She wanted to stay with Viktor during his great time of need. The lack of sleep was beginning to make her feel like she was on her last legs. She could barely keep her eyes open. She had been the only one to fight the sun's affects for so long. It must be nine-thirty in the morning by now, Kat thought.

Kat walked over to the couch Viktor was quietly sleeping on, once again putting her palm on his face. She caressed his cheeks and forehead with her fingertips. No longer able to bear being away from him, she climbed onto the couch and wrapped her arms around him.

The couch wasn't as comfortable as the bed he had upstairs with the one thousand thread count sheets he loved. It was even worse than the couch that stood over by the wall she was using, but it would do. As long as she could be near him she would endure anything. "I love you Viktor, I'm pretty sure I fell in love with you the first time I saw you attacking the Hunter that was after me at the hospital. I fell in love you again at the club, and then more deeply when you were stalking me in my apartment." She giggled as she nuzzled her nose against his cheek. "I know you can make everything all better. You're brother isn't getting any better. I know this. And I know what that means to you."

Earlier, the prince and princess discussed bringing her to the palace, solving two problems at once. Grailen would be able to get the treatment he needed from the palace healer, and she would be brought to the palace as the king had ordered.

"I need you, I need you to be with me, I need you to be ok, you know you said you would spend forever with me, you promised. And I fully intend on holding you to it." She whispered into his ear and brushed her lips against the side of his face.

Kat fell asleep after another hour. Viktor remained in his death sleep, unable to respond to her. He heard every word she said to him though.

Grailen too had fallen into his death sleep. Finally, he received a rest from the pain of his injuries. The pain wasn't strong enough to keep him conscious during daylight hours. The draining power of the sun was just too strong to be ignored.

The antidote Thomas had made and given to Grailen seemed to have eased his discomfort a bit, but his wounds hadn't stopped bleeding. Spyder and Thomas continued to give him unit after unit of blood. It seemed to pour out of him almost as fast as they could give it.

Thomas, Spyder, Viktor, Dave, and the Royal PIAs, pains in the asses, as Kat had named them, were all in the kitchen. They were arguing about what to do when Katrina walked in. Oddly enough, even vampires tended to congregate in the kitchen even though none of them needed to eat food.

They all quieted when she entered the room. "Wow, can you make a girl feel anymore welcome with the warm and fuzzies you guys give off?" she said, annoyed as she grabbed one of the stools and sat down at the serving bar. Once seated, she looked at everyone and waited, the situation was getting a little irritating, she thought. Everyone always wanted to keep her in the dark about things, things involving her, her future, and Viktor.

"Princess Katrina, we were just going over what the next plan of action should be. As I'm sure you noticed when you awoke, Grailen is no better after giving him the blood cocktail I made. We have come up with a solution that may help us in many ways." It was Thomas that finally spoke up since no one else would.

"Well, let's hear it," she replied with a little reluctance in her voice. It always seemed like they stalled when they were about to say something she didn't want to hear. She just needed them to spill their guts. She knew she wasn't going to like whatever they were about say.

Prince Evan piped in, "Well, since Thomas's miracle medicine didn't work for Grailen as we had all hoped, his best chance to survive is for all of us to take him to the only place where there are doctors. Vampire doctors much more advanced than Thomas. They have better facilities and resources at their disposal. They will be able to heal your Viktor's brother." Kat noticed the prince emphasized the word your and winced. She knew full well she would be reprimanded for bonding with a commoner, even though she had no idea what was happening at the time. Even if it was through Viktor's punishment, she was still going to suffer.

Kat looked at them all in exasperation, "Why haven't we taken him there already? What the hell are we waiting for?" Furious with everyone in the room for holding back these miracle doctors from her until now, what could they possibly have been thinking?

"It's at our home, at the palace of King Alexander. He has also demanded that we return to the palace anyways, as quickly as possible. So taking Grailen there will serve two needs, having you brought to the palace, and to give Grailen a better chance at survival." Princess Anna finished, waiting for another smart comment from her newly found cousin.

Kat stared at her dumbfounded, the palace? She closed her eyes and took a deep breath. She knew that was coming. Was she ready for it? To face the king himself, the man who it was more than obvious everyone respected and was totally afraid of? Well, except for his children. The prince and princess seemed to only be a little worried. The only punishment they would be worried about was if the king took away their super expensive outfits or something.

"Oh. The palace."

"We spoke to the king. He would allow us to bring Grailen to the palace for care on one condition, that you are brought with. The king will not allow us entry without you, and he said we were lucky the Judges have been preoccupied until now. Otherwise he would have dispatched them two days ago. Even now, if we don't arrive tonight with you in tow, they will be sent to kill us all and retrieve only you and his children." Viktor spoke in such a low tone. Kat wouldn't have been able to catch a word he uttered if it hadn't been for her enhanced hearing.

She knew he was serious. Defeat was written clearly across his face. She didn't think Viktor, out of all the people here at the mansion, would ask her to go to the palace willingly. He knew that was her greatest fear, besides loosing Viktor.

Viktor knew by telling her that, she would have no choice but to go along with the plan. Otherwise they were all dead. The king acknowledged the Council as a very important entity in the survival of their race and the protection of the entire royal family. But they were expendable. He did not tolerate anyone going against what he said, and it seemed he felt it necessary to make examples of everyone who did so. He did everything in his power to ensure insolence did not occur often, which it didn't.

Kat felt like she was going to pass out. She never liked being put in a corner with no way out. Everything rode on how she responded. Did she want to put everyone's lives in danger, not give Grailen the best chance he could have to get better? Did she want to be hunted the rest of her life by Hunters and the High Council? No, she didn't. Most of all, she loved Viktor and that was what gave her the strength to do what she needed to do. Kat got up off her stool and looked at everyone, feeling a sense of resignation and hopelessness. "Ok, I'll play nice and go along without a fight. Just so you all know that if anything happens to Viktor, if the king orders these Judge demons after him, I won't play nice anymore." With that being said, she left the kitchen and headed up to the room she shared with Viktor to gather her nerves before her trip to the palace.

CHAPTER 22

Kat was fuming upstairs in her room. She knew it was time to go, that everyone would be waiting for her so they could begin their trek to the palace. She heard from one of their conversations that it wasn't a golden walled structure like the European royalty. It wasn't positioned on hundreds of acres of beautiful green fields, perfectly manicured lawns, and intricate flower patterns. Vampire royalty preferred the security of underground facilities.

Being ready to leave wasn't a problem for Kat, she was born ready. Yet there was a nagging feeling eating at her that when she got to the palace and met the new family she recently acquired, things weren't going to go her way. What was to come, she wondered? On that thought, she took another deep breath, trying to relax her mind and body. She had the habit of having panic attack symptoms; heart racing, chest feeling tight and heavy, when she was under stress. This situation was no different. She felt her chest tightening with every beat of her heart.

Being in a code situation at work when someone was dying, that was no problem. It didn't cause her to stress out like she was doing now and make her want to run away. She knew what she had to do in codes, and the order that it needed to be done. In the vampire world she found herself immersed in, she had no idea what her role was. How was she was supposed to act? Did she really have to do everything the king said? And what would happen to her and to Viktor if she didn't? She wished she had the answers to her questions before they left for the palace. She knew that once they were at the palace, she had no idea what or who she would run into. Once she was there, there was no turning back. Kat remembered someone mentioning the palace was an underground structure, a nuclear fallout shelter or something the local government's military were coerced into getting rid of. They gladly handed over the keys and forgot about its existence.

The night before, while Kat lay on the couch in the basement of the mansion with Viktor sleeping his death sleep beside her, her body finished its change. Her hair grew longer and thicker, her natural highlights intensified. Her incisors thickened, and lengthened. Her teeth looked like she spent hours at the dentist receiving whitening treatments. Her vital organs finished shifting into their new positions, making her a more efficient predator. She now had better control of blood flow to her muscles during times of exertion. It would allow her to move faster than detectable by human eyes. Her heart strengthened. Each chamber increased the total volume of cardiac output, making each breath of air more efficient. She didn't feel the majority of the change because it happened while she slept with the length of her body pressed up against Viktor's.

She had gone back up to her and Viktor's room on the second floor of the mansion to get ready for their trip. Not knowing how long she'd be gone was driving her insane. She wasn't sure what to bring. She didn't really have any of her personal belongings from her apartment. There really wasn't anything she absolutely needed. Well, besides the beautiful necklace Viktor gave her during their precious time together, before she ran from him and created the giant mess they were now both in.

She remembered how he had come back to their room with the necklace, hoping that she would let him in and welcome his warm embrace. That night he was right, she wanted nothing more than to spend every second in his arms. That was when he presented her with the necklace she wore. The chain was a delicately woven gold chain link. The pendant was filled with small diamonds surrounding a large pink ruby. The color of the stone was something she had never seen before. It was the most beautiful piece of jewelry, and he gave it to her!

Kat wasn't normally one to melt when a person gave her something, but this was beyond anything anyone had ever done for her. When she opened the box, she didn't know what to say. Thinking of the memory, she laughed at herself, remembering how she had to hold back tears. She didn't want to embarrass herself during their special moment.

Reality came swirling back to her conscience. Her job at the hospital was surely gone by now. Everyone probably thought she was lying dead in a ditch somewhere or burnt to a crisp in Carmen's kitchen. As for all of her possessions in her apartment, Kat figured she could kiss everything she had goodbye too. Hopefully Carmen would take care of her things. Hopefully she would be given the chance to get her stuff back someday when things cooled off, if they ever did.

Thinking of the changes her body underwent overnight, there was one thing she couldn't stop focusing on. Dave noticed it while she slept near Viktor and devised the necessary clothing to accommodate her new physique. The change had shredded everything she was wearing on the top half of her body. She couldn't wait to try them out. They were one of the only exciting features of the bad experience, that and Viktor. Unfortunately, there was no time for fun and games, but that was the way of her life. She was always the serious and focused one of the bunch.

Kat took off her makeshift shirt. Dave had fixed her a swath of material while she slept so nothing would get caught on her wings. Wings!! Yes, she had wings. No one else did, as far as she knew and from what Viktor had told her while he went over the special abilities of the vampires he knew. Holy cow! That's all she had to say.

Kat walked to the mirror sitting on top of Viktor's dresser and turned halfway so she could see her back. There they were, in all their sparkly, iridescent glory. She wondered if the serum Malice gave her mixed with her royal vampire blood and her wings were the end result. If he was trying to kill her, it backfired.

The serum did just the opposite. It made her being a vampire more spectacular than she could have ever imagined.

Out of all the possible unique abilities she heard about during her stay in the mansion, especially those of the royal families, Kat thought her wings were the coolest. Dave talked to Kat while she lay in her bed recovering from the ordeal and told her interesting facts about her new royal cousins. Prince Even was able to hear the heart beat of a human from over a mile away and his skin could change tones to become more like the environment to blend with. Princess Anna's special ability wasn't as cool as Kat's or her brother's. The princess could change her form into that of a wolf. She couldn't hold the form for any length of time. That ability was pretty lame, Kat thought. Or maybe it was because she didn't like her cousin, Kat wasn't sure.

Dave didn't know what any of the other royal family member's abilities were. He couldn't tell her what her father's, Prince Eric, or King Alexander's were. When she was given the opportunity, Kat would have to find out. Her curiosity on the subject was overwhelming. Now that she thought about it, Dave never mentioned what Grailen could do. Kat knew Viktor was able to transport from place to place with a mere thought, but all royal vampires could do that. Being a royal vampire meant that you were immediately given the generic abilities that not all common vampires had. She had a lot to learn.

The fact she had to drink blood totally stunk. She would have a problem with that for the rest of her existence. The other benefits were becoming more obvious to her, far outweighing the downsides. Being able to spend forever with Viktor and traveling the world together sounded great. Depending on how strict they were going to be with her movements, the traveling was a big maybe for now.

Those perks of vampiredom were what kept her will strong, allowing her to be able to go on. She needed all the strength she had to go to the palace and face her worst nightmare. Those thoughts of Viktor and their future together gave her the strength she needed to go to the palace even though that was exactly where she didn't want to go. She wanted to do her part to get Grailen the help he needed. He would receive treatment by vampire healers who knew what they were doing with unlimited resources available at their disposal. That was important to her and she would do anything she could for him. She would just prefer to do something else.

Kat couldn't think about drinking blood from an actual human. Do you know how much bacteria was on a person's skin? Having to expose herself and her mouth to that type of unsanitary practice on a regular basis? No thank you! I'll take my overly processed, disease screened, pre-measured blood in a handy plastic bag, thank you very much.

During the beginning of her change, when no one was around when she woke up, she found the stash of blood they planned on transfusing her with. At first she couldn't find anything to puncture the bag. Finally she found a pair of scissors in the bathroom drawer, hurriedly cut the first bag open, and dove right in.

She didn't let her mind take over and gross herself out as the blood poured into her mouth. She relaxed as much as she could and let her instincts have their way. It was pretty easy downing four bags of blood in one sitting. Her thirst was painful at first, but the pain eased with each bag she consumed. That's what she focused on to keep going. What she didn't want to focus on was the fact that after the second bag of blood was fully consumed she looked forward to drinking the third. She started craving for what she tasted on her tongue. Yuck! She liked the taste of blood, but she didn't like the fact that she liked the taste of blood. Yes, she would definitely have a few things to get used to being a vampire.

Kat was ready to go. She carefully put her shirt back into place, slowly stretching the white gauzy material so her skin was covered but her wings were able to move freely. She didn't know how delicate they were. Her wings looked like that of fairies she saw in the movies. Her wings seemed to be made of a very delicate substance. She couldn't say what material because they had some type of fluid circulating through them. She was pretty sure they were as alive as the rest of her. Kat was a little worried because her wings were almost long enough to hit the floor and she would have to be conscious not to drag them in the mud or get them caught in a car door or something.

Kat headed for the door hoping her meeting with the vampire king, her uncle, would go well. She wasn't sure how he would take his long lost niece having wings, or being bonded with a non-royal. She was also worried that he may do something to her Aunt Rose.

Kat was confident her aunt didn't have any knowledge of the vampire world. Her aunt took care of Kat when her parents died as any good aunt would do. Her visit with the king was so important on so many levels. Viktor's and Grailen's lives depended on it. She would try her hardest to keep her witty comments to herself, or at least to a minimum.

Everyone was waiting in the atrium of the mansion leading to the front entranceway. Viktor was there, standing next to Grailen who was strapped to a makeshift stretcher. She noticed he wasn't moving. Kat sighed as she finally saw the rise and fall of his chest signaling that at least he was still breathing.

The atrium of the mansion was almost as big as her apartment, she thought. Her thoughts trailed to her best friend Carmen. Grailen seemed to disappear whenever the opportunity arose while she was kept in the mansion waiting to rescue Viktor. Grailen would use the times during those days to be the one to go on supply runs. He didn't tell anyone where he went on the side, but Kat knew. Heightened senses allowed her to smell Carmen on him.

Kat never had the opportunity to be alone with Grailen considering everything that was going on. She wanted to know how her friend was doing, to know if Carmen knew what was happening to Kat. She wanted to let her best friend know how sorry she was for being the cause of her house getting blown to smithereens. Kat also wanted to know what sort of relationship Grailen was starting with her friend.

Kat knew when she was first brought to the mansion Viktor asked his brother to keep an eye on Carmen. He was to keep her safe if the Hunters happened to show up at her house thinking they would get another chance to capture Kat. Another ploy the bad guys used a lot was to capture someone important to the real person they wanted to have in their mitts. It was obvious something was going on between them.

Grailen had gone alone to see how Carmen was fairing while Viktor was being held captive. He didn't take anyone else from the Council with him. Having been a part of why her best friend's house was half blown apart sort of made Kat feel bad and inspired the need to check on her. Carmen already had the construction crews out to the house and was now able to stay there while the repairs are completed.

When the king understood her feelings for Viktor, he would let them live happily ever after at the mansion. That was her goal. No one was going to tell her where she could and couldn't go. She didn't care what their title was. She would have none of that kind of bully behavior from anyone, not even Viktor.

Walking down the grand staircase of the mansion, Kat heard various discussions going on. Dave and Spyder were in deep conversation covering the basics of what needed to be done while both brothers were away from the mansion. Dave would cover the daytime chores. Spyder would go out at night and keep the mansion safe and secure, patrolling from the shadows. Thomas would accompany his leader to the palace until his punishment was decided. He mentioned being there to take Viktor's punishment for him if Viktor wanted. Viktor snorted with disbelief. He would take what was given to him like a man.

There was a possibility Viktor might not survive whatever the king decided to dish out. There was also a possibility the king would have Grailen killed as punishment. There were too many what ifs in the situation. Kat didn't know what to do, what would be best for both her and Viktor?

Word of the long lost princess had caught on the wind and was already traveling to all parts of the vampire community, local and abroad. The threat to her safety had tripled since the Hunters began stalking her. Spyder called in more troops to help secure the mansion over the last few nights. Apparently he was like Viktor, he had a squad of his very own to command. Spyder ordered his men to accompany the group to the palace entrance to make sure no one that shouldn't be there decided to try and get a glimpse of the new princess. Spyder's team would return to the mansion immediately after. The mansion would be at higher risk of attack with both Viktor and Grailen gone.

Kat walked up to where Viktor stood and held his hand. Thomas made the suggestion to keep her wings to themselves, not wanting the word getting out to the general vampire public. Publication of the new winged princess would cause something of a stampede to get to the mansion to see her. The group agreed keeping silent about her would be for the best.

"It is time to go," Viktor said. The plan was that everyone would transport to the entrance of the palace. Thomas and Prince Evan would each take one side of Grailen's stretcher. Viktor would take Kat since she had not been given any time to practice transporting herself. Princess Anna would transport herself and the royal staff.

Before they left, Kat leaned over to Viktor and kissed him on the lips. "I love you," she whispered into his ear. At that moment, their bodies began to waver into mist.

CHAPTER 23

"What the hell is going on Sebastian?" Viktor growled at the vampire standing in front of them. Spyder's men stood behind everyone else. So far, no one made an unwanted appearance, trying to get the scoop on the new princess. For that, everyone was relieved. Sebastian was wearing the royal guard uniform typical for those guarding the palace and its inhabitants. Their friend relaxed when he realized who had appeared before him.

"Palace security has been heightened since word of the princess was brought to us. His Royal Majesty made the decree when their royal highnesses, the prince and princess, left to go and retrieve her. Since the Judges were not in residence, all entrances to the mountain were to be monitored more closely, as you can see by the two checkpoints that you'll have to go through to get to the palace door. Now that word is out in the general vampire community, the princess must be protected more carefully, as well as all members of the royal family."

Sebastian, Viktor and Grailen's old childhood friend, couldn't stop staring at Katrina. As per royal decree, the guard must show respect to all royal family members and not stare directly at them. Sebastian was having trouble controlling himself. Normally, especially if the king himself had seen such an outright show of disrespect, he would be at risk of execution. They all knew why he was doing it, and also figured it wasn't going to be a one-time phenomenon. Everyone the princess encountered was going to have the same problem. She was truly a sight to behold!

"No one is allowed entrance into the palace without specific invitation by the king himself. We knew you were coming. We thought you would be here a little sooner though. I'm sure he won't mind that Thomas is with." Sebastian grinned in his mischievous way. Sebastian was not one to avoid trouble, he was the one who went out and looked for it when they were younger.

Sebastian finally took his eyes off the princess and went to the control panel of the gate. "You do know that those men standing behind you," Sebastian said as he pointed the tip of his rifle at Spyder's team. "They won't be able to go into the palace with you. You are all safe from Hunters here, nothing to worry about." He slipped a white strip into the scanner and did something Kat found very odd. He pulled out a small but very sharp looking dagger and jabbed his finger. He squeezed his finger and let a droplet of blood hit the strip. The scanner read the code of Sebastian's blood. Once his identity was verified, the locks of the doorway began to undo themselves and the door slid open along its track. Behind the door was a group of royal guards waiting for them.

Prince Evan was relieved of his half of the stretcher by one of the guards. No such luck for Thomas though, not that he would give the honor of carrying his battle injured friend away for anything.

Princess Anna led the group, taking up her usual prestigious position in front of everyone else. She snapped her fingers and the next set of doors were opened. Kat noticed there was a similar wall unit with a white strip hanging from it, just like the one Sebastian used. Kat took up the rear, behind the guard holding the stretcher by Grailen's head, walking next to Viktor.

Behind the second door, once it was fully open, Kat saw inside the entrance to the palace. Holey moley, it was just like in the movies! There was nothing ordinary about the place, despite it being completely underground. There were gold leaf accents everywhere. The furniture was oversized with large jewel colored velvet cushions and had legs carved into claws at the bottom. There was a massive chandelier hanging from the ceiling in the middle of the room, which she saw once she passed the threshold of the palace and looked up.

On both sides there were staircases that wrapped along the walls just like the one at the mansion, except there was one on each side. Kat could see through one of the doors beneath the middle where the two staircases met, one of many rooms. It was probably used as a grand ballroom. As the thought entered her mind, her stomach dropped and she gasped for air. Maybe it was a receiving room for the king?

There were servants waiting for them, ready to show Thomas and the guard where they could take Grailen for treatment. Thomas and the guard immediately started following them, the sooner he was treated, the better, Kat thought. She figured there would be activities for her to participate in while Grailen received medical attention. Viktor gave her a strong hug and kissed her forehead. He followed behind them without saying a word to her.

The prince and princess disappeared when the group walked through the main palace entrance. Figures. Kat took a step forward to go with Viktor when one of another group of servants stepped in her way. "Forgive me your highness, but his majesty has ordered us to direct you to your rooms, where you will be staying, so you can ready yourself for your first meeting with him," she said. The servant lady appeared to be hesitant when talking to Kat; as if she were afraid Kat would grab her and bite her. Maybe that happened to her before?

The servant gestured toward one of the staircases. Kat didn't see an option but to follow. She didn't want to leave Viktor's side, but she figured she had to play nice with these people until the king decided what his punishment would be. Afterwards was another story. There was no way she was going to let someone tell her where she could and couldn't go, but for now she would behave.

Kat was speechless. She had rooms, as in multiple. Each one was bigger than her entire apartment! And the bathroom, it was ridiculous! The size was unbelievable! The counters, walls, and floor were made of beautiful shades of black and gray marble, her favorite. The fixtures were nickel plated with gold trim. The tub was large enough to fit four people in it.

The king provided very extravagant surroundings for his family. That must be why the prince and princess felt so entitled. They must take all of it for granted when most people in the world had so much less. They felt it was their birthright. Somehow her cousins felt they deserved it just by being born to the king, and others didn't.

She felt a little jilted. Kat loved her life and the simple things she enjoyed while growing up living with her aunt. They were simple people with simple needs. Kat never wanted for anything. Her aunt did her best to provide for her. Unlike these people, Kat appreciated everything she had and everything anyone had ever given to her.

Yes, they struggled a little financially, but all lower-middle class families with single parents did. That was why the prince and princess had the attitudes they did. Kat didn't know if she could ever become accustomed to their way of life. The palace was a little too grand for her taste. It was definitely beautiful, but a little overly indulgent.

Even staying at the mansion, which looked like a poor man's house in comparison to the palace, made her feel a little out of place. Being with Viktor made everything better at the mansion. She didn't suppose that he would be willing to move into her little apartment with her. That was if she even had an apartment after all of this was over.

Lost in the moment, Kat didn't notice that two servants had come into her receiving room. "Excuse me, Princess Katrina. We don't mean to point such things out. But when you arrived, we noticed your additional, um, appendages. And well, we were wondering if you would like to take a bath while your clothing is being prepared?"

The female servant who spoke kept her glance towards the floor, never looking Kat directly in the eyes. That was going to have to stop. It seemed there was a major caste system going on and she didn't like it. Just because they were servants in the big man's palace didn't mean she expected them to bow before her because they weren't worthy. She was nothing like her cousins, and she would never treat people as poorly as they were used to being treated.

"Yeah, I guess I could use some freshening up." Kat looked down at herself. She had been wearing the clothes Dave picked out for her a few days ago. He was a pretty handy guy, and he guessed her size correctly, a little loose, but overall everything fit well enough. The clothes she had on, the makeshift shirt to fit her wings and the pants, were both smudged with dust and grime. Kat had worn the same clothes since she woke up lying next to Viktor.

Kat followed the servant girl, the one who had yet to speak to her, into the bathroom. When the girl started to turn the water on, checking the temperature, that was the last straw. "Um, you really don't have to do that, I'm more than capable of setting up my own bath, but thank you," she said as she tried to grab the towels out of the girls other arm.

Serving girl wasn't having anything to do with Kat not letting her provide service for her. "This is absurd. I'm a big girl," Kat said as she grabbed a better hold of the towels the servant girl didn't want to let go of. "I can take care of myself, now give me the towels!" she said a little more pointedly than she meant to.

That was one way to get them to look her in the eyes. Serving girl, they didn't wear name tags which would have been helpful, glanced up at Kat with tears in her eyes and ran out of the bathroom. Great, now she felt bad. Kat didn't need anyone to take care of her! Checking the temperature of her bath water, that was a little too weird and creepy. Kat had been doing a pretty good job of taking care of herself so far.

She would have to deal with that later, teaching the helpers not to help so much. But the servants, who Kat could smell were vampires, were too subservient. They were too docile. It was the twenty-first century. Yep, some things were going to change.

Wanting to get cleaned and dressed so she could check on how Viktor and Grailen were doing made Kat hurry through her bath. She ended up draining the water though. Kat lie back on her wings which proved uncomfortable no matter how she tried to position herself, so she ended up taking a quick shower. Grabbing one of the fluffiest towels she had ever touched, Kat quickly dried herself off. She took special care of her still very sensitive wings.

Wrapping herself in another towel, she walked out into her bedroom. There, lying on her bed, and thankfully not with anyone standing there ready to help her dress, was the most luxurious black gown she had ever seen. There was just something about famous designers and what they were able to produce, she thought.

Whoever picked out the dress had picked her favorite color. The black of the gown would be a nice contrast with her complexion. Now that she had turned into a vampire, her skin was very pale. She was always a little pale, now she almost glowed.

Kat leaned over the bed and picked up the dress. The pure blackness of the beautiful material matched her hair. She held the dress up in front of her. The front of the dress had a square neckline that would show some of the new cleavage she grew overnight, but not too much to be distasteful. The waist had an A-line cut, which would show her trim body off nicely. The length of the dress reached to the floor, which would match her almost floor length wings. She turned the dress around. Almost the entire back of the dress was missing all the way down to the waist. That was one way to avoid her wings, she thought. Kat was going to have to figure something out, modify whatever clothing she got her hands on so at least some of her back would be covered. She had never been known to be a skin flasher.

Kat noticed there was tiny, delicate, crystal like gems reflecting the light when she moved the material. The crystals lined the square neckline. Her eyebrow lifted when she noticed there was a slit going up the right side from the bottom of the dress all the way up to the middle of her thigh. She felt like she should be going to the Golden Globes instead of downstairs, even if it was to meet the vampire king. He must like flashy, either that, or his high and mighty princess daughter had a hand in selecting her outfit for the evening.

If Princess Anna did have something to do with it, Kat would have to thank her for doing such a great job. That meant the princess probably didn't have anything to do with it. Maybe it was one of the servant women?

Kat put her fingertips on the gems and ran her hand across them. "Ouch!" What the heck? Kat looked down at her finger, then back at the gems. That's when she noticed the crystals looked like real diamonds. There must have been over a thousand of them sparkling up at her!

When she jumped pulling her hand away from the dress she banged her toe on something hard at the foot of her bed. She glanced down and saw magnificent black strappy high heeled shoes to go along with her dress. Size seven and a half. Was Dave here? How would they know her size? Even though she thought the mansion and the palace service was a little over the top, she did appreciate they were thinking of her and planning ahead. So far Kat didn't have to go without anything for very long. That was something she could definitely get used to.

Once Kat dried her hair she looked in all the drawers of her powder room armoire. The powder room was not the bathroom. It was a completely different room! It was separate from her bedroom, bathroom, walk-in closet, sitting room, and receiving room. In the drawers of the armoire, she found a ton of makeup, and not just any makeup. All the labels read Elegance`. She had only read about the brand of makeup in magazines, it's what all the movie stars used. She delved right in. She couldn't let her face look plane, not while wearing that beautiful dress and those fabulous black strappy shoes.

When Kat bent over to look closer in the mirror, something seemed to be missing, her wings! They were gone. She turned her shoulder so she could look at her back. Yes, they were gone. All that was left of them were little bumps on her shoulder blades where her wings had emerged. There was no other sign of them now. Damn, she was kind of getting used to them, even liking them. She wondered if they would ever come back.

Oh well, she had to hurry up and get ready for her meeting with the king and find out what was going to happen to Viktor and Grailen. She had to decide what she was going to do about it if Viktor was punished too severely. Kat didn't really want to stay in the palace any longer than she absolutely had to. If they did anything to hurt Viktor she wasn't going to take it lightly. She had no problem with disowning the entire family she just recently found out existed. It's not like she would miss any of them.

Kat finished with her makeup thinking she would love to keep just half of the products in the dressing table drawers when she went back home. Home was a term she wanted to think about later. She would think about it later because if she did it now she would start crying again.

Kat walked back into her bedroom. Looking around, she realized she didn't have undergarments to wear with her dress. Ugh, she was never a woman to go commando, panty lines hear me roar! She didn't care. She felt not wearing underwear was unnatural, not to mention the chafing!

Thinking there might be a small chance someone might have thought of the underwear issue, she checked all the drawers in the dressers lining the closet walls. Dang, there was a ton of clothes, all with designer labels on them, but no underwear? Who did the shopping? It must have been a male servant.

If she was going to stay in the palace for a while she'd have to find someone willing to do a little shopping for her. The servants would be happy to do anything for her. Probably even paint her nails or wax her butt. That type of thing wasn't for her, be my servant and bow before me. Whatever, she was an independent woman. These royals had another thing coming their way if they thought she was going to tolerate having everyone else dictate how her everyday life was going to be.

Kat dropped her towel. She was ready besides the fact that she was naked. She grabbed the top straps of the dress, turned it around and laid it back down on the bed. She reached out to pick it up again. Cramps in her back took over. Kat cried out and buckled over onto the bed in pain. When the pain finally subsided she caught her breath and looked over her shoulder.

Her wings were back. What the heck? Was it a control problem? Obviously she didn't have control over them and they were going to come and go as they pleased. She must have done something to make them come back out. Kat did stretch out her shoulders a little while reaching for the dress. Was that it? She rolled her shoulders a little, trying to relax herself. Her wings disappeared again into the folds of her back.

Amazing! Her wings, when outside of her body, almost reached the floor. How could they possibly fit into her back? The bumps on her shoulder blades weren't large enough to hide that much material, or tissue, or whatever her wings were made of. It must be some type of vampire magic. That was as good an explanation as any, she thought. Not really wanting to experience that all consuming pain again, she left her wings hidden. When they went back in it was only a mild discomfort. Bringing them out was a completely different story.

She carefully climbed onto the bed to pick up the dress, concentrating on not flexing her shoulder blades to bring out her wings. Then Kat carefully climbed back off the bed into a standing position. Slowly, she bent over to slip her feet into the back of the dress. Pulling it up over her hips, she slid the slender straps over her shoulders. She held her breath expecting her wings to spring out again. But they didn't.

Kat stood in front of the full length mirror taking a last look, making sure everything was in the right place and nothing was showing that shouldn't be. She turned slightly to further inspect the little bumps on her shoulders where her wings were relaxing. The redness of her skin seemed to be fading. The longer her wings were tucked in, the more the color was returning back to her natural skin shade of bright white.

The bumps weren't very large but she would need to keep them covered when in the company of humans. That wouldn't be for a while though. She had to make sure she had absolute control of her wings. She couldn't have them popping out of her back on their own accord in front of a human. They could possibly rip her shirt right off her back exposing her to everyone around! No, she would have to wait for a little while.

That was just weird to say, even to her. She was still human, right? Kat had some perks to go along with her humanity; shifting locations with a thought, possibly flying, having to drink blood, oh yeah, and living forever. That didn't make her a bad person. Speaking of blood, she was getting thirsty. The last time she had any was back at Viktor's mansion. She was sure they would have some stocked somewhere on the first floor or wherever it was in the palace she was supposed to go and meet the king. It would be wonderful if she didn't actually have to drink it in front of him.

Drinking blood was kind of a personal, private thing to her. Just like shaving her legs was.

She wasn't an expert at drinking blood, not yet. Unfortunately when her mind took over, she ended up gagging once in a while. She spit blood up like an infant. That could be really embarrassing if that happened in front of the king, let alone the perfect princess cousin of hers.

Kat took a final deep breath and headed for the door that would lead her out of her suite of rooms and into the rest of the palace. She could do this. She could meet her uncle, even if he was the vampire king.

There were a line of servants waiting, for what she didn't know, at the bottom of the staircase. When Kat reached the bottom step, Viktor entered the large foyer from a door at the opposite end of the room. That's probably where they were treating Grailen, she thought. She walked quickly up to him. "Viktor!" she said. She could barely keep her tears in check. Unable to choke out anymore words without losing control, she kept quiet.

"Katrina, you look, amazing," he said while taking her hand into his. Viktor took a step back, lifting her arm to get a better look and smiled.

Kat finally got control of her emotions and asked, "How is he, how is Grailen?"

"They are still working on him. The palace healers knew about Malice's UV weapons. Although the UV pellets are new to everyone. They think that Grailen will pull through. The bleeding has slowed a bit. Their ancient remedies really work wonders."

Viktor grabbed her up in his arms and held her close. He caressed her back and asked, "Katrina, where did your wings go?"

Smiling, she looked up into his gorgeous eyes, responding with, "They seem to have a mind of their own."

CHAPTER 24

"My Katrina, my dearest Katrina," Viktor murmured in her ear smiling that charming smile only he could give her. He grabbed Kat back into his embrace and pulled her into his arms. Squeezing her tight against his chest, he leaned his chin against the top of her head. He didn't want to let go, not ever again.

An array of loud voices came from the top of the staircase ending their reunion. Together Kat and Viktor looked up to see what or who was causing the ruckus. Princess Anna and her brother, Prince Evan, were being followed by a small gang of servants. The princess was spouting orders to them, something about her needs not being taken care of. Just because she had been gone for a while didn't mean they didn't have to do their jobs when she wasn't there to oversee them. She threatened that if such poor service continued from them she was going to report their behavior to the king or rip out their throats.

Once the golden pair reached the bottom of the staircase, Kat had a chance to get a good look at Princess Anna. She didn't disappoint, that was for sure. Her gown, like Kat's, was also black. They were suspiciously similar to each other's. The main difference being Princess Anna didn't have wings to cover so she was able to have a back to her dress. The neckline in the front of the dress differed also, it was quite a bit lower.

Kat's cousins walked over to where she was standing with Viktor. She guessed there was going to be an audience of sorts when Viktor was dealt his punishment. Kat supposed this wasn't an ordinary occurrence. Finding a long lost vampire princess and having that princess bond with a vampire the High Council considered beneath her probably didn't happen much.

One of the serving women, who looked a bit more regal, more privileged, maybe even higher on the food chain than the other servants, cleared her throat. "The king would like everyone to meet him in his dining hall." While she was motioning the group through yet another door in the main foyer of the palace, Thomas came out of the same room Viktor had been in and smiled at them all. Since he was also going to meet the king, he was also dressed in a black tuxedo. Thomas's tuxedo didn't look as good on him as Viktor's did, Kat thought. But he still looked spectacular.

Following the servant lady, everyone left the main entrance hall. Kat thought it interesting that the servant was human. How big was this place? The hallway was filled with paintings, some looking really old and others looked rather new. While walking in past the paintings, Kat looked up to see what her ancestors looked like. She had no idea how old the paintings were, she figured the old ones could be centuries old. Yet the inhabitants of them may be still alive, or maybe only a small number of them were. After all, accidents did happen. She wasn't quite up to date with vampire healthcare, how long forever really meant could be up for interpretation. There was a lot she had to learn.

The group came to yet another large room. Once they passed the threshold Kat saw him, the king. She felt an all encompassing panic attack coming on. Viktor must have sensed her tensing and squeezed her hand quickly, then let it go. There he was, the king of everyone, King Alexander Caine. He was a vampire who had lived for thousands of years and told everyone what to do. Kat instantly noticed the group of figures clothed in black robes. They stood behind the king. They were made up of different physiques; some were small, others large, a few were thin, and some were wide. Not one of them showed their faces. The Judges! This was the group of demons Princess Anna talked about. They were the king's personal lackeys that dealt punishments the king gave out to the exceedingly naughty.

Impatiently ushering the group closer to the king, the servant lady fell to the back of the room but didn't leave completely. Kat, while walking towards the threshold of the elevated area, or whatever the platform thing was holding the king and his mighty thrown, tensed a little more. She could smell blood from somewhere and turned her head to get a stronger whiff. There, in the middle of the room against a wall sat an enormous table laid out with gold and bronze services. There were many decanters too. Those must be holding the blood she smelled warm and yummy. Yummy? She must really be thirsty.

Facing back to the front, Kat looked just in time to see the king rise to a standing position. When her group reached the bottom of the step, Princess Anna and Prince Evan were in front. They bowed their heads and put their right hands over their hearts, then said in unison, "Your majesty." They raised their heads first before their bodies. They walked up the platform steps and took their seats on either side of the king. She noticed neither one of them acknowledged the Judges. Their postures changed when they were near the Judges. It seemed as though they became a little squeamish when the Judges moved forward to surround the king and Katrina's group.

Thomas was next to step up. He went through the exact same motions as her cousins. The king barely acknowledged him. Kat felt his stare on her the entire time, practically boring a hole in her forehead. The man then stepped aside to allow her and Viktor to move forward. Time to meet the oldest, scariest, and most powerful vampire alive, she thought.

When it was their turn to do the bowing thing, Kat forgot about the shoulder rule. When she put her right hand on her chest, out came her wings. She began falling towards the floor when Viktor caught her by the arm. "Katrina, what's wrong?" Viktor asked in a concerned tone. He completely forgot for just a moment where he was and exactly who he was standing in front of. Viktor looked up at the king and saw the astonishment written on his face.

The pain subsided more quickly this time and she was able to catch her breath sooner than when they sprung out of her shoulders in her room earlier. Her wings felt stiffer, stronger than before. Maybe the action was like having pierced ears, the longer she had her wings, the less it was going to hurt every time they came out? She hoped that was the case. Kat thought her wings were pretty cool, but she didn't want to double over in pain every time she wanted them out, that could be very inconvenient.

Kat thought it would be best if she put them away. She was never one wanting to be in the limelight. Rolling her shoulders back, trying to relax her body, her wings began to recede slowly once again back into her shoulder blades. When they were all tucked in and she could breathe again, Kat carefully brought her right hand up to her chest. She made the motion and ever so slightly bowed her head and bent a little at the knee. She tried not to appear disrespectful while keeping her wings in place at the same time.

Katrina didn't know if it was allowed for her to look the king directly in the eyes, but to heck with protocol and all that jazz. "Hi," she said sheepishly and smiled up at him. Her fangs caught on her bottom lip making her give a little laugh in embarrassment as she brought her hand up to cover her teeth.

"Hello, princess." The king put his right hand to his chest and bowed his head ever so slightly, never taking his eyes off her. Everyone in the room gasped together. The king must not do that very often, Kat thought. Saluting someone beneath him wasn't something a king did. The king took the last step off of the platform he was standing on, making himself and Kat at a more even level. Well, she would never be on his level, but you get the picture.

"Viktor," the king acknowledged him with cool disdain without ever turning towards him. The king glanced at the hand Viktor kept on Kat's arm. He didn't mention it but obviously it didn't sit well with him. "Why don't we all have a seat at the table so we can get to know our princess better," the king said. Then he finished with, "And we can figure out what to do with you, Viktor, my insubordinate servant." He now looked right at Viktor. This wasn't going to go well, Kat could tell. Tension was coiling in both Viktor and the king. The air was becoming overwhelmingly thick.

King Alexander grabbed Kat by the other arm causing Viktor to let go. He led her to the spot on the right so she would be seated next to what could only be his place, at the head of the table. A servant came from nowhere and pulled out her chair. He waited for her to sit then helped her push the chair in.

The king was irritable. His movements seemed a bit forced and pointed when he took his place. He shooed the servant away who wanted to help him with his chair and napkin. Everyone else waited until he was seated and gave the signal with his hand. Kat's anxiety level rose. She worried about Viktor and that she couldn't keep her pesky wings in place.

Viktor sat on her right. The prince and princess sat on the king's left side, across the table from Kat. Thomas sat next to Viktor. There were about twenty seats left empty. Kat wondered if that was how many royal family members lived here at the palace? No one had mentioned anything about her other family members or where they lived. She assumed for safety reasons, they would live here with the king. Supposedly he had a say in everything and everyone.

"Now, princess," the king said to Kat. "Where should we begin? You have such an extraordinary tale to tell me, how you managed to be unknown to the rest of the entire vampire community? It baffles me, that my own nephew, Eric, would keep such a fantastic secret as having a child from me. Even more baffling is your wings, how long have you had them?" He asked in an astonished tone that sounded a little bit like awe.

"Well, they actually just came out the other night, when I was laying," she paused. She didn't want to explain how she was laying next to Viktor in the mansion basement. "Um, they just kind of came out. Dave thinks my wings might be a side effect of the serum Malice gave me. That maybe my genetic makeup interacted with the serum and my wings are the result. I haven't really had a chance to try them out yet, I don't know if I can fly." The servants moved around them pouring everyone at the table a goblet full of blood and Kat reached for hers immediately. The thirst was overwhelmingly strong and she gulped the contents down in one swallow. She tried not to belch and hoped the servants would anticipate her need and give her a refill.

The Judges, after everyone had been seated, relocated to stand at random intervals behind the occupants of the table. Yes, they were really intimidating to say the least! Looking at the king, Kat couldn't believe how young he appeared. She knew he was over a thousand years old. He had lived in the times where there were no conveniences of any kind. She wondered to herself what country was he born in? Were there countries at that time? The king looked her same age, they all did. Well, they were all vampires, so the age of twenty five was the key.

The king wasn't an overly large man, but he was still taller than both Viktor and the prince, who were both well over six feet tall. To Kat, the king seemed gentle enough. Maybe gentle wasn't the right word. He didn't seem as mean as everyone made him out to be. Expect the unexpected, she told herself.

Viktor decided it was now or never, the suspense was killing him, and addressed the king. "Your Majesty, I..." the king chose that moment to hold up his hand to silence Viktor. One of the Judges moved closer to Viktor's back to make Viktor aware he was treading on thin ice. Viktor sat back against his chair in silence. The future didn't look so bright at the moment.

"I will deal with you in a moment, when I decide how I should deal with your insolence," the king hissed through his fangs angrily as his eyes became deep red. Not the same color hers or Viktor's did. The king's eyes were darker, almost a crimson maroon color whereas hers and Viktor's were a brighter shade of red.

Kat didn't know what to say. Was she right to give the king's temper some room and not say anything in Viktor's defense? Yes. She would save that for a more opportune time. The king was a reactive man with his temper. To say that the king was a little pissed off wasn't adequately describing the raw emotion she saw in the king's eyes. Viktor sat back against his chair and remained silent and completely still. They all knew this could go one of many ways, and making the king angrier wasn't a good idea.

The king looked at Kat, thankfully taking his attention away from Viktor for the time being. "Princess Katrina, I would like for you to understand something. You, as I am, as my children are, of royal vampire lineage that goes back thousands of years, to the beginning of time actually. You have responsibilities and privileges unlike any other."

"You are different from anyone of us," he continued. "You are, as far as we know, the only child your father ever had. I'm sure what you have been through in the last few weeks has been very difficult. However, your safety is now one of my highest priorities, as is the safety of all my family. What I'm about to say may surprise you, but it is what I think is best for you, for us, and for our kind." Again, a long uncomfortable pause occurred.

Wow, this guy really likes the drama, she thought right before he spoke again. "It is very obvious that you care for this common vampire. Not knowing our ways, you can't be at fault or held accountable for what has happened before you were brought here to the palace. Viktor, however, is a completely different story. No matter, I believe Malice has done us a sort of favor by injecting both of you with that poisonous serum. You, my beautiful niece, are one of a kind. Your father's mother was a female Judge, a fairy demon. The blood that runs through you may have something to do with why you developed wings, for you are one of only two vampires that I know of who have them, and why Viktor does not. Also, my medical staff tells me. You see, Katrina, I believe in fate. I believe you and my servant, Viktor, were meant to be due to our nature and the nature of the bond. Don't fool yourselves in thinking that I approve of your bond. That is not the case. Viktor will remain here in my palace until I deal out his punishment, which still is to be decided. You will be given the run of the palace. There is no area where you are forbidden to go. Katrina, you will stay here with us, your family. The sooner you become comfortable with your surroundings, the better." Wow, Katrina thought, did the king practice that speech before she got here?

Well, she had a few questions of her own for the king. She didn't want to bring up the topic of Viktor again, because that was a sore subject with him right now. Kat wanted to find out exactly what happened to her father and if the king knew anything about her mother. Did he ever meet her? "Your Majesty, I was wondering if you could tell me what happened to my father, your nephew, Eric?"

"My dear," the king said and took a deep breath, carefully considering his words before he said them. Sadness washed over his features for a moment. "Your father, Prince Eric, was my brother's son. My brother decided to mate with one of my uncle Reskin's Judges, the only female Judge to have existed. The result of their mating was your father, who is the only other vampire I have known to have wings. That is, besides yourself. Unfortunately, King Reskin sentenced my brother to death for his treasonous act. Your father disappeared a little over twenty-four years ago. Prince Eric liked to live on his own, he was a bit of a loner and didn't appreciate the finer things living in the palace with us could give him." With that long and overly drawn out decree, King Alexander stood from his seat, bowed once to Kat, showing the tips of his fangs while he smiled.

Prince Evan scooted back in his chair. The king whipped his head in his son's direction. "Evan, don't think for a moment I have overlooked your actions. Putting yourself in danger to save a common vampire is not acceptable and you know it. For this, you will be banned from training for one year."

"But father!"

"I'm saying this to you as your king and your father. Royal blood is not to be put in jeopardy for frivolous adventure."

Kat didn't know what to say. Was that it?

"Katrina, I have other issues to attend to. I'm so glad you are finally home." The king looked at Viktor and said, "You will stay here until I've decided what to do with you. I have the mind to sentence you to one hundred years of blood starvation in a slaughter house. That would give you sufficient time to think about what you've done."

He continued with, "My healers tell me your brother will pull through. When he is well enough, he will be sent back to Delta 9 headquarters. My sources tell me your brother was aware of your bond to my niece. I will deal with him when he has fully recovered." The king finished his orders to the Judges and took his leave.

Once he was out of sight, Kat exhaled deeply. She hadn't realized the entire time the king was talking she held her breath waiting for the worst. She turned to look at Viktor and said, "I can't believe this! Viktor, we're both going to stay here at the palace, together!" She flung herself into his open arms where he hugged her so tightly she could barely breathe but she didn't care. Not one bit.

The king was going to let her be with the man she was absolutely and utterly in love with! Well, for now. The future could be a different story. Kat was in total awe, she didn't realize how stressed out she had been with the thought of loosing Viktor forever, forcing her to face eternity alone, without him.

"I love you Katrina, I love you so very much," Viktor said as he continued squeezing the air out of his woman, he couldn't let her go, and he never wanted to again.

She laughed, "Viktor, my love, if you ever get captured again,

I will kill you myself. Don't you ever put me through that again!" Kat continued to kiss him all over his smiling face.

Katrina wondered how long the king would take to decide Viktor's fate. The punishment couldn't be too bad since he hadn't already decided, right? Viktor was going to live.

But, as Viktor knew all too well, there were worse things than death.

Lightning Source UK Ltd.
Milton Keynes UK
06 November 2010

162504UK00001B/34/P